BROKEN GIRLS

NICKY DOWNES

Storm
PUBLISHING

Ebook ISBN: 978-1-80508-324-5
Paperback ISBN: 978-1-80508-326-9

Cover design: Lisa Brewster
Cover images: Shutterstock, Depositphotos

Published by Storm Publishing.
For further information, visit:
www.stormpublishing.co

ALSO BY NICKY DOWNES

Detective Jack Kent

Silent Fall

To Frances Taylor.
My wonderful mum.

PROLOGUE

Pain. Intense, burning pain.

Leia clutched her mother's handbag to her stomach and bit down on her tongue. *Not now. Please, not now.* Not after such a morning. A moment of freedom. Not when, for the first time, she could be her own person rather than an offshoot of her mother.

Leia stumbled on. Squinting, she spotted the distinct shape of the bull at the edge of the shopping centre. If she headed for that, she could get to New Street station. If she got to the station, she could rest on the train and make it home before her mother returned. She realised that she'd left her glasses at the cafe, but she didn't want to go back there to get them. It would spoil it, and besides, she wasn't sure she would make it back to the cafe and still get back home. What if he was still there? He would think she was stupid – forgetful or, worse, childish.

She handled this kind of pain every day. She needed to breathe through it. Slowly in. Slowly out.

A flash of deeper, penetrating agony screamed through her broken body. Leia grabbed at her thin jumper, pulling it away from her throat as the pain radiated up her neck and into her jaw. She was suddenly conscious that people were staring at her. Mothers pushed their children in the opposite direction. A group of teenagers giggled behind their hands as they passed her. Why couldn't she be more like them?

Trying to relax, she focussed on the bull. She charged, ungracefully, towards it. A woman with purple hair, overladen with shopping, bumped into her shoulder and tutted.

Leia wished she was home, or somewhere safe like the library. Away from the crowds. No one cared what you looked like at the library. They were too busy doing their homework, reading or surfing the internet. All in their own space. She knew the rules there. Town was a different matter.

Stomach cramps stopped her dead. She grasped at the band of her flowery skirt trying to loosen its belt from the last buckle hole. The hole she'd made the night before with a sharp pair of scissors. Her clothes were now all far too baggy, and she hated having to hold on to the top of her skirt, as she walked, to stop it from sliding down her slender hips.

Her vision narrowed like watching life through a timed-out seaside telescope. She remembered being seven. Her father holding her up to see the view from Weston-super-Mare's Grand Pier through the lens. Then, when the pennies ran out, he placed her gently back in her wheelchair. The one and only time she'd seen the sea.

She stood still for a moment. Remembering the waves. In. Out. One more step. Then another.

It never hurt this much before. Unrelenting agony travelled down her arm to her fingertips. Falling, she thought of him. His smile. How he'd held her hand and made her feel that she had a reason to live. And her first taste of a vanilla milkshake. It was so much nicer than she'd expected. Today was a good day. It shouldn't end like this.

ONE

'You can see why I called you, DI Kent.'

Detective Inspector Jack Kent stared at the youthful body on the mortuary slab. From the girl's face, she could have been any age between thirteen and eighteen. She was likely undernourished as her cheeks were hollow, reminding Jack of nineties fashion models back when emaciated-skinny was the vogue. Dark circles shrouded her eyes and she wore no makeup. Her dull-brown, shoulder-length hair was swept up, revealing unpierced ears. But it was clearly her heavily scarred body that caused Shauna concern. They weren't the scars of a self-harming teenager, but medical scars.

Shauna pointed to a round mark on her abdomen. 'That's from an old feeding peg.' She indicated to another, on the other side of her body. 'Until recently, she had a stoma.'

To Jack, the child looked like a rag doll stitched together by a seamstress. It was as if Shauna had started the post-mortem and had already sewn her back up. The two longest scars ran from below the girl's belly button to her pubic hair, and between her breasts to her stomach. But there were many others and Shauna gave her medical opinion on them all.

'Appendix removal.' She gestured at a small scar on the right of the girl's body. 'Possible gall bladder removal.' And so it continued.

Jack tried to ease the growing, palpable tension in the room. 'She's been in the wars then.'

Shooting a disapproving look at her friend, Shauna stood up. A gold bar raised with her eyebrow. Shauna Scott was usually the one making the jokes; the more macabre and the darker, the better. But today there was no trace of humour in her eyes – she looked genuinely concerned.

'Perhaps cancer...?' Jack wanted to be sure that everything was ruled out, so she didn't jump to wrong conclusions.

Shauna shook her head. 'She suddenly collapsed in the middle of the Bull Ring. The ambulance crew tried to resuscitate her but pronounced her dead within minutes of reaching the hospital. She was shopping on her own...no mates around. There's something just not right about this one. I mean, even if she has been seriously ill, the range and scope of medical interventions just don't fit. And I haven't even opened her up yet.'

'How do you know all this?' You wouldn't expect any detail about where she was found to be included in her medical records.

Shauna stood, stretching her back. 'I spoke to one of the nurses in A&E. This just didn't smell right so I rang you.'

Jack wasn't surprised that she'd been called in. This young girl's sudden death had *suspicious* written all over it. And after so many years working together, she trusted Shauna's gut instinct. Reaching into her bag, she popped a mint from an open packet, placed it into her mouth, and began to suck. She knew what was coming next.

Shauna smiled. 'You can wait outside until I've opened her up if you like.'

Jack didn't move or even flinch until she heard the screeching of the bone saw as it cut through the breastbone.

Soon the young girl's insides were displayed. After investigating for several minutes, Shauna frowned. 'Not quite what I was expecting.'

Jack didn't look too closely. None of what she had seen so far was expected. 'How do you mean?'

'Everything looks normal at first glance.' She switched on her mike. 'For the benefit of the tape, I can see that all organs are intact and appear to be healthy. There is some minor scarring particularly of the lower bowel.' She lifted it and examined it more closely. 'I can see that at some point part of the bowel has been removed and diverted to a stoma. There's no evidence as to the reason why this would be needed.'

Shauna turned her concentration to the intestines. She squeezed along each section. 'There appears to be no signs of blockages or damage in either intestine.'

Shauna removed the stomach, holding it upright to avoid any spillage. She tipped its contents into a large dish. It was too much for Jack; she looked away, sucking harder on the mint as her stomach churned.

'Looks like she had a vanilla milkshake shortly before her death.' The sweet tang of vanilla did nothing to hide the stench of recent digestion. Jack swallowed hard to stop herself from heaving. Not for the first time, she pondered how her friend managed to cut dead people up and remain relatively normal. Strike that. Her friend hated being described as normal. Shauna would always be queer and alternative in both her dress and lifestyle. Under her white apron she wore a Sisters of Mercy T-shirt with the sleeves roughly scissored to show off her full-sleeve tattoos. As soon as the post-mortem ended, she'd throw off the rubber shoes and replace them with Doc Martens painted with red roses complete with thorns.

Having dispensed with the stomach, Shauna moved on to the kidneys and liver, removing them skilfully with a single flick of the scalpel. They were all, Shauna noted, a healthy colour and size. No apparent signs of cirrhosis or kidney failure. She weighed them and verbally noted the weight.

'What's going on here?' Jack could sense Shauna's growing confusion with each cut of the knife.

After a moment, Shauna took a step away from the autopsy table. She folded her arms. 'I'm not getting this. As far as I can see, this child is perfectly healthy. Despite the signs that she's been repeatedly operated on, I still can't see any evidence, as yet, of disease.'

'Then how did she die?'

'That's simple – of a heart attack and I'll take a close look at that organ in a minute, but, my guess is, there'll be no obvious sign of heart disease either.'

Shauna spent the next twenty minutes closely examining the heart. Each chamber was measured and checked; any signs of abnormality noted. 'There are some mild indicators of myocarditis. This could suggest that this is a case of Sudden Death Syndrome. I'll need to look at her medical history.'

Jack was familiar with myocarditis. Heart disease ran in her mother's family. That side of her family was rather more sedentary than her father's. Adventurous outdoor pursuits were the norm for the past few generations of the Kents. Jack was a hereditary mountain climber rather than the first in her family, though she was the most accomplished by some margin. 'Are you saying that's the cause of death – myocarditis?'

A dropped scalpel rattled into a petri dish. 'The enlargement is slight. It might be nothing. But I really do need to find out what she's been treated for.' She gave a heavy sigh. 'None of this makes sense.'

The post-mortem continued without any further revelations. Eventually, Shauna motioned for her technician to sew up the body. She went to shower and change, leaving Jack to walk back to the office. On a chair, next to Shauna's desk, was a large clear plastic bag. It was labelled *Leia Thompson* and contained the poor girl's effects which had recently been transferred to the morgue. Jack wasn't sure whether it was the trainers or flowery pair of knickers that made tears prick in her eyes. She undid the knot at the top of the plastic bag and opened it up to see if she could find the girl's purse and phone, in the hope they would offer more clues as to who the girl was in life. Jack rummaged through until she found a black, patent handbag. She pulled it out and held it up. It wasn't the type of bag that you'd expect a teenager to carry. It didn't match the girl's plain, casual outfit and was more the kind of thing that a middle-aged person would own. The detective in Jack wondered if she'd stolen it.

Jack opened the handbag's metal clasp. Inside was a purse shaped like the face of a cat. That was more like it, she thought. Unzipping it, she found a few coins and a library card. The photograph matched the dead girl – even her hair was swept back in the same rough ponytail. Her name and address were clearly printed on the right-hand side.

Before Jack could search for her phone, Shauna walked into the office. 'The mother's coming in shortly. You'll probably want to be here when she identifies her.'

'Wasn't she with her when she died?'

'She arrived just before they pronounced, but I thought you might want a formal identification. I also thought you might want to meet her. I got some interesting reports from the nurses upstairs.'

Jack *was* interested in meeting the mother. She didn't have many other leads to go on. It would have all been different if Leia had died at the shopping centre. The scene would have been preserved and procedures followed for a sudden or suspicious death. Dying at the hospital made everything seem less official. Of course, it made sense for a formal identification to occur. Just because the girl had a library card with the name Leia Thompson, it didn't mean they could be certain it was her.

Gail Thompson arrived and immediately wanted to see her daughter. When she asked Shauna if Leia was okay, it became obvious she was in a severe state of shock.

Jack moved forward and took the woman's arm. 'My colleague is just going to check that your daughter is ready to view, let's sit down?' She gently moved her to a seat.

Aside from her age, Gail looked like a carbon copy of her daughter. She had the same dull-brown hair, worn in an identical pulled-back style, although hers was speckled with grey hairs. Her eyes were red-rimmed and sunken. She grasped Jack's arm. 'What happened? Was it an accident? The police officers didn't really say when they brought me to the hospital. Then she was just lying there. As the doctors did things...'

Jack took a moment to decide how to respond. 'We don't know yet. There'll be other tests they'll need to do.'

'I came down here as quick as I could. There was some confusion. They didn't know where she was. Somebody said she had been moved to another ward. This isn't a ward, is it? I know it isn't. I know... I know...' She started to sob.

Now Jack was confused. She reached around for the box of tissues strategically placed on the table beside them. She handed a couple to Gail. 'I thought you saw your daughter in A&E? When they brought her in...?'

Gail blew her nose and placed her hands on her knees still clutching the tissue. 'I was told she'd died. They left me with her for a few minutes and then took her away. I thought maybe... I hoped they were wrong. I asked a nurse where she had gone, and they said she might have moved ward. But I know this isn't a ward.'

'No, I'm sorry for the confusion, your daughter is here.

When anyone dies unexpectedly, then a post-mortem is carried out.' Jack wondered where Gail had been for the couple of hours since her daughter's death. She hoped that she wasn't walking the wards looking for Leia. The mortuary was in the basement of the hospital. It wouldn't have taken her long to find it. Jack placed a hand on Gail's shoulder.

Before she could ask her, Shauna returned. 'You can come through now, Mrs Thompson.'

'It's miss. I'm on my own.' Gail stood and glanced at Jack. 'But Leia's never been any trouble.'

Once inside the viewing room, no word was spoken for at least five minutes. Shauna had done a respectful job of laying out Leia's body for viewing. She was shrouded in a white sheet pulled up under her chin like a nativity angel. Gail stroked her daughter's face with her fingertips. Then she leant down and gently kissed her cheek. 'Goodbye, my love.'

'Can you confirm that this is your daughter, Leia Thompson,' Jack asked trying to hide the tremor in her voice. These were the times she'd gladly give up – the very worst part of her job.

Gail didn't answer. She stroked her daughter's hair and kissed her again. Then she rose and stared straight at Jack. 'Yes, that's right. How did she die?'

Gail Thompson's whole demeanour had suddenly changed. Jack wasn't sure if this was acceptance or something else; something more sinister. Gone were the tears and the incomprehension. She seemed in control and calm. Maybe she needed to see her daughter's body in the morgue to believe she was truly gone? The few other times that Jack had witnessed a parent in this situation, they'd appeared broken or distant or, at least, you could sense the tension of their attempt to rein in their emotions. But Gail was blank, emotionless.

Jack took a breath. 'We don't know. There will need to be

further tests.' She paused. 'It would help to have a full medical history.'

Gail gave a strained smile. 'Of course. Come by the house tomorrow and I'll give you all that I have. There's a lot of files. It's been a long and difficult road.' Delicately stroking her daughter's face with her fingertip, she said, 'But she's at peace now.'

Jack found herself nodding in response despite wondering why Gail seemed so keen to show them her daughter's medical files. 'Thanks.'

'What about her things? Can I take them?'

'What things?'

'Her clothes, bag... and anything she bought.'

Once again, Jack was taken aback. Guiding her by the arm, Jack led Gail into the hallway. 'I'm sorry. We'll need to keep them a while.'

'Why?' Gail snapped.

Jack felt a sense of uneasiness return with the tightening of her throat. 'It's how it is... evidence, you know.'

'Silly me, of course. Though I'm not sure what her taste in clothes will tell you.'

Her clothes told them a great deal. Most of it speculative. Her flowery pants were the type worn usually by a pre-pubescent child while the handbag was more likely to be carried by a much older woman. Jack speculated whether they were charity shop purchases. And the fact that as a teenager she was in town shopping on her own made her appear like an outcast. Besides her strange assortment of belongings, there was lots that didn't add up about Leia Thompson. Like why, as an apparently healthy teenager, she had undergone so many operations – and why such a young woman had succumbed to a heart attack, when she had only a minor heart condition.

'We can talk more about this tomorrow. Don't worry. I'll get someone to drop you home. Is there a relative or friend that can come and be with you? Or a neighbour?' Jack wondered if she could convince her superintendent to assign a Family Liaison Officer. Maybe there was more to the mother and daughter relationship that only having someone in the home watching Gail could discover.

'No. It's just me and Leia.' Gail clutched her bag to her chest as she stood to leave. 'We don't need anyone else.'

TWO

On the doorstep of the mid-terraced house stood a woman leaning on her walking stick. She waved as Jack pulled up. Jack could see signs of concern on her face as she approached. The events of the day must have distressed the poor woman. It's not often you plan a shopping trip and find yourself witnessing the death of a teenager. They'd been lucky to find her before she slipped back into the crowds at the mall. A police car was sent with the ambulance and the PC had taken down her address.

Colleen Harris stood aside to let Jack in. She walked straight into the front room. An Xbox controller sat on a side table alongside some AirPods.

'I told the kids to wait in their rooms until we finished. I don't want them hearing this.' Colleen sat down on the armchair and pointed at the sofa.

No wonder she was so upset if she had kids of a similar age. 'I'm sorry to do this but it will help in our investigation to know what happened and whether Leia said anything before the ambulance arrived.'

'Leia...was that her...it's such a pretty name.'

Jack nodded and took her notebook and pen out of her jacket pocket. 'When did you first see Leia?'

'It was funny. I'd seen her earlier in the day. She looked lost and I thought a little worried. I was going to approach her then, but she darted off towards the rag market. There was something odd about her.' Colleen's forehead creased. She reached for her handbag, knocking her walking stick to the floor as she did, and took out her vape. 'Do you mind?'

If it helped her remember, Jack could just about put up with it. 'Go ahead. When did you spot her again?'

'I'd just come out of Next. The one at the Bull Ring – the side entrance. I saw her stagger and fall. She was right in front of me. If I hadn't got that ruddy thing...' She pointed to the stick. 'I'd have tried to catch her. It wasn't like she had much meat on her, poor bab.'

'Then what happened?'

Colleen took a deep drag on the vape and exhaled. Sweet-smelling smoke wafted in Jack's direction. 'There was a young bloke hovering around... he'd got his phone out, so I told him to ring an ambulance. It was obvious we'd need one. She was so pale. I bent down. Then thought sod it. My knee's a pain, what-ever, so I knelt down next to her. Took her wrist and felt for a pulse. It was there, steady like. Bit fast if anything. I used to be the first-aider at work.'

'Was she unconscious? Did she say anything?' Maybe it would explain why she was in town alone with no shopping bags.

Wiping away a tear, Colleen replied, 'She said, *Mum*. Just that, then closed her eyes.'

The second witness Jack visited lived in a bedsit in Moseley. There was little room to sit in the small space. Jack sat on the edge of the unmade bed and Sanjeer Bahsin sat on the floor. He physically shook as he said, 'I'm sorry she died. Poor kid.'

'Thanks for all that you did to help.' Jack smiled.

'I only called the ambulance and held her hand. Everyone else, apart from that nice woman with the stick, just walked past. It was horrible.' He sniffed. 'I was late for work too. You couldn't...'

'What?'

'Let my boss know that I did a good thing. I need the job, or I'll lose this place.' He wiped his nose with the back of his sleeve.

Jack took down his boss's email. 'Was there anything else you remembered?'

'Yeah. She looked scared. I mean really scared. And she said *Mum*. Sort of like croaked it. She wasn't like a typical girl. No pouty lips and hair extensions. Pretty though. I guess.'

Scared seemed an odd thing to say. What was she scared of? Dying? Jack asked a few more questions and thanked Sanjeer.

'Do you think I'll get my jacket back?' he asked as she stood to leave.

'Your jacket?'

'Yeah. I covered her with it.' He paused and looked down. 'When she wet herself, like.'

The next morning, Jack waited in her car on Dennis Road in the South Yardley area of Birmingham, a stone's throw away from the Swan Shopping Centre. Miriam Ngozi pulled up in her silver Golf exactly on time. Jack had already filled her in on the reasons why they were here.

'Thanks for coming.' They both climbed out of their cars and Jack nearly put her hand out to shake, but then changed her mind. You were more likely to get a hug from Miriam than a handshake. She was Jack's favourite Family Liaison Officer – a middle-aged woman with a dry sense of humour who always managed to stay calm no matter how fraught the situation became. People always talked to Miriam. Her tightly weaved hair and glasses made her look professional yet approachable.

'That's okay. It sounded like you had problems booking me. My supervisor mentioned it.'

'Yeah. It's an unusual one. Could be a case of sudden death but there's something not right.'

'I'll keep you in the loop, don't worry,' Miriam replied, and Jack had no doubt she would.

A Family Liaison Officer's role was twofold. They were there to support the family, keeping them up to date with what was going on in an investigation. But their other role was to report back to the investigating officer about anything they found suspicious or concerning. Jack knew that she couldn't do Miriam's job. She wouldn't have the patience.

Miriam tried the doorbell. Jack didn't hear any sound so assumed it was broken and rapped on the door. No one answered, so she knocked harder. A moment later, Gail opened the door a fraction. When she saw who it was, she opened it wider.

After a quick greeting, Miriam and Jack followed Gail down the hallway and into the living room. It was far too chintzy for Jack. Too many cushions on the over-sized sofa. The nets at the window were pristine white and there wasn't a crumb on the beige carpet. Had Gail hoovered the place after returning from the hospital?

'Please, sit down. Tea? Coffee?' Gail asked.

Miriam touched her arm. 'Why don't you show me the kitchen? I can help you make them, and we can introduce ourselves. Jack, shall we get you something?'

'Coffee, milk, no sugar, please,' Jack responded.

As soon as they left the room, Jack glanced around looking for clues about the family dynamic. There were photos of Leia on every surface. Some showed a healthy toddler on the swings in the playground. Plump, cheerful and excited. Others, in the same style of silver frames, showed an older child in a hospital bed, or a wheelchair. Thin, pale, emaciated. Jack didn't need to be a doctor to know that something had happened to Leia during her early childhood.

Miriam brought in a tray and passed a coffee to Jack. There was nothing in Gail's demeanour that showed that she was recently bereaved. Was she keeping it together for them? Miriam took a seat beside Gail on the sofa which threatened to engulf her in its plushness. Jack pulled a chair from the dining table and sat opposite them. Gail glanced at her with a look of disdain as if she'd ruined the living room's ambiance.

Jack took a deep breath. 'Yesterday must have been a massive shock and I'm not here to question you. We just need to try and make sense of what happened.'

'My daughter died,' Gail said in a tiny voice.

Miriam placed her hand on Gail's knee. 'We need to try and find the cause of death. I'm sure you would want us to.'

'It wasn't unexpected.' Gail looked down at Miriam's hand and she promptly removed it.

'What do you mean?' Jack asked, leaning closer.

Gail sighed, stood up and opened the front of a bureau. She took out a large photo album and passed it to Jack, before sitting back down. 'She was always ill. Premature and that.'

Jack opened the front cover. The tiny baby in the photos lay swamped in a plastic incubator. Various tubes protruded from her arms, chest, bladder. 'How many weeks was she when she was born?' Jack asked, though babies were an enigma to her.

'Twenty-nine,' Gail said, proudly.

Jack made a note in her notebook. 'That must have been worrying for you.'

Gail shrugged. 'I knew she'd make it. She was such a fighter.'

A fighter as a baby but not now? Was that what she was implying?

'And the father?' Jack asked.

Gail pursed her lips as though about to spit. 'Useless.'

'Do you have his name?' Miriam asked. 'We can inform him of what's happened if you haven't managed to yet.'

Gail crossed her arms, resting them on her stomach. 'No point, love. He's dead.'

Jack raised her eyebrows. 'Dead?'

'Yeah. Car accident. Drunk behind the wheel, no doubt,' Gail said. 'I can't see the point in talking about him to be honest.'

She showed more emotion now then she had when they walked in. Her face was puce and her fists clenched around a tissue that she'd taken from a box on the table.

'I'll still need his name and the names of any living relatives. They have a right to know what's happened.'

'His name's Terry Doughty.'

Jack wrote it down. 'Leia was premature, you said, and always ill. Can you tell us more about that?'

'I've got her medical records ready for you, as you asked. I always got copies.' Gail stood. Then turned to Jack and Miriam. 'You'll have to follow me.'

Gail led them both up the stairs, along the brown carpeted corridor and to a room at the front of the house. Gail opened the door. The shelves were full of neatly stacked box files. A folded wheelchair was propped in a corner alongside a pair of hospital crutches. There were also hospital-like stands for drips and other machines that looked medical but Jack couldn't name.

'What's in the files?' Jack asked.

'Starting from when Leia was born...' Gail dragged her finger along the edge of each box, down and across each row. '...

until a month ago.' She stopped at the last box. 'These are her medical records.'

They'd need a team of officers to come and collect them. That is, if Gail gave her permission. Otherwise, they might need a warrant. 'Can we take these away?'

'No... I mean, only if you promise to return them. I need them. They are, well, Leia.' Gail started shaking. Tears began to fall down her face and Jack watched as she crumbled in front of them.

Miriam gently took her arm and led her back downstairs, leaving Jack on the landing. The medical records could hold vital clues that might either explain Leia's death or make it more suspicious. They would need to be scrutinised in detail. Taking out her radio she called the station's duty sergeant. 'Can you send a van to 5 Dennis Road, please. I need you to transport some medical records.'

With the arrangements agreed, Jack tried the doors on the other upstairs rooms. The first bedroom had the same old-fashioned feel as the rest of the house. The bed was neatly made and covered not by a quilt but an eiderdown. It was pretty, if you liked that sort of thing, embroidered with butterflies and emerald-green leaves. All the furniture was white, including a dressing table which carried only a comb and brush set that looked unused.

Jack closed the door softly and moved onto the other bedroom. She assumed this was Leia's and expected to see the usual teenage mess of clothes on the floor, fairy lights, and homework strewn on a desk. Instead, the room was almost a carbon copy of the other bedroom, only the eiderdown was covered in hares rather than butterflies and the dressing table had some books on it, at least. Jack walked over to pick one up and read the spine. *Pride and Prejudice*. The book underneath was *The Canterbury Tales*. Maybe this was the girl's English homework, Jack thought. She opened the cover to see a template pasted on to it. *Property of Leia Thompson.* Moving on to the white wardrobe, which was larger than the one in the adjacent room, Jack opened it to find that one side was taken up with shelving that held books, hundreds of them, mostly classical literature. On the other side were clothes: jeans, trousers and blouses. No sign of a school uniform.

Jack took a quick look in the chest of drawers which held her pants and socks, and a few plain coloured jumpers. Nothing of significance. It was only when she was leaving that she looked properly at the bed and realised it had a metal frame and could be lowered and risen. It was a hospital bed. Jack shivered.

Downstairs, she found Miriam and Gail in the kitchen. Gail was washing up the mugs and Miriam sat at the kitchen table. Jack took a chair next to her. 'What school did Leia attend?'

Gail removed her hands from the bowl, shook them and reached for a tea towel. 'She didn't.'

'She didn't attend school. Why was that?'

'Because she was homeschooled.' Gail sat opposite them, her back straight and shoulders tensed.

'As it's a sudden death, it would be helpful to have all her electronic devices, her phone, tablet, laptop, etc.,' Jack said. They hadn't found a phone with her which was strange in itself. What teenager didn't carry a phone?

'She never had any of those things. Wasn't interested.'

Jack tried to hide her surprise. After a moment, she went on. 'I notice that she likes to read.'

'You went into her room?' Gail's voice sharply rose.

'Yes. I did.' No point in denying it.

Miriam smiled. 'We're trying to help, Gail. In any incidence of sudden, unexplained death, we look for reasons and that sometimes means having to pry a little.'

Gail stood with enough force to knock over her chair. 'You're not suggesting she killed herself!' She started to wail. An inhuman sound like a cat being strangled. Miriam stood and took the woman in her arms as if sweeping her up like this was the most natural thing in the world. Jack just wanted to cover her ears. Instead, she stared at the mother falling apart in front of her and wondered what she was hiding. Jack felt like she was watching a stage play. All this drama was a distraction. She wondered when they'd meet the real Gail Thompson.

THREE

DS Nadia Begum pressed the doorbell beside the label that read GERALD CHAMBERS and waited.

It wasn't Marcus Barnet that answered the door. It was a young woman with braided blonde hair, wearing a tailored navy suit. 'Follow me,' she said brusquely.

Nadia was led inside and up an oak staircase to the first floor. The inside of the chambers was as austere as the front door had been. A short, dark passageway led to a waiting room. 'You can wait here. Marcus will be with you shortly.'

Nadia took out her laptop from her rucksack. On opening it, she spotted an email from her boss, DI Kent, outlining a new case. A quick glance told her it was the unexplained death of a child. After flagging it for future reading, Nadia reviewed the notes for the Sara Millings case. It was a rape case and the first that she'd taken from investigation to prosecution.

At least ten minutes passed before Marcus Barnet QC appeared, carrying his robes over one arm and a hat box in his right hand. Nadia guessed it contained his off-white wig which she could easily imagine him wearing. It wasn't much of a stretch. It would fit perfectly on his shaven head. Tall, Black and muscular, he could have been a model. No wonder Jack once had been in a relationship with him. Nadia could feel herself blushing under his gaze.

Then he smiled. 'So sorry for keeping you. I was in court, Detective Sergeant Begum. May I call you Nadia?'

He held out his hand. She still had her laptop on her knee. Instead of shaking his hand, for reasons of modesty, she put the laptop back into her bag and stood. 'It's fine, I managed to get some work done.'

'Great,' Marcus replied with a grin, before leading her to a room on the other side of the landing.

His office was vast. At one end sat a desk surrounded by shelving that held several weighty legal tomes. At the other was a large wooden table surrounded by eight solid chairs. In the middle of the room sat a well-worn patterned sofa and a coffee table. Marcus dropped his gown on the arm of the sofa as he passed and indicated for Nadia to take a seat at the table.

As Nadia did so, the sun from the leaded window shone straight into her eyes making it difficult to see, so she changed seats to one with her back to the light.

'Sorry about that. I'm always on at the clerk to get us some blinds, but it will ruin the look of the place apparently.' Marcus opened a box file that had been left out on the table. 'Now, the Jacobs case, correct?'

Nadia nodded. She was here to help Marcus go through the evidence, as well as to practice answering any questions that both sides might throw at her when she took the stand. He seemed assured and put her at ease as he talked through the initial interview that she'd had with Sara Millings, which was the part she dreaded.

'Sara told you that she asked Steven back to her student flat.' Marcus tapped his pen on the relevant page.

'Yes. They'd met at a pub, and he'd offered to walk her

home. She lived nearby.' As she answered, he made notes on a yellow legal pad.

'Did she ask him to come in?' He sucked the top of the pen. 'I mean, the flat was on the second floor so she could have said goodbye at the entrance.'

'I asked her that question...' Nadia turned the page of her copy of the statement. 'On the next page, second paragraph. "Did you ask Steven to come up to the flat?"'

'Ah, yes, and the response was, "No, not specifically. We were talking about a band we both liked, and he just followed me."' He continued. 'Do you think she was attracted to him?'

Nadia squirmed in her seat. 'You'll have to ask Sara that. When I met her, she was scared, distraught even. She clearly hated him. There was nothing in her statement to suggest she was interested in him sexually. She thought he was being friendly.'

'She invited him up to her flat, made him coffee...'

Nadia took a deep breath and bit her lip. 'And he held a knife to her throat and demanded that she took him to her bedroom.'

'We only have her word for that.'

What the hell was he doing? He's the prosecuting barrister. 'No, we have the knife.' Nadia tried to find the page in the evidence bundle with the details of the knife.

Marcus beat her to it and held up the photo. 'This could have been anyone's knife. It's the same as many young men might carry around, particularly if they did certain hobbies, like fishing.'

Nadia scowled. 'You really think Jacobs is the type to go fishing?'

Marcus put down the photo. 'You got angry... flustered. You can't do that. The defence is going to claim black is blue. You need to be ready for them. Good, quick response regarding the knife, though.'

'But you can't prove that – about the fishing, I mean,' Nadia muttered.

He followed up with several other questions arising from the interview and the investigation. And then he stared straight at her. 'What about Sara? Do you think she'll cope under the pressure?'

Nadia was silent for a moment. All she'd thought about recently was how Sara would cope when her rapist stood before her in court. 'I don't know. Have you met her yet?'

He nodded. 'Once. She held things together well. But I got the impression it was a struggle. You've met her more than that. What do you think?'

'I think she's been through a great deal. Especially with the publicity about the murder of Jacobs's father. But she does want this...her day in court.'

Christopher Jacobs had been murdered three months before. He was the local mayor and a nasty piece of work. A vigilante killer had taken exception to his dodgy dealings on the council and thrown him from his apartment's balcony. Good riddance, in Nadia's view.

Marcus stood up and walked over to her. 'Of course Sara does. Thank you, that's all my questions for now. I think we'll need a couple more sessions over the next day or so before the court date. I'll get Fiona to email you some possible times.' He led her to the door. 'Oh, and say hi to Jack for me.' The look in his eyes as he said this made Nadia wonder if he still had feelings for her boss.

FOUR

When Leia Thompson's medical records were delivered to the station that afternoon, it was clear that the officers who collected them hadn't noticed her mother's system of storing the boxes in date order. Jack decided there was little point even starting to look at the files until the mess was undone, so she set out to place each box alongside the back wall of the office in chronological order, from birth to death. The first box she examined contained doctor's files from January 2019 to April 2019. That box went near to the end of the poor girl's timeline. Jack had opened the tenth box of the evening when Nadia arrived. Jack quickly explained what she was attempting to do, and they both got stuck into the task.

'December to March 2017?' Nadia asked.

'Before the second-to-last box.' Jack took out another pile of folders. 'How did it go with Marcus?'

'He's a smooth operator.' Jack raised an eyebrow, and Nadia blushed. 'I mean he's good at his job. Had me questioning myself by the end of it.'

'He's smooth, all right,' Jack muttered. Their relationship had never been a serious one. A few interesting dates, one very nice weekend in a cottage in Suffolk, and some good times between the sheets. But something never really clicked. Each of them was always trying to win the upper hand. Maybe the problem was he wasn't a woman, and that was where her romantic preference usually, but not exclusively, lay. Whatever it was, their relationship never moved further than the physical and had quickly fizzled out.

It took them an hour to reorder the boxes. 'How sad that this child's life is summed up like this,' said Jack. It was the pure volume of medical notes that concerned her. 'It must have been bloody awful for the poor kid, going through so many procedures.'

'So, remind me, why are we investigating?' Nadia stood, rubbing her back. 'She was ill and she died. Surely this is more of a coroner's issue or one for the Safeguarding Board.'

Nadia had a point. It reminded Jack that she needed to prepare questions for her meeting that afternoon with Dr Jennifer Pride, the Lead Paediatrician on the case. She'd been concentrating on preparing the briefing for her staff, but a child's sudden death meant multiple agencies were involved; all with different agendas and priorities. This whole case could rapidly become a nightmare if she didn't get a quick handle on it. 'Let's just concentrate on our investigation and worry about all the other agencies later. It's going to be a circus before we know it. I just want to be clear that there's a criminal element to this case before we discuss it more widely.'

Nadia sat down on the floor and grabbed a chocolate bar from the front pocket of her rucksack. 'Do you want some?'

Jack shook her head. She was calorie counting. Her next big climb was only nine months away.

'So, what are you thinking, boss?' Nadia took a chunk out of the bar.

'Have you heard of Munchausen syndrome by proxy?' Jack asked.

'Where a parent deliberately harms their child for attention?' Nadia unwrapped more of the chocolate bar. 'There's been a lot in the news about it recently.'

'That's it. Though come to think of it, I'm sure it's called something else now.'

'Fabricated or induced illness by carers,' Nadia replied.

'Sorry?' Jack's stomach growled so she placed her hand on it, willing it to stop.

'That's what it's called now. We covered it in our training. I did a module on child abuse.' Nadia ate the last of the chocolate bar and screwed up the wrapper. 'It's a mental illness where a caregiver deliberately causes the symptoms of an illness.' She glanced over to the boxes. 'All this though. Someone would have noticed, surely.'

'The autopsy was bizarre.' Jack told Nadia about the scars and lack of disease. 'We need to speak to the doctors involved in her care. It's going to take forever. But you're right, if her illnesses were fabricated or induced by her mother, I just don't get why it wasn't picked up.'

'Maybe she saw lots of different doctors, looking for different causes of symptoms and pain?' Nadia stood up and lifted the first box. 'We should start by listing the specialists she saw. Have you got a list of her GPs too?'

Jack had asked Miriam to support Gail in making a list of her previous addresses and doctors. She sent her a text to see if that was complete. After pressing Send, Jack checked the time and felt a surge of guilt for disturbing her colleague at one in the morning. Then she checked her email and was surprised to find that Miriam had just sent her an email with an attachment marked **GT further information**. Clearly, she was burning the midnight oil too.

As Nadia listed the consultants and hospital doctors that Leia had seen, Jack went through the addresses and GP details. Gail and Leia moved on average every four months, always staying within the area of the West Midlands. Most of their addresses were in Birmingham, but they'd also lived in Wolver-hampton, Walsall, Coventry and Solihull. Jack made a note of Leia's latest GP and planned to ring him as soon as the practice opened.

By 2:30 a.m. Nadia had sifted through three of the boxes, barely making a dent in the row. Jack, meanwhile, had mapped out a timeline of addresses and GPs. She yawned, debating whether to go home or pour herself yet another coffee. 'We probably should take a break. The briefing starts at nine a.m.' Jack needed to get her thoughts together before then.

Nadia nodded. Before she left, she paused and looked back to the boxes.

'What is it?' asked Jack, rubbing her tired eyes.

'Nothing,' Nadia replied. 'I just can't imagine the life this girl had.'

Jack slept for a couple of hours and left her flat at 7:30 a.m. to travel to Danny's Climbing School. Though she was exhausted, she needed to stick with the strict regime she'd set herself or would have to cancel the Kanchenjunga expedition. Balancing her work as a police detective and her climbing was always an impossible task. The nine months until the expedition would pass quickly and there was plenty to do beforehand, not least to make sure she was fit. She completed her stretches in the changing room and went to look for her coach.

Danny was washing chalk off some of the lower holds on the climbing wall. Jack gave Danny a quick hug which she prob-ably needed more than he did.

'You've had someone in already today?'

'Yeah. Eliza's in town.'

A month ago, Eliza Summers had won a bronze medal at the Summer Games. Danny coached her whenever she was in the Midlands. Fortunately, she'd been able to use the route that Jack had been practising on ready for her trip. It was supposed to be a rough proximation of some of Kanchenjunga's rockier sections. Attached to the wall were a couple of extra-large climbing volumes that stuck out at such an angle to give even the most seasoned climber palpitations. This morning Jack would only have time to attempt the climb a couple of times. She chalked up her hands as Danny attached the belay rope to her harness.

Through the first easier section, Jack managed to move quickly and easily from one hold to the next. She felt surprisingly supple and alert considering her lack of sleep. Danny had added a trickier stretch in the next section which tested her strength. Holding on with a fingertip crimp, even for a few minutes, strained the tendons in her hand. But she fought through it and managed to use a knee bar to rest for a moment. Pushing off for a tricky hold, she misjudged the gap and her fingers slipped. She leant back into the swing, annoyed with herself as she dropped from the wall.

Her impatience with completing the climb, and her subsequent fall, reminded her that she couldn't rush her newest case. Getting to the truth about Leia was imperative. Having a time limit with the upcoming trip made that even more urgent.

Jack arrived at Lloyd House police station just in time for the start of the morning shift. There were several constables clogging up the stairs as she rushed to her office. The briefing she'd prepared was short and perfunctory. Jack had assigned every member of her small team a period of dates to concentrate on. She needed them to study each file for that period, listing all of the doctors and procedures that had taken place. They had to establish a firm timeline before they could proceed any further.

Within twenty minutes every person in the room was engrossed in this activity.

Meanwhile, Jack prepared for her afternoon meeting with the Lead Paediatrician. What she didn't want was for them to argue that this was purely a medical or social services problem. Whatever had happened, a child had died in suspicious circumstances. It was everyone's issue, but particularly a legal one.

Firstly, she opened the post-mortem report sent from Shauna. Every scar had been mapped; every procedure labelled. Jack created a spreadsheet with all of these on. She wanted to be ready to correlate procedures with dates and doctors, which was why the team were hunched over the medical records in silence. She assumed that Dr Jennifer Pride was doing the same with the records at the hospital. Jennifer, of course, had a distinct advantage in knowing what each procedure meant. Jack meticulously listed the medical terms that she didn't know. After an hour, she called Georgia over. 'Do me a favour.' She held out the sheet of paper. 'Can you find a medical dictionary online and see if you can explain these procedures.'

'Sure, boss.' Georgia took the paper off her as though it was a red card in a football match. This was a rare moment. Detective Constable Georgia Steele was usually bubbly and keen. Had she been pulled away from some significant event in the medical file she was scrutinising? Before she turned to go back to her desk, Jack asked, 'What period are you looking at?'

'December 2009 to April 2010.'

Jack did a mental calculation. Leia would have been three years old. 'Anything important?'

'She stopped walking.'

Jack leant forward in her chair. 'Excuse me.'

'She just stopped walking. One day she was fine. I mean she had asthma, eczema and other allergies. But apparently that's more likely in a premature baby. Then she was referred in January 2010 to a consultant because she stopped walking.'

'Do you have a name? Of the consultant, I mean?'

Georgia nodded. 'I'll email you my notes.'

When the email came through, Jack wrote down the consultant's name in her notebook. Mr Jarvis Taylor, Paediatric Consultant, Heartlands Hospital. Dr Pride would probably know the doctor, despite being based at a different Birmingham hospital. Perhaps she'd already spoken to him. After all, this was surely a key event in the life of Leia Thompson.

Jack looked back through her notebook and spotted the note that she'd made to call Leia's current GP. After spending a few minutes getting past their gatekeeper on reception, Jack was put through to Dr Min.

'Hello, can I help you?'

'My name's DI Jack Kent from West Midlands Police. I don't know if you have been made aware, but one of your patients, Leia Thompson, died suddenly two days ago.'

'Bear with me. I'll just get up her file.'

Jack tapped the table with her pen and waited for a response.

'Ah, yes. She was only fifteen. What a shame.'

'Have you seen her as a patient recently?'

'No. To be honest, I've never met her. She's a new patient. The practice nurse will have registered her. I can see here that Leia's also regularly seeing a paediatrician, so you might be better off speaking to them. Do you have their details?'

'Yes, I do. Thanks for your time.' It was symptomatic surely of her mother's wish not to have too many questions asked about her daughter's health that she'd had many different GPs and few had met her. Maybe she was moving from medical practitioner to practitioner and bleeding that person's empathy dry before moving on to another.

. . .

The foyer at Birmingham Children's Hospital was modern and inviting. The walls were freshly painted in bright colours. Sofas were strategically placed to enable families to sit together and there was a large football table game in the centre of the hall, although no one was playing on it. The noise, however, wasn't as inviting. The size of the space only seemed to exacerbate the shrill cries and shouts of the waiting hordes of children.

Jack strode up to the desk, ignoring the queue which earned her the wrath of the receptionist. The tall, imposing woman stared through her as though she wasn't there and shouted, 'Next!'

Instead of making a fuss, Jack placed her warrant card on the counter.

The woman sighed. 'Can I help you?' She didn't look as though she had any interest in doing so.

'Sorry. I'm late for a meeting with Dr Jennifer Pride. Could you direct me to her office and I'll get out of your hair.'

'Take the lift, third floor, second door on the left.' Then she pointedly turned to the next person in the queue and happily cooed at the baby they held in their arms.

It didn't take long to find Dr Pride's office. The door had been painted pink and adorned with a life-size Disney Princess. Jack knocked sharply on the door.

A soft voice came from the other side of the door. 'Come in.'

Jack strode in, smiling at the woman sitting behind a desk that filled the cramped space. Looking flustered, Jennifer rose out of her chair and proceeded to clear the mess on a chair for Jack, then she sat back down. Putting on her reading glasses that she'd been wearing on a chain, she said, 'Now then, Leia Thompson.'

'Yes. I'm deeply concerned about the cause of her death.'

Jennifer nodded. Her untidy blonde bun bobbed up and down. 'I agree. The post-mortem results are worrying. I haven't had a chance to request her medical records, but what I'd usually do in these circumstances is visit the parent with a local police officer, like yourself, and ask some questions.'

Jack coughed. 'I've got her medical records or at least those that her mother acquired over the years. We were kindly given them by her, and she has been...well, quite helpful in that regard.'

Jennifer took her glasses off and started to chew one of the arms. 'I guess you haven't had chance to look at them yet.'

Maybe she was being unfair expecting Dr Pride to have scrutinised Leia's medical notes as thoroughly as Jack had. The doctor would have had plenty of other patients to see in the last forty-eight hours so why would she be ahead of her in this case? But where was the urgency?

She might as well get straight to the point. 'Something odd happened when Leia was three.'

'What?'

'She stopped walking.'

Jennifer sucked in her cheeks. 'There can be a number of medical reasons for that. As I said, I'll need to look at her full medical records. But look, if I'm being frank, having looked at the autopsy report, this could just be a case of Sudden Death Syndrome. None of her previous conditions may be important here. Let's start with the obvious first. Rule that out and then move on.'

The hairs on the back of Jack's neck stood on end. 'Let's get this straight. If it turns out that Leia died of this Sudden Death thing, or say a heart attack, then we're not even going to look at the potentially fabricated illnesses that led to her medical procedures? Just how many young women die in this way?'

'There're about five hundred deaths a year from SDS. I couldn't tell you how many are young women. There could also be a valid reason for the medical interventions she underwent, such as phantom pain. All I'm saying is, let's not jump ahead.

We're here to find a possible cause of death for the coroner. Nothing more at this stage.'

'But wouldn't there be warning signs of something like myocarditis? I don't know... palpitations. That kind of thing?'

'Possibly. But she was a teenage girl. So, she could well have ignored them.' Jennifer started tapping the table with her pen. Jack gritted her teeth to stop herself raging at the doctor despite it not being her fault that Leia was dead.

'And her medical records, would they normally be shared with the patient's mother? Gail had everything including copies of heart traces.'

Jennifer started rearranging the files on her desk. Could she, at least, try to hide her impatience?

'It's not uncommon in paediatric cases for parents to request copies of their child's medical notes, DI Kent.'

'What about social services?' She must want to involve them, at least, in case there were previous reports of cruelty or abuse.

'Let's look at some dates.' Jennifer opened her laptop. 'Afternoon of the twenty-fifth?'

'What for?' *The multi-agency meeting, perhaps?*

'To meet with...' Jennifer looked towards the ceiling. 'The mother... Gail Thompson, isn't it?'

That was over a week away. 'I've already met her and we have a FLO in place. I'm sure we could arrange a meeting with her before then.'

'I have surgeries booked in. That's my first available date. Hopefully, the blood tests will be back from the autopsy, which will help. But I will contact social services to see if a multi-agency meeting is in order.'

Now we're getting somewhere. 'And you'll take a look at her medical records?'

'I'll make a start. Good job I can get by on a few hours' sleep a night.'

Jack could empathise with that. Of course, Jack was lucky enough to have a small team of four people currently working on the case, but it wasn't enough. If she could get Dr Pride to be more assertive about the need for a criminal investigation, then she could get more bodies assigned. At the moment, she ran the risk of having the team pulled off the investigation altogether. Why was she the only one fighting to discover what had happened to the poor girl?

Just before she left, Jack remembered to ask if Jennifer knew the first paediatrician involved in Leia's initial care. 'Do you happen to know a Mr Jarvis Taylor? He was a consultant at Heartlands Hospital.'

Jennifer shook her head. 'Doesn't ring a bell.'

'When you take a look at your records, he was the doctor that Leia was referred to after she stopped walking.' Jack rubbed her forehead with her fingertips, aware that a migraine was starting. 'How would we go about finding him?'

'The General Medical Council would be your best bet. But I will ask around and see if he's still in the Midlands.'

'Thanks. I'll contact the GMC then.'

By the time she reached the elevators, Jack's head was threatening to explode, and nausea rose from her stomach. She didn't often experience migraines, but when she did, they were bad. Fortunately, she had some strong medication in the glove compartment in her car that a doctor at Everest Base Camp had prescribed to her. Swigging from the water bottle she kept in her gym bag, Jack swallowed two tablets down. She couldn't take them quick enough.

It wasn't often that she allowed a case to get to her, but the death of Leia Thompson made her feel helpless in a way she hadn't before. Maybe this was because it involved a child. She needed one concrete piece of evidence to prove that Leia's death was unnatural, or she feared the case would be removed from her and a killer would walk free.

FIVE

Jack was on a video call on her laptop with Sherpa Norbu, one of her guides for her forthcoming expedition, when she received an incoming call from Miriam. She couldn't ignore it. Work would come first until the very last moment before she went climbing. 'Norbu, I'm sorry, can we continue this next week? I'll follow up with the sponsors, and can you sort out the issue with the Nepalese Embassy?'

Norbu nodded, waving his pen in the air. 'That might take me a longer than a week. Sure, sure.'

By the time he'd signed off, her phone had stopped ringing so she called Miriam back.

'Can you come over?' Miriam said. Jack heard an anxiety in her voice that wasn't usual for the FLO.

'Yeah, I'll be right there.' With a stomach rumble, Jack was suddenly aware how little food she'd had that day. 'Have you eaten? I can pick something up?'

'We have, but bring food if you need to.' Miriam sighed. 'Gail's not in a good place. She's holding stuff back and I thought you might be able to help her understand what's happening.'

Jack had already picked up her keys and rucksack. 'Course. On my way.'

It took half an hour to get to Gail's house, with a quick stop at a local supermarket for cooked chicken thighs and salad. Miriam answered the door. She seemed to have aged overnight. Jack noticed grey at the roots of her weave and wondered why she hadn't spotted them before.

Entering the kitchen, she found Gail sitting at the table, ripping a tissue apart into small white pieces of confetti. 'It's my fault, it's my fault.'

Jack sat down opposite her, taking her hands in hers. 'What is?'

Without warning, Gail stood and screamed, 'Out! I shouldn't have let her out!'

Miriam stroked Gail's shoulders, urging her to sit back down. Gail stared at the tall woman but didn't move. Miriam muttered, 'It's okay, it's okay,' over and over.

Jack waited, watching Gail's face begin to relax, then she said, 'Why do you say that? Wasn't Leia allowed to go out?'

'I knew this would happen.' Spittle flew from Gail's lips. 'I just knew it.'

Jack decided to take another approach. 'Tell me about a usual day with Leia,' she coaxed.

Taking a deep breath, Gail stared at Jack and said, 'The alarm goes off at seven and we both get up. Leia waits for me to have a shower first, because I make breakfast.'

'What does she do while you take a shower?' Jack wondered for a moment what normal teenagers did. She expected them to be difficult to rouse and when they did get up, they'd spend ages scrolling through their social media to check they hadn't missed any gossip. But Leia wasn't your average teenager.

'She'd take her pills,' Gail continued. 'I leave them ready for her on the bedside table every night with a bottle of water.'

Jack gave what she hoped was a reassuring smile. 'That must have been hard for her. Taking pills every day, I mean.' She nodded at Miriam, who understood this as an unspoken cue to check the pills on the bedside table. 'What would happen next?'

'We'd have breakfast. Leia can't have too much sugar, dairy or gluten so we usually had gluten-free toasted bread with a little vegan spread on it. It wasn't to my taste, but needs must.'

Talking about breakfast made Jack's stomach rumble. She tried to avoid looking at the plastic bag holding her food that she'd left on the table. 'Then what did you usually do on, say, a Saturday?' She wanted to know their routine on the same day as the week that Leia died. Was it usual for her to go to town on her own?

'Leia would read while I did the housework. Later we'd watch a film.'

'Did Leia not help with the housework?'

Gail snorted, eyes bulging. 'She was always too ill for that kind of thing. I looked after her, fed her, did all of the cleaning. She just couldn't, it would kill her.' Tears came first, then chest-wracking sobs. Jack passed her more tissues from the half-empty box.

It became obvious that Gail wasn't going to say much more. Miriam returned and started rubbing her back, before suggesting that Gail might like to take another of the pills the doctor had given her and have a lie-down.

Jack watched them both head upstairs before reaching for the carrier bag. She opened a drawer in search of cutlery. Instead, she found boxes and boxes of medication. Forgetting her hunger for a moment, Jack turned each packet and bottle over and took a photo of the labels with her phone. When she was finished, she opened a few more drawers until she found a fork to eat her salad with.

Miriam came down the stairs a little while after. 'She's asleep. Thanks for coming. She was literally climbing the walls until you got here. I think she just wanted to say it.'

'Say what?' Jack asked before taking another bite of a chicken thigh.

'That it's her fault Leia died.' Miriam rubbed her finger over an imaginary mark on the kitchen work surface. 'Did you notice how everything she described to you came back to her. *I made the breakfast. It wasn't what I liked.* Implying that all that she did was for her daughter, and she had to give things up. Do you know I eat Weetabix every morning because it's all my son will eat? No, of course you don't know that because my kid's needs come first and it's not something I'd mention.'

Jack knew she'd have to do more research about fabricated illness, but she'd always thought it was an extreme kind of attention seeking. 'I went to see Dr Pride, the Lead Paediatrician that the coroner appointed, today.'

'And?' Miriam raised an eyebrow.

'She hasn't even looked at the case yet. I get the impression that she'd be happy to find a simple reason for Leia's death, so it doesn't impact on her workload.'

Miriam nodded. 'Must be difficult dealing with dead kids though. She also works at the children's hospital, doesn't she?'

'Yeah, she does...maybe I'm being unkind. Her workload must be as crazy as mine.' Jack shovelled the last of her salad into her mouth. She glanced at her watch. It was nearly 10 p.m. An early dinner for her. 'Is there anything else I need to be aware of?'

Miriam paused for a second. 'Oh yeah. I took some pictures of the pills on her bedside table. They were already laid out for the next doses.' Miriam showed Jack the photos on her phone.

'Can you forward them to me? Oh, and thanks for calling

me. We need a better picture of what's been going on here. Can you contact social services if you get a chance too? I don't think we can wait for the safeguarding meetings. We need some concrete reasons why we can continue investigating Leia's death or we'll both be assigned to another case.' Jack stood to leave.

Back home, Jack fell asleep on the sofa at 2 a.m. Her laptop screen was left open on a pharmacy website. Her notebook had fallen to the floor. Her dreams were full of doctors wearing stethoscopes and feeling for her pulse. One doctor in particular was stroking her arm and making her heart beat at a furious rate. Jack jolted awake with the face of Dr Emily Fisher firmly planted in her mind.

Emily, with her blue eyes and thick blonde hair, had been a short-lived crush which turned into an even more short-lived relationship. Jack hadn't thought about her for months, not since Emily helped her with a case involving suspected organ trafficking. While she was still half asleep, Jack allowed herself to imagine Emily sitting next to her, helping her to decipher the medical aspects of the case as Jack lazily stroked Emily's thigh.

When she woke, it struck Jack that contacting Emily wasn't a bad idea. After all, she had majored in Paediatrics, though she was now doing a stint in A&E. Nadia had bumped into her just the other week on a trip to Casualty with her father. Reaching for her phone, Jack found Emily's number. She let the call ring out until she reached the answerphone. *This is Dr Emily Fisher, or just Ems if we're mates. I'm busy right now but you know what to do.* Jack didn't wait for the beep, she cut the call. Emily was probably on shift; she'd try again later – or at least that's what she told herself.

· · ·

The next morning, the office was buzzing with activity. Each member of Jack's team had been assigned a job to do by email, while she stared at the list of medical conditions on the wall. Georgia had checked them in a medical dictionary and started grouping them into designations – autoimmune, hereditary, allergies and a couple of other categories that Jack wasn't aware of.

Georgia appeared at her side in front of the board. 'I thought grouping them might help.'

'When did you get your medical degree?' Jack asked.

Georgia grinned. 'I Googled stuff. It's pretty elementary.' She paused, her smile waning. 'I haven't told you before, but they've diagnosed my daughter with an autoimmune condition.'

Jack turned to face her. 'Why didn't you mention it?'

'It's why I'm still working part time despite her starting nursery. I need to take her to regular appointments.' Georgia pointed to one of the conditions listed on the board. Juvenile rheumatoid arthritis. 'I did wonder if that might explain Leia's walking issue. But the other symptoms just don't add up.'

'Who would do this to a child? Put them through unnecessary medical procedures and pain.'

Georgia sat back onto one of the desks. 'When Caitlyn was first ill, they tested for so many things. We were in and out of the hospital, often staying overnight. We just wanted to know what it was and we wanted to know that she would be well again.' Georgia coughed as if to cover her emotion. 'We wanted to know that she wasn't going to die.'

'I'm sorry you're going through this.'

Georgia shrugged. 'To be honest, it makes you grateful for small things. Caitlyn loves to go to the sensory play area and when we help her to climb over the felt blocks. She's never going to climb mountains though.'

Georgia resumed her work categorising the conditions Leia had been diagnosed with, and Jack headed for the back stairs, reaching for her phone. If she was lucky, Emily would have been on the early shift and she might just catch her. Jack dialled her number and was met with an immediate, brusque, 'Hi.'

'It's Jack.'

'I know, I still have your number stored on my phone. Is this some kind of medical emergency? Have you found some more organ traffickers?'

Hearing Emily's soft laugh, Jack's legs began to shake. 'How did you guess? But seriously, I was wondering if you could help me with a new case. It may involve a fabricated illness... It's a child, so I thought you might have some insights to share?'

'What time is it?' Jack imagined Emily checking her watch. 'How about brunch at Mandy's, in half an hour?'

'That would work. See you then.'

Before leaving, Jack fired off an email to the General Medical Council. Maybe they could tell her where Mr Jarvis Taylor now worked. If he was, in fact, still practising medicine, as he wasn't showing up on the public registry.

The streets near Emily's apartment were very different to how Jack remembered them. The shop beside Mandy's Cafe was now a furniture shop with various modern chairs on display. The street was at the edge of the latest round of gentrification. How did she miss all these changes?

Through the cafe window, she saw Emily sitting in a booth, digging into a salmon and cream cheese bagel. Jack wasn't surprised that she hadn't waited for her arrival to order. Emily was always starving after a shift. Jack watched fondly as some of the cream cheese slid down her chin, and Emily's tongue flicked out to meet it. As Jack entered the cafe and ordered an expresso and a bacon bagel at the till, she hoped Emily was staring at her in the same way.

Sitting opposite each other in the booth, they ate in a

comfortable silence. Jack was conscious of the heat of Emily's legs that were close to her own under the table. Occasionally, their eyes met causing them both to smile.

Emily finished her food first. After drinking a slurp of her coffee, she said, 'I wondered if we'd cross paths again.'

Did she wink? Jack wasn't sure. 'I hoped we would too.' The statement was almost muffled by her next bite of bagel.

'Fabricated illness then. It's not really my field.' Emily dabbed the corner of her lips with a paper serviette. 'I've had a fair share of anxious mothers convinced their child has meningitis because they have a slight rash, that kind of thing. But nothing more serious.'

'Even when you were in Paediatrics?' Jack tried to work out how long Emily had worked in that field. She was a paediatric resident when they first met, but since then she'd moved to Accident and Emergency.

'I'm still in Paeds. I'm the specialist registrar for the Emergency Department.'

Jack didn't have a clue how medicine worked. She probably should have listened more to Emily when they were seeing each other, but their relationship had been far more physical than cerebral. As she thought about old times, she hoped Emily didn't notice her blush. 'How do you know if someone is abusing their child by fabricating an illness?'

'Good question.' Emily swept her hair away from her face. 'I guess if I had a patient that presented with idiopathic pain and the caregiver was behaving unusually, for example, trying to point me in a particular way or was just too pushy, then I might take pause. A repeated medical history of similar event, perhaps. Lots of unnecessary surgery.'

'Sorry. You lost me at idiopathic pain.'

'Oh, that just means pain without a determinable cause.'

'Got it. Leia had undergone a whole string of unnecessary

operations. Surely that would have raised red flags every time she newly presented.'

'I'd have to look at her medical history, but it's possible that it did. There could be some coding on her notes that a layperson might not get. Frequent flyers at emergency departments do get labelled. I even heard of one US Emergency Department that drew airplane symbols on their notes.' Emily touched Jack's arm, grinning. 'I've never done that.'

'So what do you do, if you think someone is medically abusing a child?'

'First of all, I'd raise my concerns with a colleague and we'd use our safeguarding protocol. Our DSL would contact social services, for example.'

'DSL?' Jack never worked with minors other than the odd young scrote who crossed her path during a case.

'Designated Safeguarding Lead.'

'And what would happen next?'

'We'd keep the child and adult in the department and ensure they had a nurse with them at all times. Then, when the social worker arrives, we'd discuss our concerns. In extreme cases, the social worker would seek an order to remove the child from the adult's care. Although, that is rare.'

'And if that happened, it would be on their medical records?'

'Some notes would be. The referral to a social worker, for example.'

Jack didn't recall seeing any referrals in Leia's notes, but she'd not met with anyone in social care yet. 'Would they always report a concern? I mean, how on earth did this child keep slipping through the net. If you'd just seen her body—'

'To be honest, a lot of health professionals would treat the symptoms as they present. Say the child presented as having an appendicitis. That's what the clinician would concentrate on, and only that. They wouldn't question previous operations etc., unless they thought it was relevant.'

'But wouldn't the child need to have the correct symptoms for the doctor to diagnose an appendicitis?'

Emily sat back in the booth and Jack realised, for the first time, that she looked exhausted. Of course, Emily was probably thinking the same about her. Thanks to their chosen professions, lack of sleep was killing them both. Emily finally answered, 'All of the symptoms including a temperature could be faked by an accomplished abuser, to be honest. They couldn't make anything appear on a scan, but if they caused enough fuss, then they'd likely go ahead with the operation rather than risk a burst appendix. Bloodwork can't be faked, but results can take time and at busy periods...' Emily shrugged. 'It's a very complex relationship.'

'What is?'

'The relationship between an abused child and their abuser.'

SIX

Sara Millings sat on the chair in front of Nadia. Her blonde hair was much longer than Nadia remembered and she'd stopped incessantly curling it around her fingers. Nadia wondered how soon she'd adopt that habit again once the court case started.

'Why can't I be in the court every day?'

This was the third time Sara had asked that question. 'You can watch after you've given evidence but not before.'

Sara nodded. 'I just want him to see me every day and I want to be there when they say guilty.'

Hearing this made Nadia nervous. The evidence pointed to his guilt, of course, but anything could happen in court. Nadia had told Sara this countless times. She hoped Sara would get the justice she deserved, but she hated to think about how it would destroy her if she didn't.

Sara picked at a loose thread on her jumper. 'I've made the right decision, haven't I? Not recording my statement, I mean.'

'Yes, of course.' Nadia thought she was brave deciding to read out her statement herself. Doing so would be more powerful; she could look the jurors in the eye as she explained what that bastard did to her. The statement was already impactful on its own. Sara didn't pull any punches, particularly, in terms of how she felt. *I wanted to die*, she'd written, *I needed this to end.* Nadia knew how that felt. She knew from her own experience that at a certain point your mind switches off. It's like the rape isn't happening to you, it's happening to your body, while your mind is numb. That's why the struggling stops, the screaming ends. You're dead inside.

Neither woman said anything for a while, each lost in their own private thoughts. Then Sara shot out of the chair, making Nadia jump. 'Coffee. I haven't even offered. Sorry.'

'Thanks. Milk, two sugars.'

While Sara made the coffee, Nadia considered whether she could be as brave as Sara, if she were in her shoes. Justice had never happened for the crime committed against her. No suspect had ever been charged because she'd never reported what happened to her. The shame on her family would have been too much. She always wondered how many Muslim women and girls kept their rapes and sexual assaults secret, like she had. She knew that many would never report it, whether the rape was committed by friends or family members, or by a stranger, as hers was.

Returning with the drinks, Sara smiled as she placed them on the table. 'Tell me again what happens at court, from the beginning,' she said as she sat back down.

'We're going there for the run-through tomorrow.' Marcus had arranged a day at the Crown Court so Sara could see where she would wait to be called as well as the inside of the courtroom.

'I know, but I need to be prepared. I don't want to show Mr Barnet that I'm upset. He might try and persuade me to do the video.'

Nadia explained again how they expected the trial to run, still worried that Sara wouldn't get the justice she deserved.

. . .

An hour later, Nadia pulled into the university and parked in front of the seventies concrete-built administration block. She didn't need to show her identity badge. The receptionist shouted, 'Dave!'

The head of security appeared. He motioned her to his office. Handing Nadia a file, he said, 'Those are the ones we had in.'

Nadia didn't open the file, just popped it into her backpack. She was right. There had been others. But it didn't give her any comfort. It could all be too late for Sara if the trial didn't go well.

SEVEN

Every muscle begged her to stop, but Jack refused to listen. Her gym routine was already suffering from neglect and, no matter what, she wasn't going to postpone the climb until later in the year. Kanchenjunga could only be ascended in either May or November. The weather and ice conditions would make the mountain too dangerous to climb in most other months.

Jack had requested ten weeks leave for the trip and was still awaiting final approval from on high which would only come a month before she left. Half of her time away would be unpaid, but luckily her sponsors paid for the trip itself. Though that also meant she'd have to make time to give them something back in terms of promotional tours and photo opportunities. Grimacing at the thought of the trappings of celebrity, she pulled down the weights on the lat pull-down machine. Just another ten to go.

Taking out her phone afterwards, she saw two missed calls. One from Sherpa Norbu and one from Miriam. She quickly got dressed and headed for the cafe. After buying a juice, she found Miriam's number and pressed dial. 'Everything okay?'

'Yeah. Sorry for the early call.'

Jack glanced at the large, metal clock in the cafe. It was only 7 a.m. 'No worries, what's going on?'

'It's just that Gail keeps mentioning Leia's current doctor. A Dr, err... Sharma. She wants to know if we'd like to meet him.'

Jack tried to recall that name from the medical record she'd read, but drew a blank. 'Sure. How quickly can it be arranged?'

'Today, she reckons. Shall I set it up?'

'Please. Oh and, Miriam. How is she?'

Miriam's voice dropped to a whisper. 'Quite cheerful. Too bloody cheerful, if you ask me.'

At the station, Jack took the last medical file off the pile on Georgia's desk. Georgia had taken it upon herself to scan all the files and place them into Leia's folder on the shared drive, and this folder was the only one that hadn't been entered yet.

Jack skim read each page for Dr Sharma's name, but she didn't spot it on any of the fifty pages. There were records of visits to Dr Davies, the GP before Dr Min, where Leia had reported experiencing pain in her legs and arms, and ongoing head and backaches. Were those symptoms forewarning the heart attack to come? Jack made a note to ask Dr Pride. Further in the file there were records of procedures which seemed to be written in Gail's hand. It made her wonder again how Gail managed to have so much of Leia's medical history? And why did she feel that she needed to have such thorough records? Most of Jack's own medical history had been recorded by expedition doctors, with copious notes covering injuries and illnesses she'd endured during climbs, that were sent back home to her GP. But Gail had far more than this. Jack made another note to ask Dr Pride exactly which medical notes were made available to parents in these circumstances.

Eventually, Jack returned the box to the pile. All the other members of her team had their heads bowed staring at laptop screens. 'Anyone come across a Dr Sharma? I'm assuming he's a hospital consultant.'

A few people, including Nadia, shook their heads. No one looked up from their screens. Jack wondered why Nadia had been quiet all morning, then she remembered that the court run-through with Sara Millings was taking place later. The case had deeply affected Nadia, leading to a period of sickness absence. Only when Nadia had been ready to discuss her own rape, was she able to move on. It couldn't be easy dragging it all up again.

'That's odd.' Jack stopped scanning through one of the files and looked up.

'What's up, boss?' Jayden, one of the PCs, asked.

'Come and have a look at this.' Jack held up a report of a scan. 'Read it through for me.'

She waited as Jayden did this. Finally, he shrugged. 'What's the problem? Leia had an infected gall bladder that needed removing.'

'But she didn't.'

'What do you mean?'

Jack waited to see if he'd catch on.

'The autopsy... you mean the gallbladder was healthy?'

'Yep. And still in situ.' What on earth had happened to this young girl? Had they got as far as operating and found that the organ was healthy so left it?

A half hour later, after searching through her notes, she couldn't find any answers. Her phone vibrated. A text from Miriam.

Sharma will meet with us. 5pm Tudor Manor Hospital, B13 8SQ.

Let's see what the mysterious Dr Sharma had to say for himself, Jack thought. She typed Tudor Manor Hospital into Google Maps and discovered it was a private clinic that specialised in teenage mental health, like CAMHs. This surprised her. Gail didn't appear to have the wealth to have a private consultant. Had she been referred from the NHS? Vaguely Jack recalled that when her sister had a varicose vein, she was referred to a private clinic for treatment at a weekend. This was all paid for by an over-stretched National Health Service, but Clare, being Clare, had told everyone that she'd paid to go private.

Tudor Manor Hospital sat in the middle of expansive grounds. The lush green lawn in front of the mock Tudor building looked freshly mowed. Jack imagined a gardener perched on a sit-on mower carving out the perfect lines, while plastic bins beside the automatic doors at the entrance gave the building a tacky edge.

Inside, Jack found Gail and Miriam sitting next to each other on shiny black sofas. Gail looked up from a glossy magazine. 'There's a picture of you in here,' she said, by way of greeting. 'You're advertising a watch.'

Jack didn't need to see the advert. Her reputation as a climber meant she had to do advertising shoots like this, but she avoided seeing them as much as possible. She did know climbers who had all of their publicity photographs framed and decorated their homes with them. She would never be one of those.

A tired-looking nurse approached them. Jack wondered if nurses in private medicine were as overworked as their NHS counterparts. 'Dr Sharma will see you now,' the nurse said, gesturing for them to follow her.

They were led to an office at the back of the building where, as you crossed the threshold, the smell of leather upholstery hit you smack in the face. A middle-aged man stood and motioned for the three of them to sit on armchairs in front of his tidy walnut desk. The rest of the office was a different matter. Piles of what could only be described as tat adorned the top of the filing cabinets. Perhaps this was the clinic's lost property.

'How are you, Gail? I've not slept since I heard the news,' the man said, his face etched in concern.

Gail took a handkerchief out of her bag and blew hard on it. 'I'm taking it day by day.'

Jack leant forward in her chair. 'Dr Sharma...'

'Call me Kish. Everyone does.' The doctor smiled.

Jack squirmed. The leather was too hard for her liking. 'Dr Sharma, what were you treating Leia for?'

'We treat the whole child here, Jack.'

DI Kent to you. Fake charisma never worked on her. She'd met plenty of this guy's sort on the mountain circuit. The type of character who wanted a piece of her fame but never did anything to earn it. 'What did that involve in terms of Leia? Was she an in-patient?'

'No. She wasn't,' Gail snapped.

Miriam moved her chair closer to Gail's. Jack wondered if they were about to witness another of Gail's outbursts.

'Then perhaps Dr Sharma could explain his involvement in her care.' Jack stared at him and waited.

He spent a few seconds brushing back his mop of jet-black hair before answering. 'Leia displayed some symptoms of a minor personality disorder. Not surprising considering her medical history. She'd been in and out of hospital for many years. Had mobility issues in the past. Her lack of regular attendance at a school meant that she spent little time with her peers, so I was treating that and supporting Gail with her care.'

'How did the personality disorder manifest itself?' Jack began making notes. As far as she was aware, all the other doctors had only treated her physical medical needs.

Gail spoke in almost a screech, loud enough to make Jack jump. 'She hit me. Okay. Are you happy now?'

'Gail. It's fine. No one is judging you.' Kishran stood and walked towards Gail. For a moment Jack thought he was going to hug her, but instead he sat on the front of his desk.

'How often did she hit you?' Jack asked.

'Once or twice. Does it matter? She was hurting inside and Kish was helping. He was so good with her. She listened to him. He even came to visit...'

'It was my job, Gail.'

Jack could have sworn he was blushing.

'So, who paid for her treatment? And what did it entail?'

'Well...'

Before Kishran could reply, Gail butted in. 'The NHS. Leia was referred by them. Wasn't she?' More tears flowed, then she began to howl rendering further conversation impossible. The session was over.

Miriam led Gail out of the building to her car.

Jack shouted after them, 'I'll see you tomorrow.' The meeting booked by Dr Jennifer Pride was to take place then. She turned, hoping to have a few more words with Dr Sharma, but he'd gone. Tempted as she was to ask the receptionist to fetch him, Jack decided that the meeting had thrown up more questions than answers. She would speak to Dr Sharma again, but maybe at a time of her choosing, when he wasn't expecting it.

That evening, Jack hoped to have a catch-up with both Sherpa Norbu and Martin Dereux, one of the climbers in her team. But not for the first time, Martin couldn't find the time for the call. Jack was beginning to regret choosing the French climber for the trip. If only Danny or even Ted had agreed. Danny had refused to leave his family, while Ted still wasn't properly talking to her after she'd falsely accused him of being a murderer a few months back. She couldn't say she blamed him.

Instead, Jack concentrated on catching up on emails from her team. Georgia had emailed her a list of the names of young people who had died of Sudden Death Syndrome in the Midlands in recent years. It was tagged – *worth following up?* It certainly wouldn't do any harm. Jack was shocked to see how long the list was. There was a brief description next to each one. Three boys died in separate incidents whilst playing football. A quick search of Google and she found that young people dying suddenly while playing a sport wasn't unheard of. Besides, they were found to have heart defects on post-mortem. She crossed those off the list and then emailed Georgia to ask her to follow up the rest. She'd highlighted three. All girls, a similar age to Leia and all unexplained deaths. It was probably a coincidence. But worth checking.

Jack's back began to ache. A message from Shauna asking her to the pub came as a relief. It meant she didn't have to spend the whole evening staring at her laptop screen. Of course, she had plenty of work to do – her emails were stacking up in their hundreds and the Thompson medical files still needed to be trawled. But she'd spent most of her afternoon preparing questions for the meeting with Gail tomorrow and prioritising the other work, so a night out at The Fox would be a healthy distraction.

Her friend had already bought them both pints of IPA. You could always count on Shauna to read your mind. Jack sat in their usual seats under the painting of Amy Winehouse, where they could scan the small bar for friends and those that they wished to avoid. It took two gulps of beer before Jack asked, 'Any news?'

Shauna shook her head, immediately knowing what Jack was referring to as if she were telepathic. 'I swear Toxicology are becoming slower and slower. Took three weeks for my last request. I kid you not. Unfortunately, the lazy shit of a detective didn't even try to chase up.'

Jack didn't bother asking the name of the detective. She'd only get a diatribe back about how little they deserved to be on the force. 'I'll chase them tomorrow.'

'I invited Fran too. She said that she's got planning to do.'

Fran was one of the few regulars that both Shauna and Jack had time for. She was an English teacher in a local secondary who'd transitioned over half term, expecting the school to have a heart attack. Instead, she'd mostly been met with warmth from students and adults alike. Jack picked up her phone and texted her. Jack was keen for a catch-up with her friend to see how things were going at school. As a teacher, Fran might also be able to help get more of a feel for Leia. Jack really needed to get to grips with what this young girl was like. At the moment all she knew about her was that she had a love of literature.

Jack's phone buzzed minutes later, and she smiled. Fran was on her way, after all.

Shauna stared at her. 'So, how's your love life?'

'Same as ever.' Jack turned and glanced around the bar. There were few other customers in.

'I hear that you met Emily the other day.'

Jack nearly spat out a mouthful of beer. 'And where the hell did you hear that?'

Shauna raised her pierced eyebrow. 'I have my sources.'

'Seriously, you freak me out sometimes,' Jack said. 'Anyway, it was just a work thing. I wanted to get her views on the Thompson case.'

'Just a work thing? She's single, attractive and, if I'm being honest, if I wasn't with the love of my life, I *would*.'

'Love of your life? This week's crush, more like.'

They sat in silence for a while. Jack tried not to think about Emily. It was ridiculous that just thinking of her made her blush, but maybe it was a sign that she was starting to heal after the loss of Hannah, her previous climbing partner and lover who'd died in an avalanche on Annapurna. The nightmares about her falling from that mountain had finally stopped. She still dreamt about her, but now they were good dreams.

Fran arrived ten minutes later. She walked in and plonked herself down on a vacant seat, looking flustered. Seeing her usually perfectly styled hair flow wildly in all directions made Jack smile.

'Sorry, my loves. I was grappling with Key Stage Four coursework. Believe me, you don't want to hear about it.' The bartender, Alice, must have spotted her arrival and seen her general state, and brought over her pint instead of waiting for her to go to the bar. 'Thanks, bab. I'll pop up and pay shortly. Did you two...?'

Both Jack and Shauna shook their heads; they still had half a pint remaining and it was a school night. After Fran had filled them on her life and how she was struggling with such a busy workload, the conversation moved to Jack's work, and she decided it was the right time to bring up her case.

'Actually, Fran, I'm glad you're here. I wanted to ask you something.' Jack was pleased that she could change the subject. 'I'm dealing with the sudden death of a teenager.'

Fran shuddered. 'We had a death of a pupil last year. Cancer. The school and particularly her classmates are still not over it.' She seemed lost in thought for a moment, and then a tear fell. Fran brushed it away.

'Sorry to hear that.' Jack placed her hand on top of Fran's. It wasn't often that her friend showed such public emotion.

'She was only fourteen. Fought courageously for years. Everyone loved her. School shut for the day of the funeral. We got counsellors in and built a memorial garden. So sad.'

Jack's heart sank. This was what normally happened when a teenager died – a public outpouring of grief from her peers. But Leia had no one in her life. No one to talk to about the anxiety of being a teenager, no one to share her life with other than her mother. When Jack was a teenager, she'd had Danny and other climbing friends to speak to. They'd talked for hours on the phone, or in chat rooms. Her school friends viewed her as a bit of an outsider, but she did have two close friends that shared their notes from missed lessons when she'd been away climbing. If she'd fallen from a mountain, there would have been others that would have grieved.

'Leia loved reading.'

'The girl that died?' Fran asked.

'Yes. She had all the classics in her room. *Pride and Prejudice, Frankenstein*, you name it.'

Fran smiled. 'How lovely. Her mother must have cared a little if she bought her all those. Books are expensive.'

'But she had no one. Didn't attend school. Had no friends.'

'Didn't attend school?' Fran's brow creased. 'Then you might want to talk to her welfare officer.'

'Welfare officer?' Jack asked.

'Yes. Someone from the Local Authority will know the family. I can give you a number later to call,' Fran said. 'How dreadful though. That poor girl.'

As Jack took another sip of her pint, she had a sudden thought. She would need to check it out. But there was one place Leia likely visited regularly.

EIGHT

That poor girl. The words entered Jack's head as she pulled up outside the Thompson house. The curtains were still drawn which was unexpected. It was just before 9 a.m. and Gail knew that Jack would be visiting then with Dr Pride.

Jack strode up to the front door, but before she knocked, the right-side neighbour's door flew open.

A woman with ash-blonde hair, smoking a cigarette, scowled at her. 'She's kept us up half the night with her screaming.'

'She has just lost her daughter.'

A toddler with a face covered in chocolate peered from the space between the doorframe and the woman's hip. 'Do you think she gave a damn about her poor kid. Always yelling at her, she were. And then she'd take her outside in a wheelchair. Just looking for sympathy if you ask me. Whenever I knocked to see if she'd keep an eye on my pair so I could nip to the shops, she weren't sitting in one.'

'In one?'

'A wheelchair.' The woman waved her cigarette at Jack. 'I don't reckon she ever needed a chair. And her mum kept her prisoner. She barely went out alone. It's not right. Not at her age. I reported her, you know. Not that anyone would listen.' Jack could hear a baby scream. 'I'd better see to her, she wants feeding.' The woman ushered her other child away from the door and slammed it.

Miriam must have heard the commotion. Gail's door swung open before Jack knocked again. Lines of worry were etched across Miriam's forehead. 'You'd better come in. Gail's not having the best day.'

In fact, Gail was in the kitchen wrestling with the hoover. 'I need to bloody clean. I have visitors.' She dropped the hoover and pointed to Miriam. 'And you. You're no help at all.' She stumbled then, as though tripping over an invisible obstacle, and fell to the ground. She lay curled up on the kitchen floor, rocking. 'I can't do this. My baby...my baby.'

Jack felt like she was watching a pantomime. She let Miriam help Gail to sit at the kitchen table. As Miriam went to the sink to get her a glass of water, there was a knock on the front door.

'I'll go,' said Jack. She opened the door to find Dr Jennifer Pride on the doorstep, holding a rather large briefcase.

'Sorry I'm late.' She stepped into the hallway. 'One of my patients took a turn for the worse overnight.'

Minutes later, they were all sat with biscuits, coffee and tea in the kitchen ready for the meeting. Miriam played the host, while Gail lay slumped across the table. Jack wondered how fruitful today would be.

Dr Pride started the conversation. 'Mrs Thompson, I'm so sorry for the loss of Leia. We're here today to try to make some sense of her death. We all want to know what happened, don't we?'

Gail didn't respond. This time she didn't even correct the title she'd been given.

Jennifer reached for her briefcase and took out a notebook

and her laptop. 'Now, I have Leia's medical records here. She was premature, I see.'

Gail looked up, reached for a tissue and blew her nose. Then said, 'Yes. Yes, she was. But she was a fighter.'

Jennifer smiled. 'I can see that. Did she have any ongoing health issues after that?'

'Nothing I couldn't handle.' It was interesting to watch Gail change as she spoke about the medical history of her daughter. Jack took a backseat and made notes not just of what Gail said, but also her demeanour. She perked up as she listed some of Leia's medical conditions. 'She had problems with her lungs so long-term asthma, eczema and her eyes were never good; she wore glasses from an early age.'

Jack didn't remember any glasses in the evidence bag. She made a note to go back and check.

Jennifer nodded as she wrote her notes. 'Then, at the age of three, Leia stopped walking. When did she start walking and did she meet her other milestones?'

'I don't remember. They've got the files.' Gail shot daggers at Miriam and Jack as though they were the enemy. All of her focus was now on the doctor.

'Ah. Let me see. I've got the notes from your health visitor here somewhere.' Jennifer opened her laptop and started pressing keys. A few moments later, she said, 'It appears that Leia reached her milestones in the expected sequence but was three to six months later than the average child. Of course, no child is actually average, and this would be expected with a premature baby. Does that ring a bell?'

'Oh yes, of course.' Gail wiped her nose again.

'Good. So at what age do you remember Leia walking?'

'She must have been about nineteen months old. She let go of the settee and just took a few steps before dropping to the floor to get her teddy bear.'

'Lovely. And her gait, the way she walked, that was okay?'

'Yes. It was. Once she got over the awkward foal stage.'

Jennifer looked up from her notes. 'Tell me about when Leia stopped walking. What happened leading up to then?'

'She woke up screaming. She couldn't get out of bed. And there was nothing I could do. Her legs wouldn't move.'

'She was paralysed?'

'No, she could move her toes, her feet, but not climb out of bed or stand properly.'

'Did anything happen in the days before? A fall or even a change in the daily routine?'

Jack could guess where Jennifer was going with this. Maybe it was a physical disorder or maybe something psychological.

'Nothing odd I can think of. We'd visited the nursery that had a place for Leia a couple of days before. I really liked it. The teachers were friendly and Leia played happily with other children.'

'And you took Leia to mother and toddler groups, playgroup prior to this?'

Gail slumped back in her chair, her voice rising a notch. 'No, not really. We moved a lot.'

'That wasn't an accusation.' Dr Pride smiled, tapping Gail on the hand. 'I just need to understand what happened. The medical notes show that no cause was found for Leia's inability to walk. And she started again a few months later.'

'That's because I trained her. I spent hours helping her. The doctors did nothing. They didn't understand.'

'What didn't they understand, Mrs Thompson?'

'It's miss, Miss Thompson. As usual, you don't give a jot about me and what we went through.' Gail stood, knocking her chair back in the process and stormed out of the kitchen. Miriam followed her.

'What do you think?' Jack asked Dr Pride when they were alone in the kitchen.

Jennifer shrugged. 'It could be an abusive relationship. It

could be that the child had psychological needs that have never been properly addressed. I'm not sure we're going to get much further today. Let's book in a multi-agency meeting. The coroner is pushing for an early meeting too.'

'You agree then that we should continue the police investigation.'

'We'll discuss it at the multi-agency meeting.' Dr Pride stood to go.

Jack remained seated. 'I just think there's something going on here. And I think the mother knows what happened to Leia because she caused all of this.' Was she the only one thinking that Gail was hiding something? How could she be? Her behaviour since Leia's death certainly made her look guilty.

Turning around to face Jack as she left, Jennifer said, 'It pays not to jump to conclusions.'

Jack was going to respond, but the doctor was right. To prove Gail's guilt, she needed more evidence.

A few minutes later, Miriam returned to the kitchen. 'Gail's taken some of her tablets. She'll be out like a light. Has the doctor gone?'

'Yeah.' Jack leant forward. 'What's your gut telling you?'

Miriam sat down. 'Honestly? I think Gail's an attention-seeker. Maybe even a narcissist. She's kept her daughter so close. Not letting anyone in. Not even the father. All she does is moan about herself when I'm alone with her.'

'Could she have harmed her daughter?'

'I wouldn't put it past her. But then where's the evidence? Her daughter was ill, she took her to the doctor. Isn't that what she's supposed to do? But none of the doctors she saw could find the cause of her illness, so is it the doctor's fault? Unless there's some physical evidence of neglect or abuse, well, we're kind of stuffed, aren't we?'

'The neighbour said that Leia hardly ever went out alone.'

'So?'

'I don't know why I didn't see it as significant at the time.'

'What?'

'Leia had a library card on her when she died. She loves books.'

Jack rushed upstairs to check and sure enough in the pile of books on the dressing table were some stamped with the name of the local library.

Manor Park Library was about to shut when Jack arrived. She held up the books in her hand. 'I'm returning these.'

A woman wearing a bright-red cardigan and a multi-coloured hairband motioned towards the grey bin at the front entrance. 'Just pop them in there.'

Jack held up her warrant card and the woman left her place behind her desk. 'Sorry, I didn't realise you were the police. Is it about that girl?'

'What girl?'

'Leia, the one that died. We only found out today. Finn's so cut up about it.'

'Finn?' Jack passed the librarian the books and she put them down on the desk.

'Yeah. Thick as thieves them two. Often had a natter when she came in.' The librarian leant forward and whispered conspiratorially, 'I reckon he had a crush on her.'

'Is Finn here?'

'He only works Tuesdays, Thursdays and Saturdays.'

'Can I have his address?'

'I'll have to ask my manager.'

It could wait until the morning. 'I'll be back tomorrow, then.' Jack had a strong feeling she was onto something. Maybe she would finally discover who Leia really was and learn more about her relationship with her mother.

. . .

When she got back to the station, Jack found Nadia in the breakout room. She needed her sergeant to check through the evidence bag. The lack of any glasses in Leia's possessions was another thing bothering her. 'You okay?'

'Not really, boss. You gotta minute?'

Jack involuntarily glanced at her watch as if that could tell her the answer. 'Sure. What's up?'

'The court run-through with Sara didn't go well yesterday.'

'Ah. It's probably nerves. I'm sure she'll be okay on the day.' This was Nadia's first big court case. Were her own worries about it rubbing off on Sara? It would be understandable, if so.

'She can't remember certain key bits of info when examined. I mean really key bits like about the knife.'

'Her statement is clear though. She just needs to have some more run-throughs.' Jack sighed. 'You can do this, Nadia. Is Marcus playing the accusatory prosecutor a little too hard?'

Nadia nodded.

'In the actual court, Marcus will call the prosecutor out on this. It will be easier.'

'But what if she can't do this? What if she clams up or makes a mistake? Do you think I should ask for her to do a video statement?'

'Check in with Sara and then decide. She's probably kicking herself and just needs some support. You can do this too, Nadia. Have some faith in yourself.'

Jack met Nadia's eyes which had now lost their look of desperation. 'Yes, boss.' Jack then told her what she needed from the evidence store. Seeming happier than before, though still stressed, Nadia went off to get it.

Jack was relieved to find that when she returned to the office the rest of her team were busy with their tasks and didn't need a pep talk as she was too tired to offer another one. She added her case notes to the day's log. Then she checked some of her emails and sent one to the path lab chasing up the toxicology samples. An email response flashed on her screen two seconds later. It was an automated message:

We are currently experiencing an unprecedented number of requests. We will strive to respond to you within five working days.

Sod that for a joke. Jack reached for her phone and dialled the number for the laboratory.

A young woman's voice answered. 'Hello. This is Annie Tolson. How can I help?'

'This is DI Jack Kent. I need to speak to the person tasked with the Leia Thompson case as a matter of urgency.'

'Hold the line, please.' The tinned music began and Jack swore under her breath.

An age later, the call was reconnected. 'I have Indira Jenkins for you.'

The call was connected.

'Hi. This is Indira. Is that DI Jack Kent?'

'Yeah. I'm enquiring about the Leia Thompson samples.'

'Yes. Yes. They are on my list. But then so are many other cases.'

'She was just a teenager, and we need a break on this case, Indira.' There was no harm in appealing to her. 'Could you rush it through?'

'I've had three detectives asking me the same thing this week. And, to be honest, they've waited much longer.'

'I'm sure. Are you a mum, Indira?'

'That's a little unfair.'

Jack bit her lip. She wouldn't normally do this, but... 'Imagine if your child suddenly died, you'd want answers as quickly as possible.' God strike her down. This was unfair and she knew it.

'I'll see what I can do, but as I said I have lots of cases, lots of tests to do, and if officers keep ringing me and distracting me, then they'll never be completed.'

'I understand. Thank you. As soon as you can and I won't bother you again.'

Indira had already ended the call, leaving Jack feeling like she needed a good wash.

An email came in from Dr Jennifer Pride with dates for the multi-agency review. Jack chose the first one and sent her reply. It was only a few days away. Would social services have more information? They hadn't yet answered Miriam's request. One of the issues holding this case back was the overload that all the public services suffered from. And it wouldn't be long before Jack's boss would expect her to tie this case up in a neat bow.

The last person she expected to see walk into the station that afternoon was Shauna. The pathologist occasionally attended case reviews but then only when invited, so having her storm into Jack's workspace looking ashen was more than a surprise.

'I've got a sister,' Shauna managed to blurt out before Jack questioned her presence.

The whole team stared in their direction.

'I'll take you for a coffee.' Jack led her friend out of the office and downstairs into the canteen. It was usually quiet at this time of the day. The new shift had just swapped over and the 9–5ers would be preparing to leave or already would have left the building.

Shauna was still shaking when Jack brought over a cup of the bitter machine coffee. 'Here.' She passed her the drink. 'Start from the beginning.'

'She just turned up at the morgue. And I have to say she's the spit of me. Minus the red hair, tattoos and piercings. She stood there and said, *I'm your sister, Michelle.*'

'I thought you were an only child.'

'So did I! Seems my dad had a whole other family before he had me. I wonder if there's anything else the bastard failed to mention.' Shauna took a gulp of the coffee and spat it back out. 'Jesus. Is there no sugar in it?'

Jack picked up the cup and went back to the machine and took two sachets of brown sugar from the bowl. When she got back to Shauna, she seemed a little calmer.

'Michelle wants me to go round to hers for dinner tonight, will you come?'

Jack couldn't think of anything worse than gate-crashing someone else's family reunion. 'I'm really busy right now.'

'Please, Jack. I don't think I can face them on my own. They're so, well, normal.'

Jack giggled then. Instantly regretting it, she tried to hide it with her hand.

Shauna glared at her. 'Oh, I'm sorry. Am I a joke to you now?'

'No, course not. Sorry.'

'I mean, Michelle's married with a child. Lives in Dickens Heath of all places. It is right by the canal so that's its only saving grace.'

Dickens Heath was the height of suburban Solihull. You had to have a decent income to buy a brick there.

Jack tried to get Shauna to look at the bright side. 'They haven't invited me, just you. And it will be great for you, having a family, I mean.'

'They said I could bring a friend if I wanted.'

'They meant your partner, not me.' Jack hoped she looked a little less shocked than she felt at being asked.

Shauna leant forward. 'I don't want them to know I'm a lesbian. Not yet anyway.'

'It's not illegal.'

'They might, well, not like lesbians.'

Shauna had always been a loud and proud queer woman.

This was a side of her that Jack had never seen. In fact, at times, Jack had envied the fact that Shauna didn't have any immediate family. Jack's relationship with her mother and sister was strained, to say the least. They just didn't get on. But she still made time for them, like she enjoyed the torture.

'Okay. I'll come with you.' Had she really said that out loud?

Shauna grasped her hands across the table. 'Thank you, mate. And you can drive us there, yeah?'

Of course, that was another reason she wanted her to go. Shauna didn't have a car, just her narrowboat and an account with the local taxi firm. This was going to be a long evening.

83 Moorings Drive was a new-build box with far too many windows for its narrow size. It also had a newly laid front and back lawn which Jack imagined would cause the owners problems later on. Many a weekend would be spent arguing about who'd mow the lawns.

Michelle opened the front door to welcome them and Jack gasped. Shauna was right. This woman was the spit of her. Her nose, eyes, mouth and chin were the same shape. Even her eyebrows and hairline. Obviously, the hair colour didn't match. Michelle's was a dark brown, Shauna's a deep red. And Michelle didn't have a tongue, lip, nose and eyebrow piercing. Nor did she have her neck and arms tattooed. But apart from that they could be twins.

A child appeared at her side. At least this one was free of chocolate stains. In fact, she was a tiny version of Michelle wearing a floral dress and plain cream tights. Noticing the visitors, she darted behind her mother's legs. 'This is your aunt, silly. I told you about her.'

'You must be Bella.' Shauna ducked down to the child's height, but for some reason, the girl was staring at Jack.

'What am I like? Come in, come in.' Michelle stood back from the door.

Bella continued to stare at Jack as she chose an armchair in the open-plan living area to sit down. Michelle and Shauna immediately began to talk ten to the dozen. Every time she looked back at Bella, she was still watching her but had appeared to have moved a few feet nearer like one of the Weeping Angels in Doctor Who.

A man who had to be her husband appeared at Michelle's shoulder. 'Can I get you a drink?'

'Do you have wine?'

'White or red?'

Having her father there must have given Bella even more confidence as she was now right beside Jack. 'White.' Jack didn't know what to do. She really didn't understand kids or know how to talk to them.

'Sauvignon or Pinot.'

'Whichever's open.' *Please, don't let this child touch me.*

It was too late; Bella thrust a toy in Jack's face. If an adult had behaved that way, she might have handcuffed them. Instead, she said, 'Thanks.' It was a doll. What was she meant to do with it? Could this doll like climbing? She began climbing the doll up the back of the sofa. To Jack's surprise, Bella laughed and cheered as her doll summited.

Michelle glanced over. 'There's some more dolls and other stuff in the box over there. Thank you for keeping her occupied. We have so much to chat about.'

Jack hoped Michelle didn't spot the daggers flying in her direction. Of course, Michelle didn't know that she'd put her only child in the hands of the world's worst babysitter. But she followed Bella to the box and found a more suitable outfit of shorts, T-shirt and pumps for Climbing Barbie. Bella chose another doll in a ballgown and copied Jack as she taught the doll how to traverse a chimney.

There was no one more relieved than Jack when the husband announced that dinner was ready. He placed Bella in her booster chair at the table, next to Jack, which she could have killed him for. Michelle and Shauna were still chatting about the times they didn't share.

Of course Jack was pleased that Shauna had a new family but couldn't help feeling worried that she'd somehow lose her best friend. As they all tucked into the butternut squash soup, Michelle asked, 'Jack, do you have kids of your own?'

Shauna snorted at this. 'Believe me, this perfect babysitting performance is a first from Jack.'

'I'd never have guessed.' Michelle smiled. 'Bella already adores you and she's very picky. How do you two know each other by the way?' She gestured to Shauna and Jack.

'Dead bodies,' Shauna answered. 'Jack is a detective inspector in Central Brum. We meet over dead bodies mostly.'

'Wow. Really. How interesting. And how long have you been a couple?'

Shauna was loving this. 'Ha ha! We're just friends. I mean, neither of us is straight exactly, but even so.'

What was she suggesting now? Jack was somehow not good enough for her? 'I've got more taste,' Jack interjected.

Shauna stuck her tongue out at her which Bella copied for the rest of the dinner. Jack was relieved when Shauna finally said, 'Thanks for the meal. It was so lovely, but I guess we should leave you now to put Bella to bed.'

Michelle glanced Jack's way and made her wonder whether she was going to ask her to put Bella to bed and read her a story, but she didn't. Instead, she said, 'We'll need to do it again soon and you, Jack, you must come too.'

Jack already knew she'd be busy that night, though she smiled politely.

Shauna must have read her mood in the car. Even so, she

continued to dig at her. 'When are you getting one of your own? You clearly have the knack.'

She changed the subject. 'You and your sister had a lot to talk about.'

'Do you know she only lived a few blocks from me growing up and the bastard used to pop round there every other weekend. I didn't have a clue, yet he told Michelle and her mum all about me. Even that I was a lesbian and how he'd thrown me out.'

'Bloody hell, Shaun.'

'I know. But Michelle couldn't say anything. She's like three years older than me, but she hated him too. He never hit her or anything, not like me, but then he never really needed to.'

Jack couldn't help comparing Leia's situation with her friends. At least Shauna got away from her abuse. How had Leia slipped through the net? Why was no one looking out for her? Everything pointed to her mother as an abuser. But there still wasn't enough to convict and there were too many unanswered questions. The glasses? The odd scans? Jack needed to get answers and soon.

NINE

On the way to Sara's flat, Nadia didn't care if she broke the speed limit. She didn't even think to use the blue lights that were attached to her back and front windscreens, and she didn't call for assistance. It was her job to protect Sara and she may well have failed. A car screeched in front of her as she passed a third set of lights just as they turned to red. The fist-waving occupant barely registered on her periphery. She just had to get there.

As she pulled into the road for Sara's flat, she calmed a little. 'Call Jack.'

Her mobile sprung to life. The call picked up on the first ring. 'What's up, Nadia? I thought you were in court all day.'

'It's Sara. I think she might have done something stupid. She sent me an email saying goodbye. I'm just arriving at her flat I think she's done something to herself.'

Reaching the apartment block, Nadia didn't wait for an answer from Jack; she stopped her car and flung open the door. Sprinting, she ran up the stairs to Sara's apartment and slammed on the front door with her hand, not even noticing the bruising she was inevitably causing. There was no answer. Just as she was about to attempt to break down the door, with the full force of her shoulder, it opened. Sara stood there wrapped in a blanket, pale and tiny. 'I took some pills,' she muttered.

Nadia threw her arms around the young woman. 'How many? Show me?'

'Just a few of the paracetamol.' Sara gestured to the open packet on the coffee table.

'How many's just a few.'

'Four? I don't know. Maybe more. Then I stopped myself.'

Four was too many, but it wouldn't kill her, surely. Even so, Nadia had to be sure she was safe. 'I'm taking you to the hospital.'

'No, it's fine. Honestly. I'm fine.' Sara burst into tears then. Nadia sat next to her on the sofa and hugged her, not caring if she was missing her testimony. She ignored the constant vibrations of her phone as Jack called her back.

Nadia knew what Sara was going through and couldn't blame her for her actions. She'd been there herself.

TEN

Finn sat in front of Jack, fiddling with a hole in the sleeve of his hoodie. If you ignored what he was wearing, he looked like one of the heroes from a classic novel. Pale skin, piercing blue eyes and floppy dark hair.

'I'm not surprised Leia's dead,' he muttered.

'Sorry. Can you explain what you mean by that.' The cupboard that was the only office space started to feel quite claustrophobic.

'She was always ill. Weeks would go by and I wouldn't see her. Then she'd be wheeled in by her mother and left while she went to the supermarket.'

'Gail would bring her here?'

'She used to until she found out that Leia was talking to me, then the bitch stopped bringing her. Leia had to sneak out.'

'What was their relationship like: Gail and Leia's?'

Finn shrugged. 'Leia used to tell me stories. I don't know whether they were true.'

'Stories?'

'About a princess that was imprisoned in a tower and a witch who fed her porridge that made her sick.'

'You think this was a true story about what was happening to Leia? Her mother was making her sick.' Finn should have told someone. This was a safeguarding issue.

He shrugged again. 'There were times when she missed coming because she had stomach pains and cramps. She was always making things up, but mostly she just sat and read books. She liked it when I suggested stuff for her.'

'Books, you mean.'

'It's part of my job. To recommend what to read next.'

Jack began to wonder what books he recommended. But there was nothing in the books Leia had borrowed to suggest that she was reading anything inappropriate.

'Let's go back to Gail. You said she was making Leia sick.'

'No. I said Leia made up stories. She was just sick. I think her dad told the staff she had cancer and we needed to keep a special eye on her.' He stood up. 'I've got to go now or I'll miss my bus home.'

'Wait. You said Leia's dad told you that she had cancer. When was this?'

'Dunno. A while ago.'

'Did Leia see a lot of her dad?'

'She emailed him sometimes. He was around more since he started lorry driving.'

So, she was in contact with him. 'Using the computers, here?'

'Yeah. I've got to go.' His voice rose with just a hint of anger that didn't go unnoticed by Jack.

That evening Jack couldn't sleep. The conversation with Finn played on her mind. Was Gail poisoning Leia? They needed the results from Pathology to prove that. Without thinking, she reached for her phone and dialled Emily's number. It rang three or four times before she answered. 'Hi... Jack. Do you have any idea what time it is?'

'Sorry... no. Quick question.'

'I'm on call, so was only napping, otherwise, I'd probably not speak to you again.'

Jack took a deep breath in an attempt to stop her heart racing. 'Leia came down with cramps and nausea on the occasions that she wanted to leave the house. Her health on other days, when she conformed to her mother's wishes, I guess, was better. Could she have been poisoned? What might that be with and how soon would it take effect?'

'It depends what she was given. If it was without her knowledge, it probably wasn't a pill unless her mother lied about what it was. More likely it was something she ate or drank. I'm not a poisoning expert, but surely it would show up in her toxicology?'

'We haven't had the results back yet. There are things that don't show up in blood tests though, aren't there?'

'Yeah. Did your pathologist do a hair sample too? Long-term poisoning might show up there. But look, Jack, much as I like talking to you in the middle of the night, I'm not your personal physician and the police aren't paying me a consultancy fee, so your best bet might be talking to the lead physician on your case.'

But their voice wouldn't give her palpitations. Christ, she was becoming more like a lovesick teenager by the day. 'I'm sorry, Emily.' Jack bit her tongue. 'Let me buy you breakfast to apologise.'

'I'm up now so you might as well.' The quick response.

How early was it? Jack glanced at the clock on her phone. 4:45 a.m. and she'd had no sleep. 'I'll meet you at Mandy's at six-thirty?'

'Great. And I want a full English with extra toast.'

.   .   .

Emily didn't look like she'd been woken up by the mad wonderings of a police detective. Her blonde bob looked freshly washed. You couldn't tell that her hair was shaved underneath until she swept it back behind her ears and became every lesbian's crush. Jack couldn't help smiling as she approached. 'I've ordered yours.' She passed Emily a mug of coffee. 'And this has just been brewed.'

'Good job I didn't fall back to sleep then.' Emily took a long gulp of her coffee.

Mandy, or at least the woman everyone called Mandy, arrived and plonked down a full English in front of them both. Neither spoke as they started to eat. Jack dared not to think about the calories and how much damage another missed gym session would do. At this rate, she wouldn't be able to run around the block, let alone climb up a mountain.

As if reading her mind, Emily asked, 'When do you start your expedition?'

Jack finished chewing her toast. 'End of April.'

'I don't know how you do it. Still, it keeps you in good shape.'

Jack could feel the blush start in her neck. 'Thanks,' she managed to mutter.

'Remind me, why did we split up?'

Really? Was she really asking this? And more importantly why, why was she asking this? 'No idea. Biggest mistake of my life.'

Emily took another bite of sausage, chewed and swallowed it. 'I think it had more to do with us not keeping office hours.'

That was probably true. Their time off never matched. Jack was working a nasty domestic violence case at the time and Emily had recently started her residency in Paediatrics. It was no wonder they never got to see each other. Neither spoke again for minutes. Jack began to wonder if Emily was weighing up whether it was worth giving it another go, or at least that was what she hoped.

They finished eating too soon. Mandy didn't waste any time grabbing their empty plates. They were still the only ones in the cafe. Maybe she thought she could get a smoke in before anyone else arrived. Emily took this as a cue and stood. 'Thanks for the breakfast. We must do it at a more civilised hour sometime.'

'Are you working today?' Jack asked. 'I thought you were on-call last night.'

Emily glanced at her phone. 'On shift in twenty minutes.'

Jack didn't need to look at her phone to know that there wasn't time to go to Danny's or the gym and, since she'd eaten, it wouldn't be a good idea either. 'I'll ring you...soon.'

Emily just smiled, got up and walked out the cafe.

Jack sought out Georgia as soon as she arrived at the station. The place she normally sat in the open-plan office was empty. Nadia sat in the seat next to it. 'Have you seen Georgia?' Jack asked.

'It's Friday,' Nadia answered, without looking up from the screen.

It took Jack a moment or two to work out the significance of that fact. 'Oh, yeah. She's not in today.'

'Did you want her for something special?' Nadia looked up this time.

'Aren't you giving evidence later?'

Nadia shook her head. 'One of the jurors took ill so the judge decided that we needed a long weekend. Either that or the judge did. Maybe he'd booked a weekend away?'

'How's Sara?' Jack sat down expecting a longer conversation.

'Better. She got the all-clear from the hospital. The doctors say she was lucky not to have done any damage. I'm going there after I've finished this.' She nodded at the screen.

'Umm. What day's her testimony due?'

'At this rate, after Christmas.'

Nadia could be right. This often happened in trials. Particularly ones that they expected to take a while to complete. 'I'm sure it will be sooner than that.' Jack sighed. 'I need you on this case too.'

'How's it going? Are we making progress?' Nadia asked.

'Yeah. We're only just discovering more about the real Leia. From what I've learnt so far, she felt trapped. I'm also wondering if she was poisoned.'

'Is there enough to go on?' Nadia bit her pen. 'Can we bring her mother in for questioning?'

'I've put a rush on with Toxicology and I'm thinking of having an early conversation with the Crown Prosecution Service. If she was being poisoned, then it would seem likely that it was her mother giving it to her as she barely went anywhere else except for the library.'

Nadia nodded. 'I'll finish this and I'll contact Toxicology again.'

'What is it that you're finishing off?'

'I'm checking some of the unsolved rape cases around the time of Sara's assault.' Tapping a file next to her, she continued, 'I know it might seem too late now the case is in court, but if I can find just one more person. One other young woman, a student maybe, then it will be less pressure on Sara, and Jacobs'll have less of a leg to stand on. I've already spoken to Security at the university and there were some suspicious incidents before her attack.'

'What's Marcus's view?' Jack wondered if for once he lacked confidence.

'He doesn't know I'm looking.' Nadia leant forward. 'You won't tell him?'

'When do I see him?'

'Thanks. It's not that I don't think we can convict Jacobs, it's more just to be sure. Just in case it's not enough. And if there are other victims out there, they deserve justice too.'

Jack gestured towards the laptop. 'Show me what you've got?' She was beginning to wonder herself if they'd done enough at the time. Maybe they should have looked for more evidence, witnesses, similar crimes.

Opening the lid of her laptop, Nadia opened a document. 'It's not much.' There was a list of dates and a string of complaints about a Peeping Tom.

'Where's this?'

'It's in the area of the student flats. There're about four different reports of a guy staring in through the window or following students home after a night out.' She opened one of the reports. 'A woman named Teresa O'Hara had been followed for half a mile from the pub. She managed to get hold of one of her friends who came to meet her. The guy then ran off.'

'Go and speak to her and take a photo of Jacobs.'

'You reckon it's worth it?'

'Won't know until you've spoken to her. Take one of the PCs with you. You might as well see if you can speak to all the women on your list.'

'What about this case?'

'It'll still be here when you get back.'

Jack couldn't afford to admonish herself or her team for missing the possible links with the Peeping Tom case. It might still have nothing to do with Jacobs, but as soon as she saw the document on Nadia's screen, a shiver passed down her spine. Call it police intuition. Nadia had also explained how the reports had been wrongly tagged by a police constable. When she'd originally

looked for other cases, before they pulled in Jacobs for questioning, none of them had shown up.

Jack was so worked up about the police constable's incom-
petence, she almost forgot what else had kept her awake last
night. She searched under her desk for her rucksack. She always
kept her notebook in the front pocket. Turning back through the
pages, she searched for a name. There it was. Terry Doughty,
Leia's father. She'd not checked he was dead, just taken Gail's
word for it, and by the sounds of it, he was on the scene at some
point to take Leia to the library and she had regular contact
with him.

Palms itching, Jack reached for her laptop and typed Terry's
name into the Police National Database. If he'd died in a car
crash, there would be some record. There was a few Terry
Doughtys, mostly petty criminals and all living in the wrong
parts of the country. There was also a suspicious death, but that
was a drug overdose. 'Bollocks.'

One of the PCs looked up. 'You okay, boss?'

'No, I'm not. We need to find the father.'

'Whose father?' asked PC Brown.

'Leia's. Her mother told us he was dead. But I was stupid
enough not to check it.'

'What's his name?' Jayden sat, pen poised.

'Terry Doughty. He works on the oil rigs and also as a lorry
driver.'

Jayden raised an eyebrow as if to question how she knew
this.

'Oh, and while you're at it, can you go and check the
evidence room for Leia's glasses. I sent Nadia the other day, but
she must've forgotten.'

Three hours later, and between them, they'd rung all of the
oil rig companies that they could find names for. One of them
had heard of Terry Doughty, but he'd been laid off the year
before and they didn't have a current address.

'We can't search all of the lorry firms. There must be thousands.' Jayden pointed out the obvious.

'I'm surprised he hasn't come forward. There's been media reports of Leia's death.'

'Only on *Midlands Today*. Maybe he's left the area.'

'He could be anywhere. If he was working the rigs, he could be in Scotland, I guess. He'd have some links there.' Jack began to chew her pen. 'Contact some of the local forces near to where he worked. It's possible he stayed up north. If he hasn't died after all. If he'd died of natural causes in Scotland, for example, then there might be no record of it on our systems to access.'

Jack gave up after 7 p.m. Her email inbox pinged as she shut down her laptop. It was a message from Jayden:

no sign of any glasses amongst Leia's personal effects.

Another mystery yet to be solved.

Instead of driving home, Jack stopped off at the climbing school. Danny was locking up. She ran towards him. 'Just give me half an hour.'

Danny sighed. 'Gemma's got tea on. She'll kill me.'

'Then just leave me with the keys.' Jack put on her best pleading look.

'You know I can't. If anyone found out you'd climbed alone, I'd be shut down in a heartbeat. And god forbid you fell and injured yourself.'

'Half an hour.'

Danny pushed her out of the way and turned the key in the lock. 'I'm not married to you, Jack. Sorry, mate.'

'If only you'd married me, you'd be up a mountain climbing now instead of washing dirty nappies.'

'The gym's still open. I'll send you a training session when I get home. Best I can do.'

Jack stuck her tongue out. 'I hate you sometimes, you know that.'

'Or you could come home with me. Gemma's made a shepherd's pie.' He started to walk to his car.

After sticking two fingers up after him, Jack walked towards her Range Rover. Gym it was then.

Before she started a series of reps on the weights, she texted Miriam to ask her to meet her at Gail's at eight in the morning. They needed to question her as to why she had lied about Terry's death.

When Jack trained, she relaxed. The harder the workout, the better and the more likely that she could see things with more clarity. Of course, a jog on the running machine or press-ups didn't replace the sheer joy of reaching a summit or the determination needed to conquer the ruggedness of a crag, but it did wipe away the daily stresses of police work. It also gave her time to think about her expedition.

Her main worry, other than her lack of time to train, concerned the abilities of the other climbers on her team. There were now two others joining her on the climb. Tomas Wilczek, a Polish mountaineer Jack rated as a strong and competent climber. He wasn't a risk-taker. He was more likely to forsake a summit than risk a death on descent. But his girlfriend was a different story. Maria Brody had the skills to be a world-class climber, but she didn't have the instinct. Jack hoped that the two of them, working together under her tutelage, would make an excellent team. The problem was that they were running out of time to prepare. Tomas was a doctor, Maria a television presenter and, despite their relationship, they lived in different countries. Then, of course, there was the elusive French climber, Dereux. If he didn't start turning up to planning meetings, he was off the trip. It was time for Jack to put her foot down.

She clenched her jaw and completed another round of reps.

The next morning, Jack arrived at Gail's house, not sure which version of Leia's mother she'd be greeted with today. Miriam had sent her a message that she was running late. Her younger son had refused to get out of bed. Jack knew that he was autistic and that Miriam often felt guilty that she was leaving her elder son with so much responsibility for his care. But she could never fault Miriam's commitment as a FLO.

Gail answered smiling. She quickly ushered Jack into the living room. 'Tea, coffee?'

'I'm fine, don't worry,' Jack said, wanting to get to the reason she was there as soon as possible.

'It's no bother. I'm having one.' Gail waited for Jack's reply.

'Coffee, then.'

With Gail in the kitchen, Jack had the chance to survey the room. It wasn't as neat and tidy as usual. A few condolence cards had been opened and left on a table instead of displayed. Jack opened each one and checked if any were from Finn. No joy. They were unlikely to be from relations of Gail's. No *aunties* or *uncles* present in the signatures. Maybe they were just from the neighbours. The envelopes were still at the bottom of the pile. There were no stamps on them, suggesting her assumption was correct.

'People are so kind, aren't they?'

Clearly, Gail had noticed her reading the cards. 'Yes. Have you had many cards from your relatives?'

'I don't have any.' Gail plonked Jack's coffee down on the table spilling some of it. She didn't make any attempt to wipe it up which Jack noted as unusual.

'How come?'

'There was only my mum. She died when I was in my twenties. Before I had Leia.' The doorbell rang. 'That must be Miriam.'

Jack waited for them both to sit down. 'I've just been asking Gail about her family.'

Miriam nodded. 'There isn't anyone. That's what you said to me.'

'Nobody.'

Jack expected a tear or two. But Gail seemed unperturbed. 'What about Leia's father? Tell me more about him.' Jack moved on to business.

'I met him at a nightclub. It wasn't my usual thing. Some of the girls at the store I worked at convinced me to go out with them. He was with his mates. Everyone paired up and, I guess, we were the last ones left. Lucky me.' Gail sipped her tea without smiling.

'When was this?' Jack asked.

'About twenty years ago. Our relationship was never that great. He'd go off with other women and then always end up back at mine if he needed somewhere to sleep.'

'And then Leia was born? Was he living with you then?' Jack asked the questions and Miriam took notes.

'He'd started on the rigs. He'd turn up every three months or so.'

'And what was he like as a father?'

Gail sighed. 'He doted on Leia. Always brought her something when he returned – a book, a cuddly toy, a new dress. He'd take her out to the park and then, after a few days, he'd get bored and disappear again.'

'Was he around when Leia was ill?' She knew he'd taken her to the library.

'Yes. But he never stayed long. He'd march in claiming he knew what was best for her and then just as suddenly march out again. After he'd interrogated all of her doctors, most of them wouldn't treat her anymore. When he'd gone, we had to find new ones.'

'Are you saying that Terry was the reason that you kept changing doctors?'

Gail stood up and her voice rose as her cheeks flushed. 'He never bloody helped. Not Leia. Not me. He was useless. I'm glad he's dead.'

'But he's not dead, is he, Gail?'

Jack watched her face carefully as the penny dropped. *We've caught you in one lie. Now for the rest.*

ELEVEN

Jack didn't know what to expect from Gail. Maybe she'd still claim that Terry Doughty was dead and buried. Although she supposed it was still possible that he wasn't alive. They hadn't found him.

But she didn't do that. Instead she started to sob theatrically. Her shoulders heaved as she cried, hiding her face with her hands.

'Where is Terry?' Jack asked.

Still Gail sobbed. Jack glanced across at Miriam, who frowned and made no attempt to comfort Gail. She said in a coarse tone, 'You have to tell us the truth, Gail.'

She sat up then and wiped her eyes with her hand. They looked remarkably dry. 'He's dead.' Gail waved her arm around the room. 'If he was alive, he'd be here, wouldn't he? As soon as he heard Leia was dead. He'd be here.'

Gail was hardly being fair. 'So, are you saying he might be alive? Does he have any friends? Maybe they know where he is?' Jack asked.

'Friends. He lost all those when he fleeced them dry.' She must have noticed Jack's questioning look. 'He was a gambler and a drinker so despite earning plenty of money on the rigs, he never kept it long. You're just confusing me now. I told you he's dead and buried.'

This was getting them nowhere. Miriam held out her notepad to Gail. 'Write down all the names and contact details for Terry's family and friends. Maybe we can get some sense out of them.'

Jack left them to it and returned to the station. She was the only one in the office. There was no overtime on offer on this case and the others had clearly chosen to spend the weekend with family. Of course, Jack should really be up a mountain, training for her next big climb. Checking her emails, none of the local police forces they had contacted had got back to her about Doughty. It was like he'd disappeared into a puff of dust.

If his gambling was as bad as Gail said it was, then it was worth searching for a credit record or banking history. Jack put in a search request with the Financial Investigation Unit. As she completed the email, a new message dropped into her mailbox. It was the toxicology results. Jack felt her heart race as she opened it.

The report listed a number of drugs which Jack would need to check against Leia's prescriptions. But there were two drugs that stood out. Large doses of Citalopram, an antidepressant, and Codeine. Jack didn't recall either of these featuring on her regular medication list. Finding the right file, she enlarged it to check. No reference to either drug appeared on the list.

She reached for her phone. Miriam answered immediately. 'Are you still with Gail?'

'Yes, I was just about to leave.'

'Can you ask her if she takes antidepressants and what sort?'

There was a silence for a few moments. 'Yes. She takes Citalopram.'

'Thanks.' Jack didn't bother asking if Leia had access to them. It was possible that this was suicide or an accidental overdose. But why go out shopping if that was the case? Surely the last place a person would want to drop dead was the middle of a shopping centre. Poisoning, however, was common in fabricated illness cases and the constant upset stomachs would attest to that. She may not have enough evidence to formally charge Gail yet, but Jack decided that first thing on Monday, she was getting her in for a formal interview.

Minutes later, Georgia wandered into the office. She strode over to Jack's desk. She placed her laptop down and turned the screen towards Jack. 'I think I've found something, boss.'

Jack was about to ask why she was in on a Saturday but was immediately drawn to the video. The image was grainy, but you couldn't miss the black patent bag hanging from the chair, nor the unfashionable hairstyle of the young woman sat in the cafe.

'That's Leia Thompson,' Jack said.

'Yup. And she's sitting in a cafe in the Bull Ring talking to a man on the day she died. Coincidence, I think not.'

You could only see the back of the man's head. His hair was thick and dark. His shoulders rounded in a slight stoop, common of tall men. It could be her father. Or someone else, of course.

The girl in the video then took off her glasses. Instead of putting them away somewhere safe, she placed them on the windowsill next to her. *What was she doing?*

'Get this immediately to IT. Let's see if we can get this image cleaned up a bit.'

'Yes, boss.' Georgia stood to leave. 'Don't worry, I won't try and claim any overtime. I thought I'd pop in on the way to the hairdressers.'

'Oh, and well done. Good idea to trawl CCTV.'

Jack looked closely at the grainy picture. They'd assumed it was a man by the hair. It was grainy enough for it to be anyone. Could it be Gail? It seemed unlikely. The librarian? Her dad?

The car park at the clinic was pretty much empty. Maybe the teenagers who were residents weren't allowed visitors at weekends. Jack pulled into a space near the entrance to the clinic. When she reached the front door, it didn't slide open. She looked around for an intercom, but couldn't see anything obvious. The young people staying here weren't sectioned as far as she knew, but there wasn't any apparent route to another entrance. High hedging prevented you from accessing the back of the building. It appeared to encircle the extensive grounds behind the clinic.

Jack took a step back. Dr Sharma's office was at the back of the building. The only option was to ring him and announce her arrival. She was about to do that when the clinic doors slid open as though a ghost or the invisible man had arrived. Jack entered the building, looking around as she did, expecting to see Kishran in the reception area.

'Can I help you?'

It was then Jack spotted the nurse who stood at the reception desk. She sat behind the perplex glass and had, no doubt, been the one who'd let her in. 'I'm here to see Dr Sharma. He's expecting me.' She'd called ahead hoping he might be able to help with some of her thoughts around Gail.

'Do you know where he is? Only I should be doing the medication rounds,' she answered, looking bored.

Jack had obviously upset her routine. 'Actually you could help me with something. I'm DI Jack Kent.'

'DI, so the police?' Her eyes moved furtively to the entrance.

'Yes, that's right.' Jack moved on quickly. 'Did you know Leia Thompson? She was a patient here.'

'Was a patient?'

'Yes, she died. Didn't you know?'

The nurse visibly paled. 'No, I didn't. I'm sorry to hear that. I've got to go, though. Sorry.' She started to walk away.

'Was Leia a resident here?'

The nurse didn't answer, just kept walking.

Jack sighed. It felt distinctly as though she had something to hide. There was something rather odd about the clinic. Maybe it was the lack of noise. Despite not being a parent, Jack knew that children, even teenagers, were seldom quiet. Teenagers might spend more time in their rooms but also were quick to screech at each other and generally stomped instead of walked. The staircases here weren't carpeted and the rooms were unlikely to be soundproofed.

Before heading to the office, Jack walked up to a set of windows with a view to the garden. It was a fairly pleasant day; perhaps they were congregating outside. But no. Apart from one girl who was sat on a bench reading, Jack couldn't see anyone.

Before she could ponder this, she heard a board creak and turned round to find the doctor standing behind her.

'It's a lovely garden, isn't it? We're so lucky to have all this space,' he said.

'Where're all the patients?'

'Locked in their rooms.' Jack looked quizzically at him. 'No, of course we don't do that. It's study time until twelve thirty p.m. Then they have the afternoon free and parents can visit should they choose to.'

'Did Leia ever stay here?'

Kishran gestured with his arm. 'Shall we go to my office?' He waited until they were both sat before he answered. 'Yes, she did stay with us. Not for long. Only about six weeks. I was worried about Gail, if you must know.'

'In what way?' Jack needed to know if he had any suspicions about Gail's care.

'I find her a little overbearing. Don't you?' He smiled. 'I wanted to see how Leia would get on without her being around. She did improve, as it goes. She even made a friend.'

'And how was she physically during this time? Did her physical symptoms improve too?'

Kishran stared at her as though he was trying to weigh up what he could and should say. 'Yes, they did, as it happens.'

'How?'

'According to her mother, Leia could only eat certain foods. She was lactose and gluten intolerant. She was also vegan as she had trouble digesting meat products. When she came to us, most of the food she ate had been liquidised. Gail said it was the only way she could keep food down.'

'And did she show you any medical documents to prove her intolerances?'

The doctor looked directly at her and smiled. 'No, she didn't. And within a couple of weeks, Leia was eating a wider range of foods. We did stick to a vegan, gluten-free diet, but she was eating pretty normally with the rest of the patients. And she wasn't sick. In fact, her health improved dramatically.'

'Why was that do you think?' *Go on. Tell me you think she was being poisoned.*

'I put it down to her developing some good relationships with her peers. Her mental health improved so did her physical.'

'So you think her physical health issues weren't real?'

He laughed at this. 'Of course they were real. But they may have been caused or exacerbated by her mental illness. I see it all the time here. So many patients have IBS, for example.'

'But Leia didn't just have IBS. You must know about all the surgeries that she had.'

'Let me stop you there, inspector.' He held up his hand. 'Phantom pain can be as real as pain due to underlying conditions. I did see Leia's medical records and it was obvious that she had some unnecessary treatments because of this pain. Different doctors will look for different diagnoses. When she got to me, I was able to find the real cause and treat it.'

Jack was about to ask Dr Sharma if he thought Leia was poisoned. But something stopped her. 'Did you prescribe either Citalopram or Codeine for Leia?'

'No. We use antidepressants sparingly here. Why do you ask?'

'We have Leia's toxicology report and she had high doses of both in her blood on the day she died.' Jack read off the precise amount from her notebook.

Raising his eyebrows, Kishran said, 'And you think she might have tried to kill herself.'

'We need to give the coroner all of the possibilities.'

'I see.' He stood and started to pace the room. 'Gail came here and started, well... causing a scene. Leia agreed to go with her. She wasn't discharged by us. I mean...she continued to attend the day clinics. But they weren't as helpful.'

Jack wondered if this was why Gail had lied about Leia being an in-patient here.

There were interrupted by an insistent knocking on the door.

Kishran rushed to open it. It was the nurse Jack met earlier. 'You've got to come. Rachel is really unwell.'

'Sorry, you'll need to leave now.' He didn't wait for a response, just ushered Jack out of the room. He motioned to the clinic entrance. 'You can see yourself out.' Then he headed towards the staircase.

Jack now had a choice. She could go home and dive into paperwork or take a break and go climbing. There was no point in interviewing Gail until Monday or even Tuesday as there wouldn't be any overtime payments for her officers and they'd need time to plan the questions. She wasn't going anywhere, and if she set off in the next few hours, she could spend the day

tomorrow on a crag and the evening interview planning on her
return.

A quick call to David Cavendish confirmed that he was, as ever,
up for a climb. There were many reasons why a climb was
necessary. The main one being to bring her fitness levels up to a
good level; there was nothing worse than sitting in an office
reading files or even driving round to get to interviews. But the
second reason was to get rid of some of the stress of work and to
give her space to think clearly.

Uncle David was waiting up for her. Jack had called him
Uncle David since she was a child. He wasn't a real uncle; he
was her dad's best friend and she'd spent many hours with him
and his son, Danny, growing up. The light shone its welcome
from the living room window, and David stood at the open front
door as she drove onto the drive and parked in front of the
cottage.

'How you doing, me duck?' He took her coat and threw it
on the back of a kitchen chair then put the kettle on. She'd have
a cup of tea if she liked it or not.

'Good, I guess.' Jack wasn't sure if she said that only in
politeness or if it was true. She'd had worse months since the
death of Hannah, her climbing partner. And she was actually
looking forward to climbing Kanchenjunga despite it seeming
too close for comfort. She'd never felt so unprepared for a
climb.

'I was thinking Stanage for tomorrow. You can choose a
route. Do you need a map?' David stood over her.

She tapped the seat next to her. 'Nope. The weather's not
going to be brilliant so let's see what the conditions are like, but
I've got one or two ideas.'

'How's work?'

Jack noted the concern in David's voice. 'It's fine. Just

tricky. Family relationship stuff. If only everyone was as straightforward as my dad,' she replied.

'Umm. If only.' David's eyes drifted to the fire.

Of course, he had memories of her father. They were the ultimate climbing partners and since his death many years ago, he was following suit with Jack. The perfect surrogate dad.

As soon as his tea was drunk, David stood. 'Spare bed's set up. Breakfast at six-thirty. Then we'll get off, yes?'

'Yeah. Sounds good.'

He left the room before she could even say goodnight.

Jack didn't need the cockerel's morning chorus to wake her. She'd slept well. The bed felt familiar and comforting. David's spare room was the nearest she had to a family bedroom. Her mum never invited her to stay over at her flat. The family house that she lived in as a child had long been sold. Here she felt safe.

'I've packed a flask and some snacks for later,' David said as they tucked into breakfast. 'Now, have you decided which route or do you still want to stand before it first?'

Stanage Edge was a climbing temple so Jack could easily see herself standing before it, genuflecting. In climbing, each route was named by the climber that had first attempted it. Perhaps *The Guillotine and Off with His Head* should be the climb to go for. But it would depend on what and who they found already climbing on the gritstone crag. Jack couldn't abide a busy route and would always look for her own stretch of rock, free from too many fellow climbers. As she contemplated the best route, she realised David was still waiting for a reply. 'Let's wait. Unless you've got a burning desire to climb a particular part.'

David shrugged. 'Not up to me. It's your climb today.'

. . .

Despite arriving at Stanage by 8 a.m., they weren't the first at the crag. But there was plenty of room for all without the need to socialise. The early morning drizzle hadn't deterred anyone either, despite it making everything feel damp to the touch but not too wet to risk a climb. Some of the trickier routes might be best left for another day. Jack weighed up the options, her mind travelling along each hold as she mapped them out. There were hundreds of routes on Stanage's four-mile-long edge. Eventually she stopped walking and laid down her pack and the ropes she was carrying. 'Here.'

David looked up. Clearly trying to work out what Jack's plans could be. Jack continued with her stretches; like any form of exercise, she never climbed cold.

'Well?' David asked. 'You made your mind up yet?'

Jack picked up her harness. 'Wuthering, then Dithering Frights.' She winked. These were a good place to start. Tricky with a good stretch at the crux. The names of each route always made Jack smile wondering what the story was behind them and who the climber might have been that first planned and climbed the route. She took her time attaching the rope to her harness and chalking up.

At the start of the climb, David loosened the rope to belay. The route started with a chimney. Jack placed her back against the straighter wall on the right-hand side. Pressing against it, she felt the coldness of the gritstone rock digging into her back. It felt almost soothing like a massage on her tense muscles. Leaning forward, she placed her hands behind her and pushed upward with her feet. Moving her hands up followed by her feet, she made quick progress of the climb until she reached the buttress which narrowed the chimney.

'Nice. That was quite a stretch.'

Jack heard David's comforting words and swung around onto the front face. Then it hit her that she might not only be stretching in the climb. Perhaps she was jumping to conclusions in the case. Here was a young girl fascinated by the classics, constantly ill and possibly being poisoned. Gail could have lied about Leia's father being dead, but she wouldn't be the first estranged wife to do that. Were they really ready to interview her?

TWELVE

Instead of driving the long way via David's cottage, Jack decided to drive home after the day's climbing. The rain had started to lash down. The undulations of the roads made the drive through the Peak District more difficult in the dark. But at least she had four-wheel drive and a car that made light work of the hills.

Her phone lit up just as she approached the A38. It was Emily calling. Jack picked it up on the hands-free. 'Hi. How's it going?' She tried to hide the hope in her voice.

'I've just finished a shift and I'm starving. Fancy dinner?'

As if her stomach had heard, it made a loud growl which she hoped Emily couldn't pick up over the phone. 'I'm about forty minutes away from Brum. How about that Nepalese restaurant in Sutton Coldfield?'

There was a pause. Had she blown it? Was it too far for her to go? Maybe she no longer liked Nepalese or had only said that she did to please Jack at the start of their short relationship?

'Sorry, I was just looking up the postcode for my satnav. I should be there in about fifteen minutes. Shall I get us some wine?'

Phew. Jack could relax. Apart from the fact that her heart was now beating at a furious rate, her outdoor attire wasn't in the least bit sexy. But then if Emily was coming straight from the hospital, she was unlikely to have dressed up either. *Deep breaths. It will be okay.*

Jack managed to arrive a few minutes after Emily, who was already seated in a booth at the back of the restaurant. It took Jack five minutes to reach her as she had to be welcomed by the whole Sherpa family that ran the restaurant. She hadn't been there for a few months, and Chodak had a new girlfriend and his sister Amala had given birth to twins so, of course, Jack had to see all the baby photos.

Emily stood when Jack reached the table and kissed her on the cheek. 'Sorry to drag you away from your fan club,' she whispered in her ear. 'I've counted twenty photos on the wall of you too. How many girlfriends do you bring here?'

Only one. All the other times she'd come with friends of the platonic variety or fellow climbers who loved the tearoom vibe. 'Have you ordered?' Jack changed the subject.

'Just wine,' Emily said.

Jack picked up the menu to hide her blushes. She already knew what she was going to eat.

Chodak arrived moments later with the drinks. 'You ready to order?'

'Yes. How hot are the curries?' Emily asked.

Jack bit her lip before she could make any crass comments about how hot Emily was already.

'Not too spicy. We can bring some yoghurt too in case you want it milder.' Chodak smiled and nodded at Jack.

'I'll have the Adraki Lamb Chops to start, then the Royal Tawa Chicken with rice and bread.'

Emily shut her menu. 'I'll have the kebab and the Himalayan Curry.'

Chodak nodded. 'Perfect choices.' Then he hurried off smiling, leaving Jack wondering if he somehow knew she was on a date.

Or was she? Now Jack thought about it, she wasn't too sure. But it was a bit late to ask. Instead she mumbled, 'How was work?'

'Good. We had a self-harmer in. Really upsets me how teenage mental health has deteriorated over the last year. She came directly from a clinic so hopefully she's getting some help.' Emily took a huge slurp of the wine. 'At least the wine isn't bad.'

'Which clinic?' It would be too much of a coincidence to be the Tudor Manor.

'Can't remember, some private place.'

Was it worth digging further? It didn't actually matter that much if it was Dr Sharma's clinic. They must have a large number of damaged patients that cut themselves and would occasionally need treatment.

The conversation continued to ebb and flow with ease. After the second glass of wine and well into the main course, Jack noticed how Emily's eyelashes naturally curled at the ends and that she had a cluster of tiny freckles on the bridge of her nose. She loved the bow of her lips as she smiled and, for a moment, imagined kissing them. Chodak chose that moment to come over to ask if they wanted desserts as the restaurant would be shutting soon.

Emily looked up and stared directly at Jack. 'Shall we just get the bill?'

Jack nodded. Afraid her voice would break if she spoke. When did Emily become so stunning? She so wanted to stroke her cheek and kiss her softly on the lips. And then...

'Have you finished, ladies? Can I get you coffee or anything else?' Chodak brought her back down to base camp.

'Just the bill.' Emily grinned at Jack.

'I'll pay. It was my idea,' Jack insisted.

A few minutes later, they both left the restaurant. The

problem was they had come in two cars so there'd be no 'I'll take you home' or 'do you want to come up for coffee'. In the end, they both walked over to Emily's Mini and stood, staring at each other. Eventually, Emily thrust her hands into her jeans pockets and said, 'Your place or mine?'

Jack reached out and gently brushed Emily's blonde hair behind her ears, trailing her fingertips across the shaved undercut. 'Mine? If that's okay?' With Emily they'd never been a clear role. Hannah was easy, Jack topped. Making all of the first moves. But Emily seemed to like the fluidity of roles switching from one to the other. In some ways it had been fun, in other ways it had been their downfall. When things weren't going well, neither took control of the situation.

The next morning, Jack woke first and snuggled up to Emily's back. She slept curled up on her side. Jack spooned her, nestling her chin on to Emily's neck. She'd missed being close to someone, particularly the early morning cuddles. They'd made love the night before with Project Blackbird on low on the stereo in the background. Ming Nagel's soft, caressing voice was the perfect accompaniment as they rediscovered the contours of each other's bodies.

Jack could have stayed in that position for hours, but Emily had other ideas. She suddenly sat up. 'What time is it?'

Sighing, Jack rolled over and brushed her hand through her unkempt morning hair. She glanced at her phone. 'Six-thirty.'

'Shit. I'm going to be late for my shift.' Emily paused long enough to brush her lips against Jack's. Then she flew out of bed and got dressed, almost falling over as she slipped a leg into her jeans. 'I'll call you tonight.'

Jack lay back down on the bed, contemplating whether to make an early start at the office or go to the gym. Since she still needed to complete the day's assignments before the briefing, she chose the office.

On the drive into central Brum, Jack pondered on whether this was the start of an actual relationship. She considered phoning Shauna and talking it through with her, but knew this would be met with a degree of hilarity from her partner-in-crime. Shauna would basically take the piss instead of offering any real insights into Jack's relationship dilemma. But weighing up the evidence – the dates at Mandy's cafe, the meal last night, the sex, the promise of a call – it all seemed positive.

By the time she'd reached the station, she found herself humming 'My Baby Just Cares for Me' and smiling. That soon changed when she walked straight into Terry Doughty, risen from the dead and waiting in the station's reception.

THIRTEEN

Nadia put on her suit ready for court. Her plain navy hijab needed adjusting as, for some reason, her hair just wouldn't sit right. The trembling in her hands didn't help as she struggled with it for the second time. When she was finally happy, she laid her prayer mat down in the living room. Her morning prayers seemed even more important, and as she began, her heart rate slowed and for the first time that morning she felt relaxed.

An hour later, she was standing in the witness box swearing to tell the truth on the Quran. She closed her eyes for a moment. When she opened them, she was ready for Marcus Barnet's first question. 'Your name is Detective Sergeant Nadia Begum and you've been a detective sergeant for three years, is that correct?'

Nadia swallowed. 'Yes, three years in March.'

'When did you first meet Sara Millings?'

They'd decided not to start with Sara's testimony. Marcus felt that the jury needed an explanation as to why Sara hadn't reported the assault as soon as Jacobs had left the flat. Nadia's testimony was to offer that. The hope was, Nadia would be subjected to questioning before the prosecution laid into Sara. Marcus was well aware of the impact the case was having on Sara.

Nadia explained the first meeting with Sara at her flat, twelve hours after the crime had occurred, and after she'd showered and tidied up. She spoke clearly and succinctly, only including the facts. Then she moved onto the reasons why Sara had waited. 'Victims of rape often don't report the crime immediately after. Statistically a twelve-hour delay is actually quite short. Sometimes it can be days, weeks, months even before a victim reports the crime to the police. In fact, one in six rape survivors don't report at all.'

The prosecuting counsel stood up. The judge held out his hand. 'DS Begum, can we stick to the facts of this particular case. Statistics aren't always helpful.'

'Yes, of course.' Nadia looked down and then straight at the jury. 'Sara was in a state of shock when we arrived. We called for an ambulance crew to check her over.'

'How did you know she was in shock?' Marcus asked, his hand clasping his gown.

'She was pale and clammy. Her breathing was irregular. I thought she might faint.'

'Did you question her at this point?'

Nadia shook her head. 'No. I waited for the paramedics to arrive.'

Marcus asked a few more questions about Sara's medical state. Nadia then explained that the paramedics treated her at the scene and decided not to take her to the hospital. It was at this point Nadia took Sara to the Horizon Sexual Assault Referral Centre.

'What tests were carried out at the referral centre?' Marcus asked.

Nadia looked towards the judge. 'May I refer to my notes, Your Honour?'

The judge nodded and Nadia took her notebook out of her jacket pocket. She skimmed through until she found the right page. The SARC was considered a safe and welcoming space for anyone who had been sexually assaulted or raped. It wasn't clinical like a hospital, but it was staffed by forensic nurses who knew how to collect evidence of assault. Nadia listed the procedures they had carried out.

'And what evidence did they find?'

'Evidence of recent sexual activity, including sperm. Bruising to her inner thighs. Vaginal tears. Bruising to the arms and neck.' Nadia glanced down at her notebook. She'd added all of the evidence numbers and read these out. Allowing time for the jury members to refer to each photograph. She watched their faces carefully. Some of the women physically paled.

The questioning then moved on to Sara's interview. Nadia recalled how she'd sat with her arms wrapped around her bent legs on the sofa, her head down on her knees. She wore fresh clothes and had showered, but she kept rubbing at her hands and face, as though they were covered with dirt. She didn't mention these things, just stuck to the timeline starting from her meeting Jacobs at the student's union. 'They had a drink together then he offered to walk her home.'

'Did she mention anything about how she felt about him? Did she fancy him?' Marcus looked at the jury as he spoke.

'No. She just thought he was being kind. It was dark and it's not a long walk.' Of course, they could follow this up with Sara later. Nadia was just quoting from the statement.

'And did she invite him in?'

Nadia looked back through her notes. She wanted to get this right. 'Not specifically. They were talking about a local band Sara liked and he followed her.'

'Did she say goodbye to him upstairs, then.'

'No, but she was already starting to feel uncomfortable. She hadn't even switched on the kettle before he produced a knife.'

Nadia then found the evidence number and read it out for the jury.

'Where was the knife from?'

'He'd brought it with him. It was a Swiss Army knife. As soon as they entered the flat, he followed her into the kitchen and took it out of the back pocket of his jeans. Then he threatened her with it.'

'What did he say next?

'"You'll do exactly what I tell you. Don't scream or I'll cut you."'

Marcus Barnet then asked further questions about their inquiries and the discovery of the knife. Nadia answered as plainly as she could, referring the jury to the relevant documents in the evidence pack. She was starting to feel more confident.

'That's all my questions at this time, Your Honour.' Marcus sat down and the prosecuting counsel, Mary Stenner QC, stood up.

The judge stopped her before she spoke. 'Let's take a recess until tomorrow morning.'

For the first time, Nadia looked over towards Steven Jacobs. He glared back at her, sneering. He looked much thinner than the last time she'd seen him. His features were sharper and his hairline had begun to recede. He seemed to be changing into his father.

FOURTEEN

'Why did nobody tell me my daughter had died?' Those were the first words Terry Doughty said to Jack. It was a perfectly reasonable question.

'We couldn't find you,' she replied.

'But that bitch, sorry, my ex-wife, had my number. Did she not even give it to you?'

Jack noticed how red his eyes were. Either he'd recently been crying, or he hadn't slept for a week. 'I'm sorry. To be honest, she told us that you were dead.'

'And you believed her?'

'Let's take this somewhere quieter.' Jack led Terry to an interview room off the main reception. She waited until he sat down before asking him if he'd like a drink.

'No, I'm fine. Thank you.' The change of scenery seemed to have calmed him down a little.

'How did you find out about Leia? We were looking for you nationally. Were you in Scotland?'

'Yeah. I work on the lorries now, not the rigs. I got a job that took me Derby way, so I called one of my mates to meet up for a drink and a catch-up. He told me. He couldn't quite believe I didn't know.' Terry's head fell into his hands as he began to sob. 'The report in the papers – he read it to me. So I drove here as quick as I could. I haven't slept.'

'Are you sure we can't get you something – food, drink?'

'A coffee, then, black, no sugar.'

Jack popped her head out of the door and asked the desk sergeant to get them the drinks. When she came back into the room, Terry was crying with his head in his hands. She sat down and waited for him to compose himself. Finally, he said, 'She killed her, then.'

'Who killed her?' Jack asked.

'Gail killed Leia. It was always going to happen. I tried telling them, the doctors, I mean, but would they listen? I said, she's crazy. There's more wrong with Gail than Leia.'

'Did you tell the police, social services?'

'Are you having a laugh? If the doctors didn't believe me, then you lot and the SS wouldn't.'

Jack nodded. He was probably right. Would she have believed him if he came to the station with wild accusations about his wife? It wouldn't be the first time an ex-husband had done such a thing. 'How did you think Gail was killing Leia?'

'All the tablets she was taking. Playing with her mind, keeping her out of school. She probably drove her mad.'

'You know about the medical treatments that Leia had?'

'Yeah, I know she was ill pretty much since she was a baby. But the doctors should have done more. Helped her with her pain. I kept telling them that. Then she could have gone out more, made friends. Every time I came home, she was worse or had another condition.'

'When we did the post-mortem, we found that many of the medical procedures were unnecessary.'

Terry looked genuinely perplexed. 'You what?'

'Her appendix was removed, she had a stoma and other medical treatments, but our pathologist couldn't see a reason for them.'

'What?' Terry banged his forehead with his palm. 'She was always in pain. Always. Of course she was ill.'

'Did you think Gail was physically harming Leia in any way?' Jack didn't say poisoning. She didn't want to lead him.

'What, hitting her? No, not that. I don't think so. Leia sometimes said that she hated her mum. But she's a teenager. What teenager doesn't? I just thought she was driving her mad with her stupid rules, that's all I meant. Did Leia, did she... kill herself?'

'No. We don't think so, but it will be for the coroner to decide. She was taking large doses of tablets. We think she had a heart attack.'

'At fifteen?' The tears came thick and fast then. He held his head in his hands and rocked back and forth causing the chair to squeak.

Jack left him with a police constable while she went to type up his statement. She'd barely finished when her phone rang.

It was Miriam. 'I can't get Gail to answer the door. She's definitely in. The neighbours heard her. Can you come?'

The last thing Jack wanted was to bring Gail and Terry together, so she arranged for the constable to get Terry to sign the statement and then to find him some accommodation in the local area. She'd probably need to talk to him again when he was feeling more up to it. Maybe Miriam could meet with him too. Then she drove to Gail's.

Miriam was still pounding on Gail's door when she arrived. 'No response?'

She looked frantic. 'Nothing. I went round the back and there's water running through the ceiling. I've called for back-up and for an ambulance.'

They both heard the sirens before the convoy arrived.

Within seconds, a couple of burly officers used an enforcer to break down the door. Jack and Miriam rushed upstairs. They ran into the unlocked bathroom and almost slipped on the sodden floor. The bathroom was flooded. Gail's head seemed to be at an unusual angle under the water. Her dark wet hair trailing behind her, eyes bulging, legs scrunched up under her. Miriam turned off the tap while Jack felt the woman's damp neck for a pulse. There wasn't one. She'd clearly been dead a while. She lifted Gail's hand, finding the skin on her fingertips wrinkled and prune-like from the water. There were no signs of cuts to her wrists, or other parts of her body, suggesting that she'd killed herself.

'You can tell the ambulance crew to stand down,' Jack said to the ashen-faced officer who poked his head around the door.

Jack took out her phone from her jacket pocket and called the Centre for Forensic Pathology. Now she had two unexplained deaths on her hands.

Apart from ensuring the taps were off and preventing more of the water flowing into the dining room, and moving everyone outside, they didn't do anything else. The scene needed to be preserved. Jack sent some of the officers to do door to door. She wanted to find out just when they'd heard Gail and what exactly they had heard. Shauna arrived moments later in a taxi, quickly followed by a forensics team. Her lower arm was wrapped in clingfilm. Signs that she'd been in the middle of another tattooing session. She must have spotted that Jack had seen it. Grinning, she said, 'It's a scorpion. It represents Deanna.'

Deanna was Shauna's on-off girlfriend. Maybe it was her star sign or maybe even her personality. Jack gestured upstairs and Forensics sprang into action.

After taking photographs of the bathtub and positioning of

the body, Shauna agreed that they could move Gail from the bath. She took her temperature and conducted a search of her body for signs of initial bruising, rigor mortis, skin discoloration.

'Is it a drowning?' asked Jack.

Shauna shrugged. 'It would seem the logical explanation. But people don't just drown in the bath.'

'I wasn't suggesting they do,' Jack continued. 'I mean, is it accidental, suicide, murder, even?' Jack knew Shauna wouldn't be led. She might as well ask the question and take the ridicule.

'Are there any signs that she's taken pills or alcohol?' Shauna glanced around the tiny bathroom, perhaps looking for bottles.

Jack had already searched the house and there wasn't anything apparent. Nor was there a note. But she could have easily taken pills as there were so many in the house. The body position struck Jack as odd though. She didn't look like she'd taken a load of pills and fallen asleep in the bath.

Shauna may have read her mind. 'Some signs of bruising might not become apparent as of yet.'

'You think she might have been attacked?'

Again Shauna shrugged. 'Anything's possible.'

If she had been attacked, then who would be the likely perpetrator? Jack called the station. 'Is Terry Doughty still there?'

The desk sergeant answered, 'Nope. Left half an hour ago. We've found him a room in a guest house in Moseley.' He reeled off the address.

Jack found Miriam next door making tea for the constable guarding Gail's front door. 'We better go tell the husband.'

The neighbour stopped her. 'I heard banging and shouting early this morning. I just thought it was Gail having another of her episodes.'

'Did you recognise the voices? Male? Female?'

'Couldn't tell. It might have just been Gail's voice. She's always making a nuisance of herself.'

Jack recognised the neighbour as the one that had reported Gail to social services. For a moment she wondered if she'd finished her off in the bath, so she could finally get a good night's sleep. Jack knew of people killing for less.

The Piano Guesthouse was located opposite Moseley Rugby Club and didn't look too shabby from the outside. Jack wondered why Terry hadn't decided to bunk down with any of his local mates or family. The desk sergeant would have given him that option. They found him in his room. He let them in, no doubt surprised to see Jack again so quickly. There was a half-empty bottle of scotch on the bedside table.

There was no point beating around the bush. 'I'm sorry to tell you. We've discovered your wife dead in her home.'

'What?' Terry spluttered. The word slurred. His eyes were even more red-rimmed than earlier.

'Have you seen her since you came back to Brum?' The venom he had for Gail was so apparent that afternoon. Maybe he had gone round to the house in a fit of rage and killed her. He clearly blamed her for his daughter's death. What an alibi he'd set up for himself, then arriving at the police station playing the innocent, grieving father.

'You don't fink...?' He stumbled onto the bed and grabbed for the whisky bottle. Miriam got there first and pulled it away from him. 'I had nothing to do with any of this.'

'Where were you before you came to the police station?' Jack stood in front of him blocking his path to the exit.

'I went straight there as soon as I got to Brum. I didn't even know where Gail currently lived.'

'You didn't even know where your daughter lived?' Miriam folded her arms.

'They moved so often. Gail never answered my calls and Leia never had a phone. What was I supposed to do?' He rubbed his face with his hands. 'I'm not lying. I didn't even know Leia was dead, for god's sake.'

'And yet you were worried about her well-being. Don't lie to us. We know Leia emailed you from the library.'

'Only a few times and not for ages.'

Jack wasn't sure if he was lying. He may have blamed Gail for Leia's death, but would that have led him to murder her?

Terry began to shake. Jack wondered if they were dealing with an alcoholic. The last thing she needed was to be accused of questioning someone who was unfit. 'Do you need a doctor?'

'No. I just need a drink. It's all been a bit of a shock.'

Jack's next worry was that he'd take off. They couldn't keep him here as they'd nothing to charge him with. Gail had just died and they'd need Forensics to show what the cause was. Even her daughter's death was still a mystery. It could just have easily been a heart defect as a poisoning. Maybe Gail had even decided to kill herself after the realisation that she'd harmed her daughter hit her. 'Miriam, can I borrow you a minute?'

Miriam nodded and they both stepped out of the room. The zigzag-patterned hallway carpet doing nothing to quell the beginnings of a migraine and its accompanying nausea. 'Can you stay with him and make sure he gets some medical help if he needs it.'

Still clutching the whisky bottle, Miriam said, 'Yeah. For a while. At least until the morning.'

'What do you reckon? Think he's telling the truth?'

'Possibly. Was Gail murdered, then?' Miriam stepped closer to Jack.

'Who knows? You were with her more, is she likely to have killed herself? I mean she seemed pretty unstable to me but...'

'I'm not a psych, boss. But, yeah, she was all over the place.

Her daughter had just died though. I've seen people become catatonic, angry, inconsolable; you name it. There's no one reaction to a sudden death. It affects everyone differently.'

They both heard the bump from Terry's room at the same time. Rushing in, they found him collapsed on the carpet. A second bottle of whisky lay empty next to him. He was already snoring.

Miriam plonked herself down on the bed. 'Don't worry, I'll keep an eye on him.'

Jack rushed out of the guesthouse and bumped straight into Shauna's sister.

'Jack. I'm so pleased to see you. I was going to invite you and Shauna round for another meal.'

'Me?' Jack became aware that Bella was pulling on her trousers and grinning up at her. She wondered for a moment what they were both doing in Moseley.

'Is this strange... I guess this is a bit strange.' Michelle took hold of Bella's hand and pulled her away from Jack. 'It's just that Bella keeps asking for you. You made quite an impression.'

'I did?' Children usually gave her a wide berth, maybe it was the surly uninterested vibe she gave off.

'Yeah. You and Climbing Barbie. In fact, that's where we've just been. At the indoor play centre up the road. They've got a mini climbing wall.'

'Wow.' Jack hoped Michelle didn't spot the blush as she bent down next to Bella. She guessed it would be nice to have inspired a budding climber. 'Did you enjoy the climbing?'

The little girl nodded and bounced her hand off the top of Jack's head.

'Great. I love it too.'

'Actually. That's a thought. Why don't we meet for a coffee

one day next week at the play centre? Would that be too awful?'
Michelle asked, taking her daughter's hand.

Jack found herself saying no, that would be great. She even
managed to wave Bella goodbye for a good minute as they
walked off up the road. But even more worrying was on the
drive back, she even wondered what Emily might think of
having kids.

Fortunately, by the time she arrived back at the station, she'd
come to her senses. Jayden gave her a Post-it note as soon as she
entered the office. DSI Campbell wanted to see her.

Stepping into his office, it became crystal clear that he
wasn't in the best of moods. 'Sit down, Jack, and maybe you can
tell me why we're wasting so much time and resources on this
case?'

'What do you mean, sir?' Jack sat, keeping her back straight.

'Well, you might as well move on. Whichever way you look
at it, it's sorted itself out, don't you think?'

If it had, that would be a bonus as she could concentrate
more on preparing for her climb and completing other cases.

She must have looked confused as DSI Campbell continued. 'What have we got here? Two natural deaths, suicides
maybe? Or even the mum killed the daughter and then herself?
Whichever it is, write it up and send it to the coroner. Let them
try and figure out a cause of death.'

'Shauna hasn't even done a post-mortem on the mother, sir.
We don't know how she died.'

'But does it matter now?'

'The father's turned up and the mother turns up dead.
Might be something in that.' In her gut, Jack didn't think so.
Maybe her boss was right. Nothing to see here. Time to
move on.

'Do you think he killed her?'

Jack shrugged. 'No, probably not. He's more likely to have killed her in a rage of emotion. This was far too subtle.'

'Well, there you go. Write up what you've got and send to the coroner.' She was being dismissed. He might as well have added: 'there's a good girl'. It didn't stop her messaging Shauna and asking her to let her know the time of the PM.

FIFTEEN

The courtroom felt colder this morning, despite the warmer day outside. Nadia pulled her jacket closer to her as she re-entered the witness box. She'd spoken to Jack the night before, who'd wished her luck and filled her in on the latest developments of the Thompson case. At least it looked like that wouldn't need to go to trial.

Mary Stenner QC stood in front of her and smiled. But Nadia knew this wasn't going to be a pleasant experience. She prepared herself for the first question. 'You said that Sara Millings had tidied up and showered before she called the police, is that correct?'

'Yes. That's correct.' Nadia cleared her throat.

'And yet you found evidence of semen. What about the sheets on the bed?'

'They were washed. The bed had been stripped. But there was still semen found on the mattress.' Mary must have known this.

'When someone has been the victim of a crime, is it usual for them to dispose of the evidence?'

'What do you mean?'

Mary Stenner turned to the jury. 'Well, there could have been blood on the sheets or other forensic evidence and Sara washed them. Maybe because she'd just had consensual sex and everything looked well...too clean.'

'Was that a question, Ms Stenner?' the judge interjected.

'No, Your Honour. Apologies.' Mary turned the page in her notes. 'Did you ask Sara if she already knew my client?'

'Prior to that evening?'

'Yes.'

'I did. She said that she hadn't met him before, but knew of him.' Everyone at the university probably knew of him. He was the mayor's son.

'How did she know him?'

'I didn't ask.' She hadn't asked her directly, so that was true.

'His father had a bit of a reputation. Not universally liked. Did she mention him?'

'No. Not at all.' What was she suggesting? That Sara had lied to get at his father? This was ridiculous!

'How many sexual assault cases have you investigated, Detective Begum?'

This was easy enough to answer. 'About ten.'

'How was Sara compared to the other survivors?'

'How do you mean?'

'Well, what was her demeanour like?'

Nadia hadn't given that much thought. She'd gone with Sara to the SARC, taken her statement and stayed with her throughout. 'Similar, I guess. She was upset but gave a good account of what happened.'

'So, you believed her?'

'Yes... Yes, of course...and we found the knife which corroborated her statement.'

'A knife that wasn't found at her property and could have been thrown away at any time.'

'Steven Jacob's DNA was found on the knife. It was also found in the vicinity of Sara Millings' flat.'

Mary turned over more pages in her notes. She looked calm and unflustered. 'Did you ask Sara any questions about the incident itself?'

'Yes, she gave a full account of that which I recorded in her statement.'

'I know, I've read the statement and it's been made available to the jury. But did she make it clear at any point that this wasn't consensual?'

Nadia looked over at Marcus, who frowned back at her. 'He held a knife to her throat.'

Where was she going with this?

'Putting the knife to one side for a moment. What explicitly did she say or do to show my client that she didn't want sex?'

Marcus stood up. The judge motioned to him to sit down and said, 'I'm not sure where you are going with this line of questioning. I will allow DS Begum to answer purely on what the witness said at the time.'

Nadia bit her lip before answering in an attempt to calm herself down. 'She repeatedly said no, until it was clear that he wouldn't listen, and that he wouldn't ever stop. Then, like many rape survivors, she closed down.'

'You can't know how she felt, DS Begum. That's all my questions, Your Honour.' The prosecutor sat down.

The judge turned to the defence. Marcus shook his head. 'You can stand down now, DS Begum.'

Confused, Nadia didn't move for a moment. *Was that it?*

SIXTEEN

For the first time in Jack's long history of knowing Sherpa Norbu, he appeared concerned on their weekly video call. 'We're running out of time. We need the visas sorted and I've heard nothing from the rest of the team. Just you. You're the only one organised.'

'I've got more time now. I'll chase them up.'

Gail's death had been a blessing of sorts. The post-mortem hadn't shown up anything unexpected. Gail had likely overdosed on prescribed medication and drowned. Bathwater had been found in her lungs consistent with drowning. There were no defensive injuries. They just needed the toxicology results which could take weeks. But it seemed likely that Gail had killed herself due to the guilt of killing her own daughter, despite there being no note found to categorically prove that. Many of those that took their own life didn't leave a note. Guilt may have lain heavy on Gail, but perhaps she didn't have the words to express it. It was the most logical explanation.

Now Jack felt freer to concentrate on her expedition. She could book in regular sessions with Danny and at the gym. That morning, she'd even drawn up a dietary plan and had ordered the supplements she needed. But something niggled her. She had a dreadful feeling that she was the only one preparing for the climb apart from the Sherpas.

'I'll need all the passport information this week, Jack. You know what the Nepalese government is like.' Sherpa Norbu brought her back to the moment making her wish this was a solo climb, but that brought its own dangers.

'Can we concentrate on the route for a bit. Have you checked the level of erosion on the trail to Pang Pema?' Jack was still unsure whether to take that route as landslides made the trek so difficult.

Norbu attempted a reply that Jack couldn't hear. The video link had frozen and his words scrambled. Jack waited for a moment to see if it corrected itself, but instead his connection dropped altogether. Shutting the lid of her laptop, Jack sighed. There were plenty of other things to be getting on with. A trip to see Dr Pride, for one.

The reception area at the children's hospital seemed emptier than on her previous visit. There were no queues even at the main desk, but Jack didn't bother to stop there; instead she headed straight for Jennifer's office. She was just about to climb the stairs when she felt a hand on her shoulder. Before she could turn, the hand moved across her eyes and a seductive voice whispered in her ear. 'Guess who?'

Her distinctive perfume had already given her away.

'Ruby Rose, if I'm not mistaken,' Jack said.

The hands fell from her face. Jack spun around and faced Emily, who scrunched up her face and muttered, 'Really?'

'Guilty crush. I'll not deny it,' Jack said, running her hand across the shaved part of her head.

Emily squinted. 'To be honest, in a certain light, you do have the look of her.'

'I do queer androgyny really well. You won't be the first to say it.' She was tempted to stroke Emily's face as there were so few people around, which shocked her as she never normally showed affection publicly. It wasn't to do with the fact that Emily was of the same sex. She was just as private with men. Changing the subject, Jack asked, 'What are you doing here anyway?'

'I had to accompany a child on a medical transfer. You?'

'Meeting with Dr Pride. Do you know her?'

'Yeah. She's well thought of. One of the best paediatricians in the country, specialises in cancer.'

In that moment, Jennifer went up in Jack's estimation. She could forgive her for her lack of time and apparent aloofness. Her thoughts were with the living not the dead. 'I'd better go. It looks like my case might have run its course so I'll have more free time. Shall we book something? I mean, if you've got holiday owing, shall we go away for a weekend somewhere?'

Looking thoughtful for a moment, Emily cocked her head. 'Yeah. I'd like that. Somewhere by the sea.'

Jack was going to suggest somewhere mountainous as she never really understood Midlanders' obsession with the coast. Maybe it was living so far from it that made every Brummie desire a seaside trip. 'Why don't you decide where you'd like to go and we can rent a cottage?'

'I'm so glad you said that. I had a horrible feeling you were going to suggest camping in the hills. I don't do accommodation that doesn't have an en suite.'

A few weeks ago, Jack might have run away from anyone saying this, but Emily could have suggested anything and she would still be interested. It was scary. 'I better get going.'

Emily kissed her on the cheek and turned to leave. Jack caught hold of her arm and pulled her back into a hug, kissing her on the lips before letting her go. A boy pushing a toy car spotted them and covered his face with his hands. Jack pulled her tongue out at him. My god, this woman was turning her into a child.

'Actually, have you got a minute?' Emily looked at her with playful glee.

'For you? Of course.' She hadn't made a specific appointment with Dr Pride.

Emily took her by the arm and led her to a door marked PRIVATE. She opened it and in front of them was a set of stairs.

'Don't tell me there's a sex dungeon down there.'

Emily giggled. Her nose crinkling as she did. 'You'd be surprised.'

At the bottom of the stairs was a long, dark corridor. Once their eyes adjusted to the lack of light, Emily led Jack to an open doorway. Finding a light switch, Emily flipped it. Jack gasped. The room was full of medical equipment. In the centre of the room was a hospital bed covered in a white sheet.

Emily winked at her. 'I will if you will.' She hopped up onto the bed.

'Don't you think this is a little creepy?' Next to the bed was an unopened package marked surgical equipment and one with a set of syringes. The room had an air of being long forgotten but at the same time had what looked like fresh supplies.

'Nah.' Emily spotted that Jack was looking at the package. 'I'm not going to cut you up. I'll bet one of the nurses has got a sideline going of delivering Botox.' She stroked Jack's face and pulled her closer to the bed. 'Ignore all the shit in here. I was just thinking we could...you know.'

Jack wasn't feeling it. Her investigative mind had images of illicit surgeries and serial killers. For a second, she even wondered if this was where Leia was operated on. She shivered. 'Sorry. This whole medical vibe isn't doing it for me. I just don't get why a room like this is here. Why isn't it being used? And why is it arranged like this?'

Getting down off the bed, Emily stroked the metal case

of instruments. 'I know it looks odd, but you'd be surprised how much stuff just gets moved around in hospitals when there isn't enough staff to use it, especially in old hospitals like this. And apparently the lift down here has been broken for years, making it unusable for surgeries. I'm sure it's nothing sinister. The medics all talk to each other, or I wouldn't have known about it. I mean, I don't even work here.'

'You said that sometimes staff do their own operations off the books like cosmetic procedures.'

'I've heard of it happening.' Emily glanced around and shrugged. 'It could be what's happened here. In fact, it was a nurse that told me about this place. It's been like this a while, she said. Sometimes they store things down here, but most of the time it's forgotten about.'

Jack wasn't convinced by Emily's explanation. This setup could explain the operational scars on Leia. Could they have been done illicitly? Did they need to get SOCO down to have a look at this room? The bed and the instruments didn't appear to have been used. The sheet was pristine white.

Emily looked disappointed that Jack hadn't seen the romantic side. She glanced at her watch. 'I'd better be getting back.'

Kissing her on the cheek, Jack took one last look around the room. It was a basement with a few pieces of hospital equipment. Creepy as it was, she was letting her imagination run away with her.

Jack headed for Waterfall House after a male nurse had informed her that she'd find Dr Pride on the Oncology Ward on the second floor.

The wind gusted as she turned the corner, she pulled her leather jacket closer around her and leant forward into it. She didn't notice the nurse until it was too late and she'd almost collided with her. 'Sorry,' she muttered.

The woman stood still in front of her rather than sidestepping out of the way. They stared at each other for a moment, causing Jack to ask, 'Do I know you?'

The nurse's eyes darted towards the street and, without answering, she pushed past Jack to get around the corner.

'Charming.' Jack stood and watched her stride off up the street. Leaving her wondering where she had seen the woman before.

Dr Pride was sat at a table playing cards with a bald teenage girl when Jack found her. Jennifer kept laughing and throwing her hair back. This must be the place that she felt most at home. Jack stood and watched her, wishing for a moment she could be as relaxed around children. Of course, the teenage cancer patient was far older than Shauna's niece, but then all kids were an enigma to her.

Jennifer spotted her and looked even less pleased to see her than all the other medical staff that she'd seen that day put together. Did working with children lead to a contempt of adults? She strode up to Jack and said, 'You'd better follow me. We'll go to the staffroom.'

There were no offices on this floor. The staffroom consisted of a kettle, a fridge and a dining table and chairs. The money had been spent on the facilities for both children and parents. It explained why Dr Pride had an office in the main building. Where else was she supposed to do the reams of paperwork that haunted all public sector professions?

Jack sat down on one of the seats. 'I wanted to speak to you before I sent you the final report for the coroner on the Thompson case.'

'I heard her mother had died.' Jennifer went to the sink and poured herself a glass of water. 'Sorry. Where are my manners, do you want anything?'

Jack shook her head. 'Although I'd still like a meeting with social services. And the notes from the Mortality and Morbidity review.'

'Why? Don't you think we have enough for the coroner? The inquest is coming up.'

But something still niggled, biting away at her like a flesh-eating bug. It would be easy just to leave the decision on cause of death to the coroner. Let them decide whether they should continue to investigate. But even if it was a case of neglect or poisoning, then the fact that the likely perpetrator was now dead would mean the police case would be closed. The coroner could decide that it was an unlawful killing. They didn't need a living suspect for that. It would be so easy to stop investigating and tie everything up in a report ready to be considered at the inquest, but what if she was wrong and there was another party involved, or if they had both committed suicide? That wouldn't be fair on Gail. She'd be branded as, at least, a neglectful mother and, at worst, as a killer.

'I just need to consider all the evidence, so can you arrange a case review and copy the M and M report?' She might be able to sleep at night then.

Jennifer nodded, sipped more of the water and for the first time during their meeting, smiled. 'In terms of my report to the coroner, there are a few inconsistencies in her medical records that I've added which might help you.'

'Go on.'

'The myocarditis, for example. I think it wasn't a factor in her death. She would have died because of the drugs in her system. That's my view. Obviously, the unwarranted medical procedures will need to be investigated. I have reported these. But there's also records that I think belong to another individual included in Leia's.'

'We've noted those too. Do you think they were misfiled?' Jack bit her lip. Her view was that these were added by a medical professional or someone with medical expertise. If they were in her main hospital files, then they couldn't have been added by Gail.

'Possibly. We're understaffed and underfunded. Mistakes happen.'

A cursory glance through her file and a doctor might think that these procedures were all perfectly necessary. Who would want to open her up to check why a procedure had actually taken place? Maybe the medics assumed that there were legitimate reasons for each operation. Even if nothing was removed or fixed, doctors did do exploratory operations. It's only now she's dead that these were being questioned. When it's too late for Leia.

Instead of going back to the office, Jack headed to a nearby cafe. She might as well get some lunch and there was a wholefood deli nearby that served some of the best sandwiches in Brum. She needed time to think.

Sitting at the table looking out over the local park, Jack enjoyed the time away from the case. The world outside always appeared to be running on a different timeline. Less manic than her life. Young mums pushed their babies up to the lake to show them the swans and ducks, throwing bread into their greedy waiting mouths. Jack vaguely remembered Shauna telling her that bread was bad for them, but these birds hadn't got that memo.

Of course, her peace came to a sudden jolting end. A new text message pinged on her personal phone. It was from Martin Dereux.

Something's come up and I'm not going to
make the climb. Sorry. I've also spoken to
Tomas and Maria. They wish to pull out too.

Jack grasped the phone so tight, she risked crushing it. 'For god's sake.'

A woman with a toddler on the next table turned around and glared at her.

'Sorry.' Jack held up her hand. And bit on the other choice words that bubbled to the surface. How could that idiot fob her off with a text? And Tomas and Maria hadn't even bothered contacting her themselves! Jack could finish them all for this. No one in the climbing world behaved so appallingly. There were protocols. If you were considering dropping out of a climb, you at least called a meeting or discussed it amicably, weighing up the pros and cons. You didn't just drop someone with a text or a message through a third party. What the hell was she going to do now? Taking a deep breath, she stood up, careful not to send her chair scraping backwards. She'd disturbed the clientele enough.

Danny didn't answer the front door at the climbing school straight away so she hammered on it again. When he did finally open up, she nearly gave him a black eye as she was about to knock again. 'I've got a client. What're you doing here? Did we have an appointment?'

It flooded out of her to the point that Danny had to tell her to slow down. When he got the gist, the blood started draining from his face.

'What the hell do I do now? Cancel? Let my Sherpa team down? They won't get paid for six months. Don't they realise that's how the Sherpas feed their village let alone their individual families. The arrogance...'

Danny waved at her to stop. 'Take the keys to the office. I'll meet you there. I just need to finish off the session with Eliza.'

Now Jack felt as though she was breaking up a date. Eliza, if she knew the reason why, would understand. Danny wouldn't tell her. He knew when to keep a secret and letting it slip would mean the whole of the climbing community in the UK would know by teatime – and the rest of the world by the following morning. You could almost say that the climbing community were telepathic when anything bad happened.

It took Danny twenty minutes before he entered the office. Jack was now wired from drinking another coffee. She fought back the tears as soon as they were alone. 'I can't not climb next year. It's my last chance.'

Danny hugged her. 'Don't be bloody stupid. You've got years left in you. We'll sort it. You always reckoned the lot of them were a liability anyway. There must be someone who can step in.'

Jack pulled away and raised her eyebrows.

Danny shook his head. 'I didn't mean me. You know what would happen if I left my kids for more than a day; Gemma would kill me and they'd all join in with their own mini ice picks.' He wouldn't look at her then.

'There must be someone who's climbed a similar mountain that wouldn't need to worry about getting the training in.' Jack slammed her hand on the table. 'Who am I kidding, of course there isn't!' She was shouting now. Not that it did any good.

'You can do it solo.' Danny said it in a whisper. Then coughed and said it again.

She could, but it would make everything more difficult and much more expensive. With an international team, she at least hoped that some of the costs of the expedition would be met by the others through their individual sponsorship. This didn't even have to be cash. It could be food for the trip, new gadgets to try, branded clothing. A one-person expedition was far more expensive and could be far more dangerous. Or was it? The other climbers didn't match her ability and she'd spent enough sleepless nights worrying about that.

At least when she climbed with Hannah, she felt safe. Hannah knew her weaknesses and was never too arrogant to ask for help. She was also as competent as Jack was at fixing ropes or ice climbing. Better, in some regards. Jack's thoughts drifted back to their training and planning sessions. Hannah had been beside her all the way. For a brief moment, Jack could sense Hannah's perfume. So many days they had spent sitting close to each other discussing possible routes or the equipment they would need. A knot started to form in her gut. 'I can't do this on my own.'

SEVENTEEN

Nadia swallowed hard. *You can do this. Deep breaths, remember.* Sara looked terrified. Even from ten metres away, Nadia could see her trembling. And Mary Stenner QC just smiled at Sara like a snake mesmerising its victim before striking.

'Sara. Can I call you that?' were her opening words.

Sara nodded. Nadia sat on her hands, willing Sara to get through this. Marcus had warmed her up with carefully chosen questions that Sara knew were coming. This would be different.

'You've said in your police statement and in your answers this morning that you didn't know my client, Steven Jacobs, well, but this isn't quite true, is it?' Mary bit on the arm of her reading glasses. 'You had coffee with him before, a few days earlier.'

Where was this coming from? Nadia felt the muscles in her back and neck tighten, forcing her to lean forward. Sara looked confused, her eyebrows knotted together, and for a moment the courtroom fell into an uncomfortable silence.

Then, in a quiet voice, Sara said, 'I've no idea what you are talking about.'

The judge leant over to her. 'If you could speak up a little. The jury and the court reporter may not have heard that.'

Sara took a deep breath. 'I've no idea what you are talking about. I hadn't even spoken to Steven before that night.'

'But you were studying in the same faculty for a term, were you not?' Mary continued.

'Along with a few thousand others. I was studying Fashion Design and he said he was studying Art History, so very different courses.'

Sara seemed more assured now. *But what did the defence know?* Surely this wasn't a fishing expedition?

'You met with Steven Jacobs at the Costa in the High Street on Thursday 17th April at approximately two p.m. We have a witness that we will be calling who will corroborate that. What did you talk about at that meeting?'

'I... I've never met with him. Why would I?' Sara turned towards the jury.

That's it. Look at the jury, not at him. Never look at him. Taking Nadia first had meant that she could tell Sara where to look and even how she could appear to be looking directly at the defence counsel without meeting Jacob's eye. Nadia knew what Jacobs was doing, and so did the judge and jury, as he smirked and nodded his head when Mary asked questions. Sara couldn't see him and so wouldn't be distracted by his stares and dirty looks.

'Mr Jacobs did not wish to out you in court, but you've left him with no choice. You met him to discuss a consent agreement for a play session.'

'A what? I'm not a child.' Sara clearly had no clue what she was talking about, but the squirming on the jury bench made it clear which jurors did know.

'A BDSM play session.' Mary Stenner turned to the jury. 'Participants in BDSM, that is those that partake in dominance and submission sometimes called kink, refer to those sessions as play sessions.' Then, she turned back to Sara. 'What happened to you was a play session, not a rape, wasn't it? It was an agreed and consensual role-play that fulfilled one of your many fantasies.'

Nadia groaned whilst others in the courtroom gasped.

Marcus immediately stood up. 'May I approach the bench, Your Honour?'

A few minutes later, the court was cleared. No doubt to hear arguments relating to the late evidence and line of defence. It could take hours. Nadia found a quiet spot outside the courtroom and called Jack. It didn't take much of an explanation for Jack to appear to get the gist of what had happened.

'Seriously, they're clutching at straws here,' Jack said.

'But the jury could well go along with it since they have a witness.' Nadia sighed. 'The rough sex defence wasn't even on our radar, or we'd have discussed it with Sara.'

'It's becoming more prevalent though. I blame those stupid books. *Fifty Shades* or whatever.' Her boss changed the subject. 'How's Sara doing?'

'Not too bad. She's nervous but in control. She looked genuinely shocked by the line of questioning. Let's hope Marcus can get it struck off the record. And if not, that the jury see that it's just the defence's feeble attempt to get Jacobs off.'

'You could be out for the rest of the day. See if you can find out more about what they are suggesting. We have Sara's internet browsing records. Might as well see if she's ever visited any kink sites.' Jack paused. 'But ask her directly first. I'm sure her answer will be no, she's not kinky, but she might have experimented.'

'So, what sites am I looking for?' Nadia tried to think, but her brain didn't seem to be functioning. This had all come out of nowhere.

'Anything with *fetish* or *BDSM* in the title. Look for the word *munch* too in her messages or any use of a nickname.'

Jack seemed to know all the lingo. Nadia wondered for a moment where she'd picked that up. 'Remind me. What's a munch?'

There was a pause and then Jack said, 'It's a meeting in a public place, like a pub, where kinky people hook up to chat.'

'And why nicknames?'

'Anyone into kink is likely to have a fetish nickname so they can't be outed in public.'

At least this would keep her busy while she waited for Marcus to come back with the response from the judge on his legal questions. But there were also other things Nadia could now check in relation to the reports of a student stalker. The last thing she needed was for Jacobs to get away with it.

The list of names she had from the university were mostly for past students. Nadia's first task was to track all of them down. She'd already spoken to one or two. For example, Teresa O'Hara had been spoken to but didn't identify Jacobs as it was too dark and the stalker had hidden his face. Some had moved on and were hard to track down. One of the witnesses, she had managed to find, worked evenings at a pub in central Birmingham.

Nadia rarely frequented pubs. She considered alcohol haram. The Gin Palace had its own gin-making still apparently which didn't appeal to her, but it did mean that at 6 p.m. in the evening, it was full of office workers. She adjusted her hijab and walked up to the bar. A young woman who was waving around her credit card moved to the left to let her in.

Nadia shouted over the noise. 'I'm looking for Simone!'

The barman nodded towards a waitress serving customers by the window. Nadia thanked him.

Simone turned and stuck her pencil in her messy bun and nearly bumped into Nadia who was heading towards her. 'Sorry,' she muttered.

Nadia smiled. 'I called you, I'm from the police.'

'Oh crap, yeah. It's really busy, but I'm due a break.' She waved her hand towards the garden. 'I'll meet you outside in ten minutes.'

Nadia headed for a bench at the back, grabbing it as a couple left. A woman in a fitted orange suit scowled at her. She should have moved a bit quicker, thought Nadia. In about fifteen minutes, Simone joined her. 'You want to know about the stalker?'

'That's right.'

'Not sure you could call him that really. We think he followed us back from the pub one night.'

Followed from the pub. This was a definite pattern of behaviour. 'Us?'

'Me and Jude. You know when you feel apprehensive and are super-vigilant? To be honest, I'd felt like that all night. As though someone was watching me.'

Nadia nodded. 'Go on.'

'The next couple of nights I felt really uneasy. My room was in the back of the house and looked out over some allotments. An essay was due so I was glued to my desk. There was someone out there. Every time I looked up, there was some guy over in the allotment. He didn't seem to be doing anything – digging, whatever. Really creeped me out.'

'Did you call the police?'

'We did in the end. But no one came. Probably thought we were just some overanxious students. Told the uni too, but as it wasn't a campus flat that we lived in, they didn't seem bothered either. It was just weird and then it stopped.'

Nadia got out her phone. 'Would you recognise him?'

'It was dark. Maybe his general size or shape.'

Scrolling through some photos, Nadia eventually found a photograph of Steven Jacobs that wasn't just a headshot. 'Is this him?'

'Isn't that the mayor's son.' Simone stared at the photo. 'It could be, yeah.'

It was becoming more likely that Jacobs stalked women before he attacked Sara. He'd moved on from following women to approaching them and talking his way into their homes. But they'd need more concrete evidence. And it was so late in the day.

EIGHTEEN

Anthony Campbell opened the door as Jack approached his office. 'Come in. That's the report on the Thompson case, I hope.' He was almost rubbing his hands with glee. Maybe the case-solved statistics were low for this month.

DSI Campbell lowered himself gingerly down into his chair. He often did this after a vigorous game of golf which would explain why he hadn't been at the station yesterday.

His right arm stretched towards her. 'Let's have it then.'

Jack pulled the folder closer to her chest. 'Actually, no. It's not complete. There are too many loose ends.' Jack stood. 'I tell you what. I'll let the coroner know that we need to postpone the Pre-Inquest Review for a few weeks.'

Campbell still had his arm outstretched. 'Just give me what you've got and I'll decide.' Then he stood up and moved around his desk so he stood next to her. His height was imposing at six foot three. Imposing to some, that is.

'Sir. Just give me another couple of weeks until we have a full toxicology report on Gail Thompson, and her husband is in a more fit state to interview. I've also asked to speak to social services.' They needed the coroner to adjourn the hearing. The worst that could happen was a verdict at an inquest of suicide or unlawful death carried out by Gail if that wasn't what happened. She just needed to stand her ground.

'If the coroner thinks that's necessary after the PIR, then so be it. But there's plenty of other work to be getting on with.'

Neither of them moved until DSI Campbell crossed his arms and took a small step back. 'I hear your sidekick isn't doing too well in court either.' He started waving his finger about, but at least he hadn't made a grab for the report. 'You've got a week to sort it out and both cases better go well. Or...'

Jack didn't bother to wait for the end of the sentence. She stood up and left.

Emily had left a message on her phone. *Working late tonight. Sorry.* They were supposed to be going to the cinema. The Midlands Arts Centre was showing a season of LGBTQ+ films. She would ask Shauna to go with her instead, but it was hard to not show her disappointment. They were so early in the relationship for broken dates, and their jobs got in the way last time they tried to make it work. Jack considered ringing Emily to check everything was okay. She was being ridiculous. If she did that then she'd look desperate and clingy. *Pull yourself together, woman.*

The phone rang a few times before Shauna picked up. 'I've got tickets for tonight's film at the MAC.'

'Oh, okay. Is it the kidnapping one? Only I've already seen it with Deanna.'

It was the kidnapping one. She could always try Fran.

Shauna continued. 'I was thinking of going to my sister's tonight. Why don't you come?'

Because she's your sister. 'Why, do you need a babysitter for Bella?'

'If you're going to be like that?'

'Sorry, mate. Feeling a bit crap. Not seeing Emily tonight. You know?'

Shauna laughed, which seemed unkind to Jack. 'You've really got it bad.' Before Jack could answer, she said, 'Listen, come and join us tonight. It will take your mind off Emily and that lovely body of hers.'

Shauna always had a knack of making you feel worse. 'I'll just see if Fran can go to the film. It'll be a shame wasting the tickets.'

'What time does it start?'

Opening a pocket on her rucksack, Jack checked the tickets. 'Eight.'

'You'll have time for food first then. Do both.'

That was true. And things were slow. There was plenty of research and paperwork she could just as easily do at midnight than at six p.m. 'Okay. Did you want me to pick you up?'

'Yeah. That would be fab.' *Babysitter and chauffeur then.*

Next, Jack called Fran, who was only too happy to go to see the film.

Jack returned to her work. They needed to know whether Terry had lied to them and had been in Birmingham on the day of Leia's death. Maybe he could be the mysterious man at the cafe that met with Leia on the day she died? They had details of both the lorry company and his own car registration. Of course, he could have come into Brum by rail or bus, but he didn't seem the type to use public transport. Too much of a petrolhead. Jayden would be good for the task of finding whether he was working that day and which trucks he had access to. She picked up the phone and rang his sergeant to see if they could borrow him back.

It was never lost on Jack that she operated a transient team. Nadia and Georgia were the only constants. The rest of the staff working on her cases had to be begged and borrowed. She didn't know of another team that had to go through that process.

All the other major squads were led either by men or straight, white women with no families. In fact, there were few women higher up in the force or running more specialised task forces. Everything was always for show in Brum. Box-ticking exercises. 'We have Black officers, high-ranking women and even a super-intendent who is openly gay. How progressive we are!' But scratch the surface and that just wasn't true.

Jack didn't bother to change and was going to go directly to Shauna's sisters, but spotted an off-licence en route. She couldn't remember whether Michelle drank white or red wine, so picked up a bottle of each. Next door to the off-licence was an independent toy shop. Jack paused and looked in the window.

A woman opened the shop door. 'We're closing in a couple of minutes, if you want a quick look.'

Jack was about to say no, when she spotted a doll in shorts carrying a pickaxe. She stepped into the shop for a closer look. When she picked up the box, it was clear that the doll was supposed to be an archaeologist, but with a few adaptions – like changing her boots for flat pumps – she could be a climber. Bella would love this. Jack handed over the money for the doll with a grin on her face. It was only when she left the shop that she took stock of what she'd just done. Danny was the only parent she knew well, and she did buy his brood birthday and Christmas presents, but those were usually not thought through. She'd just grab something at the last minute and hoped that it would suit them. This purchase was different, much more personal. And that's what worried her. Was she seriously considering becoming a parent at some point? Is that why she was taking such an interest in what Bella might like?

Shauna was waiting at the side of the road, ready to be picked up. She was wearing a dress and makeup, which was unlike her. Jack hoped that she wasn't letting her sister influence her or change her in anyway. There was no way Jack's sister ever would – they were complete opposites and didn't get on at all. But she'd grown up with her. This was different. Shauna moved the packages on the passenger seat without comment.

When they arrived at the house, Jack thrust the wine into Michelle's hand. 'I've bought something for Bella too.'

'Have you, mate? Ahh, that's so sweet.' Shauna couldn't hide her shock if she tried.

Within no time, Jack was sat on the floor next to the dining table with Bella, muffled voices from the living room providing the background noise. Bella had been quick to follow Jack's lead and had changed the doll's shoes. Michelle had given them a ball of wool that Jack turned into rope for the climb. The doll was going on an expedition up a very tall mountain.

They played like this for a while. The doll had almost reached the summit of the chair when Bella let it go. It fell like a stone. Climbing Barbie landed in a messy heap on the dining room carpet. Bella laughed and held the doll at the top of the chair mountain to drop again. *If only people could do that*, Jack thought. Then she brushed away a tear.

She'd spent less and less time thinking of Hannah over the last few months. When she did, she berated herself for forgetting her so quickly. For moving on. If she truly loved Hannah, she wouldn't be in a new relationship. She just wouldn't be ready. A young child had brought the grief pouring back and Jack suddenly didn't know what to do with it. She stood up and left Bella playing, indicating to Shauna that Bella was alone and headed for the downstairs toilet.

By the time she'd finished sobbing, she was a hot mess. She washed her face in the sink and looked at the red-eyed monster staring back at her. *Pull yourself together. You can't let a kid, and people you don't really know, see you like this. You're a detective inspector, for god's sake.* She blew her nose on some tissue and used her hand to fluff up her hair. Then took a deep breath.

If anyone noticed her change of mood, they didn't say anything, and it wasn't long before they'd finished the meal and Jack had dropped Shauna off on the way to meet Fran at the cinema. She was already waiting in the foyer and kissed her on the cheek as a greeting. Jack whispered, 'Looking good.' And she did. Her long hair had been curled and her makeup was immaculate. The long skirt, jumper and boots really suited her. A few people stared. Not many; this was a community event. But one or two. There was always someone. Jack knew it hurt Fran. They'd talked about it many times. Particularly when the gender critical brigade were on the rampage and the news was full of stories of the 'trans ideological war'. Of course, all Fran wanted to do was live her life as the person she was.

Fran must have noticed her glancing at the voyeurs. 'Let's just enjoy the film,' she said, and linked her arm with Jack.

'Shall we get popcorn?' Jack asked. Despite not long eating at Michelle's, popcorn was always her guilty pleasure.

After the film finished, they decided to go for a drink and stopped off at the nearest pub to the MAC. Jack ordered a pint of IPA and Fran, a Guinness. They found a booth away from prying eyes.

'I've been thinking about your girl,' Fran said.

'Sorry?' Jack took a slurp of her beer.

'The one that you think was being abused by her mother.'

'You mean the fabricated illness case.'

'Yeah. That one. Have you spoken to the Education Welfare Department? They might have her on their list if she was homeschooled. Oh, and social services?'

'I'm hoping to arrange a meeting. But the powers that be want me to move on as the mother's dead.'

'I didn't know that. Did she kill herself?' Fran looked unconvinced.

'Why do you ask?'

'I just wouldn't expect her to. Strikes me that she'd be happy to play the grieving mother.'

Fran could be right. Gail came across as a narcissist. Why would she kill herself? It didn't seem to fit when you thought of it like that. Before her death, she was the centre of attention as a grieving mother. 'You've come across this kind of thing before?'

'It's child abuse like any other. I mean, sometimes parents neglect their kids because of their own mental health or even their own upbringing. They just haven't got a clue how to be a parent. But this sounds more like control and manipulation. More like planned abuse. The parent gets attention from having a child that's ill. Although I don't think I've come across a case before. I can ask around to see if anyone I know has. It's quite rare.'

Jack nodded. It wouldn't harm getting some more opinions. But realistically she only had a week before her boss and the coroner would be breathing down her neck. Besides, they were still looking for the man from the CCTV; possibly her father or possibly Finn. Jack hadn't ruled him out. Maybe Leia was given the drugs at the cafe on the day she died, or maybe the man had encouraged her to take them herself? Until they found him, could Jack really write it all off as the perpetrator being Gail, her mother?

NINETEEN

The next morning, Jayden was the first to approach Jack. He opened his notebook and read out Terry's working pattern for the week that Leia died.

'So, he didn't have any jobs on the day of her death or the day before?' Jack wanted this spelt out.

'Nope. He could've been in Brum on that day and returned to Scotland for work the next afternoon. His next shift wasn't until...' Jayden checked back in his notebook. 'Two p.m.'

'And did he have access to any of the trucks or do we think he travelled in his own car?'

'The owner said that the drivers occasionally borrowed the vans, but he hadn't booked one out so I'm working on the assumption that he'd used his own transport. I've asked for any motorway coverage from Scotland to Brum for that evening and the following morning. It'll take time.' Jayden looked up and smiled.

She tapped her fingers on her desk. 'Great. See what you can find out.'

'Sure, boss.' Just as Jayden was about to turn away, he said, 'Do you think all this was him? The father, I mean?'

Jack shrugged. She'd thought the same at one point. He made such a song and dance with the doctors, but then Leia had told Finn about how much influence and control her mother had over her. She would always be the more likely candidate for Leia's death. Of course, that didn't stop both of them from being murderers. Maybe Gail had poisoned her daughter and Terry had killed Gail in revenge. They needed more evidence before she interviewed him. 'Let's not assume anything. Let me know if you find any evidence that points to Terry and we'll go from there.'

The Family Centre in Acocks Green could do with a lick of paint. The rusty metal chairs didn't look comfortable and the radiators barely breathed out heat. But Jack was happy to wait, having finally managed to pin down Amira Masih, a senior social worker, for a meeting. She sat down opposite a woman with two kids under five who were vying for her attention. Bella might have tapped into Jack's biological clock, but these two were switching it back off. They screamed and punched each other and kept pulling on the poor woman's sleeve. You could tell by the way the woman was glaring at them that if she wasn't in the office of social services, she would have clouted them.

Jack tried not to stare and waited.

Amira was at least sixty years old and walked with a stick. For some reason, Jack had expected a younger woman. All fresh-eyed and keen. Most social workers she knew only stuck it for a couple of years before moving on or up into management. 'DI Kent?' she asked, holding out her free hand.

Jack shook it. Getting another glare from the woman who now knew she was police.

'Let's go to my office. Paul Chater, the Education Welfare Officer, won't be long.'

The office was a bit battered around the edges, but someone

had tried to make it look homely with a few plants dotted about. Amira navigated towards the desk. It was slow going. Too many obstacles between her and the destination, including some randomly placed discarded toys. Jack picked them up and popped them on one of the unoccupied desks.

They were about to start talking, when a man barged into the room swinging a leather briefcase. 'Paul Chater.' He boomed, 'Pleased to meet you.' He sat down at the table making it clear he'd been here before.

Paul continued. 'Leia Thompson. Now then, she was on our books for a month or so. I must have visited the home once.'

Amira dropped a file on the table with a thud. *Did this mean that they had evidence she could use?* Jack turned back to Paul. *Get him out of the way first, then shut him down,* she thought. Particularly since he clearly wanted to dominate the meeting. 'What was your impression?'

'Leia was a quiet, unassuming girl. We talked about her love of literature. She told me about the books that she had read. I also spoke to her mother about her medical needs. Fatigue being the main symptom. Gail told me that Leia could only study for an hour a day before becoming exhausted. There was nothing to suggest any other issues if I'm honest and I'm usually a good judge of character.' He stroked his stomach as though he was pregnant.

Jack tried to remain neutral and not take a dislike to this man. She turned to Amira who put on her reading glasses and opened the file sat in front of her. 'Let's see, Leia Thompson. She had complex needs and the mother was, how can I put it, a bit of a drama queen.' Then she took her glasses off and glared at Paul. 'She knew how to drag you in, quite manipulative, I'd say. All *woe is me*. Didn't much like her to be honest and I only met her once too.'

Trying to prevent a grin at Amira's takedown of the EWO, Jack asked Amira to continue.

She opened the file again, turning back through the pages. 'Leia Thompson's been on the radar of social services since she was about three years old.' That was consistent with her medical history. The time she stopped walking. 'We assisted with some adaptions and made an assessment for some extra support for Mum, who was usually the only caregiver as Dad worked the rigs.' Amira paused. 'It's funny, in my experience, that's usually a euphemism for being in prison. But in Terry Doughty's case, it was true.'

'Did Gail tell you he'd died?' Might as well see if there were any inconsistencies.

'Yes, she did,' Paul butted in.

'No, actually. She told me he'd run off with the local barmaid and she had no idea where he was. But there are other accounts in here. Some social workers were told he was dead – the more gullible ones.'

Jack blushed. How long had *she* believed Gail's lie? 'The neighbour at their latest address, she told me that she reported Gail for shouting at Leia.'

'Let me see.' Amira flicked through the file. 'Ah, yes. It was rejected as malicious. To be honest, the person reporting has a history of causing arguments and has her own issues, shall we say.'

Jack was tempted to push this, but doubted Amira would be more forthcoming. 'You did keep an eye on the family – long term, I mean.'

'Yes. There were, however, no reasons to suspect that Leia was being mistreated or neglected,' Amira said. 'The house was spotless. Leia had a restricted diet, but wasn't underweight. Her health needs were being met, even though they were complicated. It was her mental health that caused more concern.'

'Were you aware she was seeing a psychiatrist?'

'Dr Sharma?'

'Yes. That's the one. And there are reports Leia had hit her mother.'

'I didn't know about that, but Leia did have a mental health diagnosis...a personality disorder. This may have been caused by her not having much social contact with people, especially of her own age, outside the home.'

Jack nodded. It was clear that social services didn't have anything concrete to add, other than Amira's instinct that Gail was a mass manipulator and a storyteller. If any of the adults in Leia's life were likely to fabricate illness, then it was likely to be her. 'We believe that Leia had a carer who induced her illness.'

'Her mother?' Amira asked.

'She seems the most likely culprit. We think she may have caused Leia long-term pain by poisoning her. But it's difficult to prove and now her mother is dead.'

'But you have to know the truth.' Amira appeared to be studying her. Jack shifted in her seat.

'Well, there's nothing to be gained if she's dead, is there,' Paul triumphantly announced.

'But you still need to know the truth. Good for you,' said Amira.

If Jack had any concerns about children, she'd contact Amira in the future. This woman had wisdom that only came with experience.

The drugs report for Gail Thompson pinged into her email that evening. Gail had ingested Citalopram, Codeine and another drug, Chlorpromazine, an anti-psychotic. Jack checked the medical report that they'd received from her GP. She was prescribed Citalopram, as they already knew, but not the other drugs on the list. Codeine, anyone could get from a chemist, but Jack needed to find out more from a doctor about Chlorpromazine.

Emily hadn't contacted her since breaking off the date. Jack texted her to see if she was free for a chat. Then she waited. First, she made herself a coffee and then returned to her paperwork. After half an hour, she got back up to pop a ready meal in the microwave. Some tasteless chilli con carne. Perhaps Emily was working. Although she vaguely remembered her mentioning that she was on days this week.

When it turned nine, and she still hadn't heard anything, she contemplated ringing her. This was what happened before. They had a few nights out and some great sex then it all fizzled out. Jack hadn't minded then. She liked being a free spirit and not in someone else's pocket, but she had to admit she was feeling lonely, and she really liked Emily.

She could ask other doctors the questions she had. Dr Pride, for one, and Leia's psychiatrist. He'd know if Leia had been prescribed any antipsychotics. If they had any in the house, suicide might be more likely. She searched her phone for his number.

Kishran answered straight away.

'Sorry to disturb your evening. I need some advice about a specific drug and thought you might be a good person to ask,' Jack said.

'Fire away,' he said, with no indication she was disturbing him.

'Chlorpromazine. Is it a drug Leia would have access to?'

'I didn't prescribe it for her.'

'Do you use it at the centre?'

'It's actually quite a commonly prescribed drug for a number of conditions, including anxiety, schizophrenia, autism even. What dosage are we talking about?'

Jack referred back to her notes. 'One thousand milligrams.'

'That's exceptionally high. A usual daily dosage wouldn't exceed four hundred milligrams.' A hint of concern in his voice. 'Did she die of an overdose?'

At this point, Jack realised that he was referring to Leia and not Gail. She corrected him. 'The drugs were found in Gail's blood. *She* died of an overdose.'

'I thought you meant Leia. I'm sorry to hear that. It's so hard when you've lost a child. Is there anything I can do to help your investigation?'

Jack paused for a moment. 'Actually, there is. You mentioned a girl that had made friends with Leia while she was staying at the clinic. Could you contact her and ask if she will see me?'

'Yes. Happy to. I'll contact her family now. As you can imagine, we're all still so upset about Leia.'

Jack ended the call soon after. Perhaps Leia had confided in her friend. It was certainly another avenue to explore.

TWENTY

The persistent rain matched Nadia's mood. She made a dash from her car to Birmingham Crown Court with her coat held above her head rather than worn. The last thing she wanted was to sit in the courtroom with a wet hijab all morning. Cautiously, she stepped into the revolving set of doors. Too often she'd been the one that caused these doors to stop to a jarring halt. She spotted Marcus, a few places in front of her, in the queue for the bag check. He turned just at the right time for her to smile and gesture towards one of the benches outside of court number one.

He waited for her to meet him there. 'I haven't got long. I still need to get my papers ready for court and I want to catch Sara before we go back in.'

'How did the discussion with the judge go?' It appeared to have taken a good few hours as they'd been another long adjournment. Nadia was beginning to wonder whether they'd ever get to a verdict.

'He accepted that the line of questioning did not match the statement provided by the defence prior to the trial. The defence argued that this evidence was acquired late and cited case law.' Then Marcus paused.

'And?'

'The judge decided that the line of questioning would stop, but they could include their witness and ask them questions relating to the meeting in the coffee shop.'

Nadia noticed he was sweating. Was there something he wasn't telling her? He wiped his brow with the sleeve of his gown. 'The witness details weren't shared with me. We would have interviewed them prior to court.' Nadia didn't hide her anger. They'd received the defence statement which stated that the sex was consensual. It also included their list of witnesses. She'd checked the names and they were all either character witnesses or expert witnesses.

'The woman only came forward days before the trial.' Marcus raised his eyebrows. 'If you can believe that.'

Shaking her head, Nadia said, 'They must think we're daft.' She paused, trying to work out how to phrase it without him thinking that she didn't trust Sara. 'I spoke to Sara and checked her internet activity. There's no evidence that she's ever partaken in kink.'

A grin formed on Marcus's lips. 'I'm surprised. Haven't we all tied someone up or given them a quick spanking.'

Nadia took a deep breath. 'Sara hasn't. From what she said anyway. And the defence shouldn't be questioning her on that, should they?'

'Not usually, no.'

Over Marcus's shoulder, Nadia spotted Sara coming through Security. She looked exhausted and far less confident than she had the previous evening when Nadia met with her to discuss the shocking defence. She focussed back on Marcus, while at the same time gesturing to Sara to join them. 'What does that mean?'

'I'm about to explain that to Sara.' He waited for her to reach him before saying, 'Let's find somewhere private to talk.'

Marcus led them both to an empty witness waiting room. He closed the door and waited for Sara and Nadia to sit down. 'The thing is the judge has decided that the defence can ask two questions related to rough sex or BDSM. The first is: Have you ever partaken in sexual role-play involving a rape scene and/or a knife? The second is: Did you discuss having a sexual play session, and what your parameters for that would be, with Steven Jacobs prior to the evening that the alleged attack took place?'

Nadia could understand the second question, that was directly related to the case, but the first included prior sexual history. Did they have some evidence of that? 'I'm surprised the judge is allowing the first question.'

Marcus looked directly at Sara. 'And what would your answer be to it?'

She paused, just for a moment and Nadia noticed a blush form at the bottom of Sara's neck. 'Ask me again.'

'Have you ever partaken in sexual role-play involving a rape scene and/or a knife?' Marcus asked in the same voice he used in court, clear, deep and forceful.

'No.' Sara shook her head. 'I haven't.'

Marcus stood and moved towards the door. 'You'll be fine. We start back in twenty minutes. Why don't you both get a coffee.'

Sara sat in silence for the whole time they waited for the court to restart. She wouldn't look directly at Nadia, taking small sips of coffee from the tightly gripped disposable cup.

'Is there something you're not telling us?' Nadia felt she had to ask.

'No, there's nothing.' But still she didn't look directly at

Nadia.

Nadia waited. She could now hear the persistent drip of rainwater from a broken gutter outside the window. She stayed silent, hoping that Sara would trust her enough to tell her the truth as she felt she was keeping something back. But it was soon time to go into court for the start of the session, Nadia stood. 'I'll need to go if I'm going to get a seat. You need to make yourself known to the usher.'

Sara nodded and turned her head away to face the window.

The courtroom was almost full, but Nadia managed to squeeze into a seat on the right of the prosecutor's bench. It wasn't long before the court was called to rise for the entrance of the judge. Then Sara re-entered the witness box. She looked tiny, as though she'd shrunk between visits.

The defence barrister stood, readjusting her gown.

Before she spoke, the judge turned to the jury. 'We have discussed relevant sections of the law. The defence will now ask two questions that I have agreed to. You should disregard the questions and answers from the point in the cross-examination where Sara is asked if she met Steven Jacobs in a cafe.'

Mary Stenner QC coughed. 'Did you discuss having a sexual play session and what your parameters for that would be with Steven Jacobs prior to the evening that the alleged attack took place?'

'No, I did not,' Sara answered.

Mary looked as though she was going to ask a follow-up but stopped herself. 'Have you ever partaken in sexual role-play involving a rape scene and/or a knife?'

Nadia stared at Sara. This was the question that worried her. Sara stared at the floor. Despite Nadia willing her to look up at the barrister or the jury, she didn't. 'No. I never have.'

No. It's not enough. Nadia swung her head to the right. The jury looked puzzled. And no matter how many times Nadia muttered in her head that it didn't matter, it did.

TWENTY-ONE

The long drive to the house only emphasised the wealth of the occupants. The lawn and surrounding shrubs were immaculate, maintained, no doubt, by a professional gardener or even a team of gardeners. When Jack pulled up to the house, she checked the address. It was such a contrast to Leia's two-bedroomed terrace. But it was right. This was Charlotte French's home, the young woman that had befriended Leia at the clinic.

As she got out of the Range Rover, a woman walked towards her from the already open front door. She held out her hand. 'Louisa French, you must be DI Kent. Charlotte is waiting for you in the drawing room.'

Jack shook hands with the woman she assumed was Charlotte's mother and followed her into the house. Signs of inherited wealth dripped from every surface, from the paintings on the walls to the rugs on the oak parquet floor. The drawing room was larger than Jack's entire flat. A young girl sat with her legs up on the overstuffed settee, receiving looks of disapproval from her mother. She immediately sat up planting her feet on the floor and smiled at Jack, who sat down beside her.

'I'll get you some tea.' Louisa left before Jack could say that she preferred coffee.

'Sorry. She didn't really want us to meet. I don't think she approved of Leia.'

Charlotte pulled up a sleeve of her jumper. Then quickly pulled it down again to her wrist. Not before Jack had noticed the lines of scarring on her arm.

'Why did you? Befriend Leia, I mean?' Jack asked.

'I liked her. The other girls were so...dramatic. Everything was such a struggle for them. Leia just sat and read on the bench outside and didn't get involved.' Charlotte wiped her eyes with her hand. 'They didn't like that. They used to tease her. The staff were useless. They couldn't care less what went on when he wasn't there. So, I looked out for her.'

Trying to hide her surprise, Jack asked, 'When who wasn't there?'

'Kish.'

Kish – not Dr Sharma. Jack parked that for a moment. 'Did Leia talk to you about her family?'

Charlotte shrugged. 'A bit.'

'What did she say?'

Louisa chose that moment to come into the room with a tray. She placed it on the coffee table. 'Shall I be mother?' Jack shot her a look. Of course, Louisa could insist on staying for the rest of the interview as Charlotte was sixteen and vulnerable, but Jack hoped she wouldn't, knowing full well that she'd get little out of her daughter if she did. 'Actually, why don't I leave you to your little chat.' Louisa tapped her daughter on the knee, stood and left the room.

Smiling, Jack said, 'Where were we?'

'I didn't like her mum.'

'Whose mum?'

'Leia's. She was always hitting on Kish. Everyone noticed. It was disgusting.'

Dr Sharma had a hold on these girls. It made Jack feel a little uneasy. 'What did Leia say about her mum?'

'She said that she hated her. She couldn't go anywhere apart from the hospital and she made her eat rubbish all the time. She said she might run away.' Charlotte almost spat out the words.

'Run away from the clinic?'

'No, she wanted to be at the clinic. Run away from home, if they made her go back.'

'When did she say that?'

'As soon as I started speaking to her, about a week after she arrived.' Charlotte leant over to pour herself a cup of tea. 'Do you want one?'

'No, it's fine. What else did she say?' If only Leia told her that she was being poisoned.

'Cake. I can cut you a slice.' Charlotte held up a knife.

'No, thanks.' All Jack wanted was to learn more about her friendship. 'Leia?'

'She wasn't allowed any friends or to go to school. She talked about school a lot. Asked me what it's like. I go to boarding school. I told her it's shit, full of bullies.' Charlotte took a gulp of tea. 'I think she would have swapped places if she could. I'd be up for that.'

'Did she ever mention a boyfriend?'

'No.' Did Jack notice a moment of hesitation? 'Are you sure? She might have met them at the library, say?'

Charlotte dug her nails into her wrist. 'She didn't say anything to me,'

Jack paused. She wasn't convinced by this, but Charlotte was becoming agitated. She changed the subject. 'Did Leia say anything about being ill?'

'We were all ill, that's why we were there. I can't tell you how much I hate hospitals, but the clinic was okay. Most of the time. At least it was just pills.'

'What do you mean?'

The girl paled. 'Nothing really. I've been in a few hospitals with stuff. That's all.'

She could have been referring to the self-harming. But maybe there was something more. 'Leia was ill a lot, wasn't she?'

'About as much as the rest of us. Always at the doctor's, in and out of hospitals, no one knowing what to do with us and our stupid brains.'

Without warning, Charlotte grabbed the knife off the tray and attempted to slice at her forehead. Jack grabbed her wrists.

She shouted, 'Mrs French!'

The door to the drawing room swung open and Louisa gently took the knife and pulled her daughter into a hug. 'It's okay,' she said in a calm voice. Then she turned her head to face Jack. 'I think you'd better leave.'

The whole meeting left Jack with a feeling of apprehension and concern. She couldn't help thinking that she'd messed up. Had she pushed Charlotte too far? If she spoke to her again, she'd take Miriam with her or a social worker. Not that there was likely to be a next time.

Jack took a moment to compose herself and to think about what to do next. She decided to drive to the library. It was becoming clear that Finn was far more of a friend than he was letting on. Luckily, she'd caught him at the end of a shift. He'd just left the library and was walking a steady pace towards the bus stop.

Jack pulled up alongside him and opened the passenger door. 'Get in. I'll give you a lift.'

He seemed to be hedging his bets. Maybe he thought she'd abduct him. But at least he'd save money on the fare. He climbed in next to her,

'I want you to be honest with me,' Jack said as she pulled away.

He nodded.

'You and Leia were clearly close. Did anything happen between you? Were you meeting up outside of the library?'

'No!' He slammed his hand on the dashboard. 'It wasn't like that.'

'Wasn't like what?' Jack continued. 'Leia was fifteen. You know it's illegal.'

He blushed an unhealthy shade of crimson. 'We never... I can't believe.'

'But you met her, didn't you. On the day she died, you met her at a cafe.'

He looked confused. 'No!'

Jack decided to push it further. 'You know Gail Thompson is dead?'

He nodded.

She was tempted to ask if he killed her, but that would completely cross a line. It wasn't like she'd read him his rights. 'How do you feel about that?'

'She killed Leia. She got what she deserved.' He spat the words out.

Could he have killed Gail in revenge?

The rest of the journey had passed in silence, Jack knew she'd overstepped the mark. She slammed her backpack down on the desk at the station. They'd need a witness. Someone who'd seen Finn at the cafe. Or some forensics linking him to the house. He was guilty of something. Jack was sure of it.

And then there was Dr Sharma. The more she heard about him, the more she was beginning to dislike him. The GMC would have his work history. It would be worth checking that.

Charlotte had also mentioned that Leia wanted to run away. Could she have been doing that on the day of her disappearance? Could the person in the cafe be facilitating that?

Jack reached again for her phone to call Emily. She was ready to dial and then she stopped. What if she didn't want to hear from her? Asking her about a medical issue might just make the recent distance worse. Of course, Jack wanted her as a lover not just an adviser, but asking her a medical related question might equally be the shoe-in she needed to talk about more personal things. Her hand began to shake as she made the call. It rang twice before going to voicemail. Now she was convinced Emily was ignoring her even though it was just as plausible that she was working. She shouldn't have made the call. It made her feel worse.

The GMC had a public register on its website. There were two Dr Sharmas, a man and a woman, on the registrar's list. Both fit to practice. Dr Kishran Sharma was listed as a consultant psychiatrist, registered since 2006. That seemed to fit. It stated his current employment since 2017 but no previous.

Jack's fingers hovered over the keyboard. You could type any name into the search engine. She wasn't sure why, but she found herself typing *Finn Locke*. A single line of text followed. Finn Locke was a medical student at the local university up until eighteen months ago. He'd only studied for a year it seemed. He must have dropped out. But he had some medical knowledge. Was she right? Was he wrapped up in this in some way? Could he have killed Gail? Or even Leia? But why would he do that?

They'd emailed the GMC before and had little response. Jack dialled the number to contact an adviser.

Another wait for an answer and the adviser said as soon as she mentioned she was police, 'I'll have to put you through to another department, hold the line please.'

A moment later, the call was answered. 'This is Elaine Garrett. How can I help you, Inspector?'

'We contacted you about a week ago for the full record of

Mr Jarvis Taylor, a Paediatric Consultant at Heartlands Hospital.'

'Bear with me.'

Before she could say anything else, the call was put on hold again. Only this time she was met with silence and not awful music.

'Ah, yes. Mr Taylor,' Elaine said, on returning. 'We don't have any records past 2016, I'm afraid. It looks as though he left the profession.'

Jack jotted this down. 'Did he go anywhere after Heartlands?'

There was a short silence. 'Yes. He went into private practice for a couple of years. A clinic in the South East. I can't give you the name over the phone. We'd need to do that officially.'

Jack reminded her of the *official* email that they'd already sent, twisting the pen she was holding which promptly fell apart.

'You should have the answer soon. Couple of days at most.'

Jack sighed. 'Could you look up someone else for us?'

'Of course.'

'Dr Kishran Sharma. I've used the registry on the website. Can I have his former employment?'

'You'll need to put in a formal request for that too, I'm afraid.' Jack could hear the impatience in Elaine's voice.

'Why don't you ring me back at the station, then you'll know I'm legit? We really need that information to help with a serious enquiry related to a child. Surely this information is in the public domain anyway?'

'Not when there's any investigations into their conduct.' The line went quiet. 'I'm sorry, I shouldn't have mentioned that. You'll need to put a request in through the proper channels.'

'An investigation?'

'Dr Sharma is fit to practice.'

It was clear that she wasn't going to get anymore from

Elaine, so after hanging up she fired off an official email for more information. Knowing that they would give little information about the conduct issue that Elaine alluded to.

She then asked about Finn. They could only confirm that he hadn't qualified.

There was so much going on. It was getting hard to focus. Emily; her teammates dropping out of the expedition; the lack of progress on the case. Jack was starting to feel anxious that everything was unravelling. The old fears came streaming back. She held her breath for a moment. Counting slowly, she willed herself to breathe normally again. For a moment, she'd feared she was heading for a full-blown panic attack. They'd plagued her life for over a year. Now they were more infrequent. She needed to get a real grip on at least one aspect of her life.

Her phone pinged. It was Danny.

Fancy a trip to the Ice Climbing Centre?

There was only one indoor ice climbing centre in the UK. But it was in Kinlochleven, Scotland, and would mean taking at least a few days' break. Danny knew what she needed training wise. He had a point. Eighteen months had passed since she'd ice climbed. It wasn't a skill that you lost. Like most physical activity, you could rely on muscle memory, but it would hurt if you didn't use those muscles regularly.

Before she replied to Danny's text, Jack decided to pay another visit to the Tudor Manor Hospital. On the way she called Louisa French. She was pleased when Charlotte's mother answered the phone, fearing she might blank her. 'I'm sorry about earlier. Is Charlotte okay?'

'Yes, she's fine. She's had fewer outbursts since she's been getting treatment. As you've probably guessed, she has a history of self-harm.' Louisa sounded deflated.

'I've just got a quick question. Was Charlotte referred to the clinic by the NHS?'

'No. It's a private clinic. And an expensive one at that. But Kish works wonders.'

Every time Jack had visited Tudor Manor, her interview was cut short. This wasn't going to happen this time. She spotted the flashing blue lights as soon as she turned into the clinic's sweeping drive. What could have happened now?

An ambulance was parked close to the clinic's entrance. Its back doors were left wide open with no sign of the paramedics. Reception was deserted. Jack walked in and listened out for any sign of what had happened. The lift in the far right corner pinged, the doors opened and a teenage girl was pushed out on a carry chair by an ambulance technician. Their partner followed with Dr Sharma and a nurse behind them. The girl's wrists were heavily bandaged and her head lolled to one side as though she had been drugged.

Kishran turned to the nurse. 'You phone her parents and tell them I'll meet them at the hospital.'

The entourage passed Jack, barely acknowledging her presence as they made their way to the ambulance. The nurse ran over to the reception desk. After rifling her way through a file, she picked up the phone and dialled a number. Only then did she spot Jack; she motioned to the seats opposite the desk.

Jack sat down and waited for the nurse to finish her call. As she walked over to her, Jack realised that she'd seen this nurse before at the children's hospital. It was the woman that she'd nearly crashed into when she was looking for Dr Pride's office. 'What's happened?' Jack asked, although she was pretty sure she knew the answer.

'One of the patients cut her wrists,' the nurse answered in a monotone voice as though this was a daily occurrence.

Jack nodded. 'You work at the children's hospital too, don't you?' Then added. 'I'm sorry, I don't know your name.'

'Shelley... Shelley Anderson. I do bank work there, yeah.'

Jack knew this referred to taking on agency shifts in nursing. Shelley was chewing her lip, weighing up whether to say something. 'Shelley. Is there something we need to know... about the clinic, I mean?' Jack didn't want to push her too hard, but there was clearly something bothering the nurse.

Shelley smiled. 'No, it's not about here. It's something else.'

'What?'

'I don't want to talk about it. It's not about my work.'

Jack racked her brain. What else could it be? 'Is this about another case I'm working on?'

Shelley shook her head but wouldn't look her in the eye.

'You know Steven Jacobs?'

Shelley sat back up looking like a rabbit caught in the headlights. Jack knew she was right.

Minutes passed in silence. Jack knew if she waited. Shelley would answer.

Eventually, she said in a quiet, steady voice, 'I recognised you from the TV reports about... about the case.' After a pause, she said, 'He raped me... Steven Jacobs raped me.'

'And you didn't report it?' Jack tried to stop this sounding like an accusation.

'No. I was too ashamed.' Shelley's deep-brown eyes met Jack's, who got the feeling that she was now ready to talk. Without saying anything, Jack reached for her notebook and pen. 'You're going to write this down?'

'Can I be honest?' Jack asked. Shelley nodded. 'The case hangs in the balance. If we can get your testimony heard in court, it would make all the difference.'

Shelley sighed. 'You might not think so when you hear it.'

'Try me.'

'Okay... I lived in a ground-floor student flat while I was

training, 'round the corner from Sara's. And, well, some odd things happened. There were times when I felt that someone was watching me. It got to the point when every evening, as soon as I got back from college, I'd close all the curtains even if it was still light outside.'

The reports of a stalker that Nadia mentioned.

'One night, I got home late. I had an essay to finish.'

Jack interrupted. 'When was this?'

'Sunday 4th March. Two years ago. It's not like I'm ever going to forget it.'

Jack wrote down the date. 'Sorry, go on.'

'I'd literally just turned the key, opened the door and walked into the flat. He followed me in.'

'And this was definitely Steven Jacobs?'

'Yes. It was him. I actually knew him from the campus. He wasn't a student there. But he used to hang out in the student bar.' Shelley shuddered.

'What happened next?'

'He told me not to scream. He wasn't going to hurt me.' She started to cry. Jack placed a hand on the back of Shelley's shoulder as the nurse covered her face with her hands. 'He had a knife. Little, like a Swiss Army knife. He held it up so I could see it. Then he pushed me against the wall, placed a hand over my mouth, pulled up my skirt and raped me in the hall. I still had my backpack on.'

'I'm so sorry, Shelley. My guess is that he's done this to many women who have been too ashamed or scared to come forward. I know this is hard. But we do need a formal statement from you.'

'But who would believe me after all this time?' She started to take long, deep breaths. 'I didn't scream, fight him off. How will that look?'

'He had his hand over your mouth and a knife at your throat. What else could you do?'

She started to sob again. 'I laughed when he finished.'

A silence engulfed the space between them.

This was what had caused her shame. A reflex. Hysteria.

'Shelley.' Jack pulled the nurse towards and hugged her. 'You weren't in control. Speak up. We'll take your case straight after this one. Whether he's found guilty or not. Take back control. It will help seeing him go down for this.'

'Who'll believe me?'

Jack sat back. 'I can't promise that the jury will. But it will be two women with similar stories, not one. It will make a huge difference to his overall sentence if convicted. Please come to the station and make a formal statement.'

Shelley nodded. 'I will.' She wiped her face with her sleeve. 'I can't come yet. The other girls...they'll be worried about Jo. I need to go and check on them.'

Jack assumed Jo was the girl who had cut her wrists. 'Will you come straight after?'

'Yes.'

'I'll send a car for you.' Jack didn't trust her to come on her own. Then she added, 'Why didn't you say anything when they did the door-to-door after Sara's rape?'

Shelley stood up. 'There was no way I was ever going to live in that flat after that. I went to live with my sister. I wasn't there when it happened to Sara.'

Jack knew that Nadia was tenaciously searching for more women. Some might never be found. Especially, if, like Shelley, they didn't want to come forward. The system often failed women who were sexually assaulted. It wasn't just the trauma of reliving the event, it was the fear that they wouldn't be believed. That their rapist would walk free.

And now she had to tell Marcus that he'd probably need to prepare for a second trial against Jacobs.

TWENTY-TWO

'Can't we just add her as a new witness at the trial?' Nadia asked. She'd felt completely excluded from the conversation between Marcus and Jack. She was meant to be the lead officer. Jack should have raised this with her first. Was she supposed to just be happy that she would be carrying out the initial interview with Shelley Anderson in the morning?

Marcus sighed and said, 'This will need to go to a new trial. If the CPS thinks there's enough evidence, we can charge Jacobs with this rape once this one is completed. It's a whole new complaint.'

Did he have to be so condescending? She was just checking. 'Do you think he'd change his plea at this late stage if he knows we're got evidence against him?' They needed to explore all options, surely.

'We could raise that we have another complainant with the defence. It might sway them into looking for a deal. What do you think?' Jack turned towards Marcus, who was now sitting on the edge of the windowsill.

'Let's see what she gives us in the interview.' He stood up.

Maybe he thought this was the end of the discussion as he headed for the door of the witness room.

'Wait.' Nadia raised her hand. 'There were other reports of a stalker in the area where both Sara and Shelley lived. I followed them up, but that's all it was and only one of them tentatively identified Jacobs.'

'Might be worth doing another house-to-house, but include students that lived there up to, say, three years ago and include those from the hospital too,' said Jack.

Nadia understood why this was complicated. There was a possible new case to investigate. The trial had already begun, and they wouldn't be able to link the evidence to this, but if they did decide to try Jacobs for the second offence then they needed to be sure there wasn't a third victim out there or more. 'I'll go back and interview them all formally, if you're sure the super will sanction it. What do we tell Sara?'

Marcus scratched his forehead just under his wig. 'Nothing. She's given her evidence. Let's see what the defence come up with to counter, but I think we know where this might be going.'

'Do we have a name for their coffee shop witness?' Jack asked. 'Might be worth checking their credibility.'

'I've got it.' Nadia checked her watch. 'Let's get back to the station. We need to be there to meet Shelley.'

'I'll fill you in on the afternoon session later,' said Marcus.

Next on the stand was one of Sara's flatmates. Nadia hoped her testimony would go smoothly.

When he reached the door, Marcus turned. 'Do you fancy a drink later?'

He was only looking at Jack so Nadia kept her mouth shut. Did her boss blush before saying yes?

TWENTY-THREE

Watching the video of the interview, it was clear to Jack that Shelley Anderson would make a good witness in court. She spoke with clarity and dignity. Of course, there were no guarantees. It was possible that Jacobs would be acquitted and that would make any further prosecutions twice as hard. Jack didn't want to consider that. Now they were tying the stalkings and rapes together, she expected them to find others that had gone through similar ordeals. She had little doubt Jacobs was a serial rapist. At the time of his arrest, their main aim was to get him to court and secure a conviction. With hindsight, they should have spent more time looking for other possible victims. Not that she or Nadia could be blamed for a police constable's misfiling of the stalking reports. But Jack saw this as another indicator about how ill she'd been at the time. Grief had affected her work. There was no denying it.

By mid-afternoon, she completed a good chunk of paperwork relating to the interview. Georgia sat staring at her laptop screen. Jack had asked her to look back into all of the hospital doctors and GPs that Leia Thompson had seen. The GMC would be sick of them by the time they were finished. Someone had hurt Leia, poisoned her even. It could have been Gail, it could have been her father, but what if it wasn't? What if it was someone else? There was still something about Finn that bugged her too. Whoever this was would need to have regular contact over years with Leia though and they hadn't identified a consistent family friend, doctor, nurse or social worker. Maybe they'd not looked hard enough.

By five o'clock, Jack was ready to clock off. Marcus texted just at that moment.

> Where shall we meet? M x.

She should reply: *Let's not.* Or: *Sorry, I'm too busy.* Instead, she considered going.

If it was down to him, they'd end up at a wine bar near the courts. All very exclusive and full of his middle- and upper-class mates. The food would be excellent but expensive. But she wanted him on her turf. That way she was in control, so she replied:

> The Loft in half an hour?

The beer would be good and so would the atmosphere. The food would be the very worst in terms of her pre-climb diet, but then so would any of Marcus's choices – too much cream and butter in the sauce.

Jack arrived first. The Loft was pretty much empty so she had her choice of seats. She chose one of the booths at the back. Like most of the bars in Birmingham's gay quarter, the Loft held out its arms and pulled you in with a friendly hug. And it was a Wednesday, so no entertainment, which for Jack was always a

bonus. She preferred listening to live jazz than any other performance, queer or otherwise.

The eclectic mix of beer and cocktails on offer meant it
catered for everyone. Jack chose a craft beer. Effie, one of the
regular bar staff, took her order just as Marcus arrived. Jack
watched him scan the room with a look of, not exactly, horror
but something on that vector. He spotted her and walked over,
choosing to sit on the opposite side of the booth. 'We could've
gone anywhere you know. I'd have paid.'

This comment was met with the silence it deserved. Some
women might be in awe of Marcus Barnet QC, and she had to
admit he looked stunning in his neatly tailored grey suit, but
she'd seen him at his worst. Their friendship started back when
he was a paralegal and running errands around chambers.
They'd literally bumped into each other and he'd dropped a
whole bundle of files in a puddle. Jack had finished her
'moment in court' as a PC who'd witnessed the robbery of a
corner shop, so she was able to stop for an hour to help him sort
the papers into a reasonable order.

They hadn't jumped into bed together. That came much
later. A case they were jointly working on came to an abrupt
end when the main witness jumped in front of a train. The
horror of this led them both into needing some physical
comfort. The relationship was pretty much doomed from that
moment on. Jack still couldn't work out how they remained
friends after spending so much time arguing over the most
random and irrelevant things. The sex, mind you, had always
been good. Too good.

'I'll have a glass of the Sauvignon Blanc, if you can recommend it.' Effie, having just dropped off Jack's beer, raised her
doubly pierced eyebrow at this and jotted Marcus's order on
her pad.

Jack took a sip of her drink. 'What do you reckon with the
Jacobs case?'

Marcus shrugged. 'Could go either way. Everyone knows the story of Steven Jacobs and his dad. Even the jury, unless they lived under a rock last year. It will come down to who they believe and whether there's enough evidence to support it.'

'What about a deal? The interview went well with Shelley today. We may well find other women too. Can't you approach the defence, see if they'll go for a guilty plea rather than further charges down the line?'

Marcus scratched his head. 'What's the CPS said?' he asked.

'Haven't spoken to them yet. But if they say there's enough there to charge, will you go for a deal?'

Effie brought the wine at that moment. 'Did you guys want something to eat? Or shall I give you a moment?'

Jack mumbled her order. Marcus chose the same. As Jack's eyes followed Effie retreating back, she missed spotting Shauna striding towards them.

She grabbed Jack's arm. 'Excuse us a minute.'

Not having any choice, Jack followed Shauna outside to the garden.

Shauna waved at a woman with a mass of short, blonde, curly hair. 'This is Deanna. Deanna – Jack?' Then she sat down with enough force to rock the table and the pair of beers that sat on it.

Jack sat down next to her. Shauna leant over. 'What the hell do you think you're doing?'

'I was just—'

Deanna had the cheek to smile and reach for her beer as if it were popcorn.

'He's married! Or had you conveniently forgotten that?' Shauna, for all of her alternative, keep-your-distance persona, was actually quite parochial when it came to love and relationships. Something which Jack often forgot.

'I'm having a meal with him. We're mates. It's what mates do.'

'What about Emily?'

Deanna put down her beer and said in an Australian drawl, 'Who's Emily?'

'Emily is her girlfriend, which I think Jack may have forgotten.'

Full marks for the scowl, Shauna.

'Number one. I'm an adult and I can make my own mistakes, believe me. Number two. I don't think Emily sees herself as such. Number three...' Jack was going to say that she had no intention of sleeping with Marcus. 'This conversation is ridiculous and I'm starving.' Jack stood up.

Shauna took her hand. 'You'll regret it in the morning, I promise you.'

Pulling her hand away. Jack left the two to gossip about her. Fortunately Marcus hadn't given up on her and left. He still sat in the booth looking out of place among the queer folk. As she made her way through the tables, her phone buzzed. It was Danny. No doubt waiting for an answer about the Scotland trip. Jack motioned towards Marcus that she needed to take a call and headed towards the corridor leading to the toilets.

Danny didn't bother with a 'Hi, how are you?' 'I've worked out that we can fly from Brum to Glasgow, have a few sessions at the centre and fly back the next day. Flights aren't too expensive either. What do you say?'

It wasn't a bad idea. If they went this weekend, it would give her some thinking time too. 'Go on. Book it. I'll send the money over. Won't Gemma mind though?'

'Dad'll look after the climbing school and he's offered to babysit so Gemma gets to go out with her mates. She's okay with that.'

Jack tried to imagine Uncle David surrounded by Danny's brood. She hoped that Gemma had the foresight to send them to bed before he arrived. But they were his grandkids. Something her own dad would never experience.

By the time Jack returned to the booth, the food had arrived. She got stuck in without trying to explain why Shauna had whisked her away. Marcus didn't look amused. His silence made that crystal clear. The rest of the evening was spent in polite conversation about mutual friends until Marcus said, 'It's all been a mistake.'

'What has?' She had to take the bait, not ignore him.

'Getting married.' His brown eyes bored into her, making her squirm in her seat. 'I thought the differences we had would be ironed out once we were settled. To be honest, I thought we'd have a baby on the way by now and would be busy making future plans together as a family.'

'You thought a baby would solve your problems?' Jack couldn't quite believe what she was hearing.

'Well. No... I mean...' He'd moved his legs forward so he was gripping her right lower calf with them.

Jack wriggled her leg out of his hold. 'I always thought you were an intelligent guy.'

Effie chose that moment to collect the plates. 'Another drink?'

'What whiskies do you have?' Marcus turned his tired face to Effie.

It was going to be one of those nights. She might as well join him. They both chose a Glenfiddich.

Marcus stroked the side of her hand. Jack wasn't surprised this aroused her. There hadn't been many men in her life. Out of the few, Marcus was the constant. He was in trouble and was seeking solace. She was, no doubt, stupid enough to give it him. The whisky wouldn't be enough on its own.

Out of the corner of her eye, Jack spotted Shauna leave with Deanna. Jack quickly pulled her hands away, but she could still sense her friend's disappointment from across the room.

· · ·

In the end, Jack left the Loft alone. They both chose to get separate taxis feeling heavy with either remorse or the aftereffects of one whisky too many. The usual bright streets of the Gay Village did little to lighten the mood as the taxi weaved its way towards Jack's flat.

Once home, she spotted that the hall cupboard door was ajar. Jack kept all of her equipment neatly stored there. Before Saturday she'd need to pack what she needed for the ice climb. Her three pairs of ice axes were stored away, fitted with axe guards and wrapped in cloth to ensure they were kept clean and dry. Her favourite pair had belonged to her father. The blades were longer than modern axes and the shaft was covered in a light-coloured wood. Jack unwrapped one of them and held the shaft to her nose. The faint smell of oil and varnish took her straight back to watching her father ascending the peak above her. The flash of the axe and the bottom of his boots all that she could see of him.

She wrapped the axe back up and picked up a pair of lighter ones. They would need to be sharpened before Saturday so she left them on the table next to her case files. Hopefully, she could do it in the morning if she woke up early enough.

The plane made its ascent and Jack almost grabbed for Danny's hand. She hated flying. Years of landing and taking off from 'the scariest airport in the world', Lukla in Nepal, had finished her off. It didn't help that she was flying in a similar biplane. A newer one, but still as small, and it rattled.

When they were in the air, Danny said, 'Any thoughts on your climb? Is it going ahead?'

So that's what he thought. Without support, she'd crumble and cancel the whole expedition. The previous night, she'd tossed and turned, agonising over what to do. She had an idea of how to proceed. Now was the perfect time to test it on someone she trusted. 'Well, actually, I've decided to make it a Sherpa-only climb. Just me and a Sherpa team. Not as support, as equals. That's how it will be billed and that's what I'll take to the investors.'

Danny nodded his head. 'They'll treat it as a solo climb.'

'No. I won't let them. I've even thought of looking for a film crew that will focus on the Sherpas. It might mean that we'll have to postpone, but I'm hoping not.' It wouldn't be the end of the world. She could tie up more loose ends at work. Maybe even get to the bottom of her relationship with Emily, who she still hadn't heard from.

Once the flight was over and they had left Strathclyde and hit the highlands, they were met with an imposing landscape of lush, tree-carpeted valleys encircled by mountains.

They soon arrived at the Ice Climbing Centre.

Jack realised she was starving and headed over to the cafe. A young woman, with long auburn braids, smiled at her across the counter. 'What can I get ya?'

'A black coffee and chicken salad. Thanks.' Jack took her card from her wallet. The girl put her hand over the machine. 'We don't charge for celebrities.'

'Does the boss know?' Jack gestured at the pair who were still deep in conversation with Danny.

'Who cares?' She held out her hand. 'I'm Casey. I boulder when I'm not serving the paying public.'

Jack shook her hand and caught the glint in her eye and the wide, knowing smile. 'Pleased to meet you.' She picked up the food and drink. 'Better get on to it.'

If she was cool enough, she might have swaggered, but instead Jack almost slipped on a chocolate wrapper as she went to join Danny, who'd arranged their climbing times for the day.

. . .

Cold air has its own fresh smell, untainted and pure. It stripped away your nerves when climbing but replaced them with fear. Frost bite, slipping and not stopping, ice burns. Your senses run in overdrive. Above all, you are alert and more alive than you could ever be in an office or a city.

A crampon boot shoved into fresh ice follows each move of the axe as you climb. Kick hard with your foot, get a good shoe hold and then reach up and replant the pick. One foot, then the other. It's the opposite of rock climbing. It has clear pattern and rhythm.

Two hours of climbing and Jack felt new and refreshed. Whatever dark thoughts she had about her current cases and relationships, the expedition cleansed from her mind.

Her phone rang as soon as she stopped below the ice wall to take a breath. It was Nadia. 'You'd better get back to Brum quick. There's been another sudden death. A young girl, only thirteen.'

TWENTY-FOUR

There was no quick way to get back to Birmingham. If they drove, it would take them over seven hours. There wasn't a direct flight back until the morning either. The sensible option would be to wait for that and trust her team to begin investigating in her absence.

In her frustration, Jack kicked a bin in the cafe, spilling some of the rubbish on to the floor. Casey rushed over. 'What's up? Surely your session wasn't that bad?'

Jack realised she was still wearing crampons on her boots. Bending down, she removed them before she did any more damage. 'I've got to rush back to Birmingham. Unless you know someone with a time machine or a teleport, I don't think you can help.'

'What about a helicopter?'

Jack stared at Casey, trying to work out if she was kidding. 'Seriously?'

'I'll just call my dad. Give us a sec.' Casey got out her phone; turning her back on Jack, she spoke in hushed tones. Then she hung up and turned around. 'Sorted. He'll pick you up in the car park in about forty-five minutes.'

'Your dad has his own helicopter?' Jack gestured for Danny.

'Yep. Well, it's his boss's really, but I'm sure he won't mind when he knows it's for you.' Casey couldn't hide her excitement.

Danny decided to sit the trip out and stay over. He'd fly back in the morning and at least get to ice climb again.

Feeling nervous, Jack strode towards the helicopter instinctively dropping her head before climbing in. Casey's dad, Fergus, wasn't what Jack expected. He looked more like a hippie traveller than a successful businessman.

'So good to meet you, Jack. I have to admit, I'm a bit of a fan as I'm sure Casey told you.' He eased the helicopter vertically into the air. 'Don't worry, I've done this flight a few times before.'

Jack knew she didn't look any less worried than she had before he spoke. She much preferred to spend her time with inanimate objects like mountains than anything that had the capacity to drop out of the sky.

Any hope of spending the journey planning what she would do when they landed in Brum was quickly extinguished. Fergus clearly liked to talk. Even the heavy sound of the rotor blades didn't put him off. He'd given Jack a helmet with an intercom which she had no way of knowing how to switch off.

There were some moments of interest. Passing above mountain stretches and into valleys, for example. Fergus knew which range they were crossing, how high they were, their composition. And it was wonderful seeing crag that she knew from a different angle. By the time they crossed into England, Jack felt a longing for a permanent move to Scotland.

Clouds were gathering, ominously grey. She didn't know much about helicopter flying but hoped this wouldn't lead to a choppy flight or even to grounding them.

Her phone vibrated in her pocket. It was a text from Emily:

Hey, mate. What're you up to today?

She could just not answer since Emily had ghosted her for a week. But she decided to be the adult in the relationship.

Got another suspicious death. Sorry. Will speak when it calms down.

Perhaps this was how it was going to be. All hopes of a steady relationship dashed. They would just be sexual encounters when they both had the time. Jack wasn't even sure if that was worth bothering with. Maybe it was time to call it quits.

Fergus must have judged Jack's morose mood, which darkened to match the encroaching cloud. He stayed relatively quiet until they reached the outskirts of Brum. The grim weather still following them at a distance. 'We've got an office on Hill Street. We use a heliport about half a mile away. Will that be okay for you?'

Checking the location of the suspicious death, Jack replied, 'Perfect.' She could easily get a taxi to the scene – a terrace in Small Heath. She even considered getting a taxi home and picking up her car. It would add about fifteen minutes to the journey, but she'd saved hours by using the helicopter.

As soon as they landed, Jack rang Nadia. 'Where are you?'

'Still at the house. I've made everyone hang on until you arrive. Shauna's been quite brutal about that.' Nadia sounded in control.

'I'll go and get my car. Should be with you soon. Thanks for keeping the wolves at bay.' Nadia would know what that meant. There'd have been pressure from other teams to take on the case, particularly since she wasn't in the area. But she'd learn more once she got to the address.

· · ·

The house was not dissimilar to Leia's. A typical Midlands terrace. The front door directly on the street with a large window next to it and one above. Jack put on a forensic suit and closed the boot of her car. A private ambulance was parked outside with two young men sat in it, reading newspapers. Jack nodded at them as she went past. The curtains twitched at a number of the houses opposite. This would be the cause of gossip for weeks, maybe longer.

The front door was ajar. Jack tapped on it, pleased to see that it was opened fully by a police officer with a clipboard. He noted her name and ensured that she'd changed into a forensic suit and shoe coverings. A woman, who Jack assumed was the mother, sat rocking backwards and forwards on the settee. Nadia pointed to upstairs. 'The girl, Sammi, was found this morning collapsed in the bathroom. She was a wheelchair user. The ambulance crew arrived within minutes, but couldn't revive her.' Nadia dropped her voice into a hush. 'The crew had a few suspicions of neglect or possible parental abuse so they notified the police.'

There was something not right in the house which Jack noted when she entered the property. Her instincts were generally sound about these matters. It wasn't anything you could immediately put your finger on, but the air around her felt heavy and claustrophobic.

There wasn't room for both Nadia and Jack to enter the bathroom. The door was open. Jack could see a young girl lying on her back. Shauna was in guard dog mode, hovering over the body. She smiled as Jack squeezed into the small space. 'Sammi was found on her front. Her head...' Shauna pointed to a gaping red gash on her forehead. 'Had hit the toilet seat as she fell.'

'I was told she was a wheelchair user.' Jack couldn't see any signs of a chair. Maybe someone had moved it. She was also unsure how the girl had got upstairs as there wasn't a stairlift.

'According to the mother, Sammi needed the chair if they were going out for a walk but could negotiate the stairs and the house with the aid of a stick.'

Jack couldn't see one of those either. Considering what she'd seen of the house – piles of clothes on every surface, cups and plates piled on tables, too much furniture – Jack couldn't see how the girl could navigate a chair anyway.

'Did the fall kill her?' Better to concentrate on cause of death and consider other factors, like neglect, later.

'I think...' Shauna sat up. 'She may have been dead or dying which caused her to drop to the floor. There's so little blood from the head wound.'

Jack scanned the bathroom. Shauna was right. There was a smear on the toilet lid which was a clear plastic with red hearts set in it. At first glance, Jack had thought these were blood splatter, but they were too uniform when you got closer. Even the cut on the head did not appear to have bled much and it was quite a wide gash. 'So her heart stopped and she fell. Maybe she came to the bathroom as she was feeling ill. I'll speak to the mother. See how sudden that was.'

'Nadia's spoken to her. Her mother heard her leave her room. It sounded like she was crawling to the bathroom which she sometimes does. Her mother just assumed she just needed the toilet. Until she heard the crash. I can only assume that her heart stopped as she tried to stand to use the toilet.'

It wasn't hard to make the link with the other case. But this could be a perfectly natural death of a young girl with underlying health conditions. Or it could be a case of neglect. What else had Nadia and their team picked up to call her?

'You can move her when you're ready.'

Shauna nodded and started to put her instruments back in her bag. Nadia was still standing on the landing. 'Which bedroom is Sammi's?'

Nadia nodded towards the one next to the bathroom. It was the smaller of the two facing the back of the house. Sammi wouldn't have had to crawl far. The bed was unmade. It looked as though the duvet had been pushed to one side as the girl had got up. There were piles of discarded clothes everywhere. A small television sat on a stand next to the bed. An old-style Play-Station in front of it with a well-used controller. The room smelt damp. Jack turned and spotted the walking stick next to the door. She wondered why Sammi hadn't used it. Maybe she felt too weak to even stand.

Her mother had sat downstairs oblivious to this. But that could have been normal for her. Her mother wouldn't have had time to administer any care in any case if what Shauna believed was true. If the mother did care, of course. Jack needed to talk to her too.

Before she did that, she took a look in the mother's room. It looked as though any money she had had been spent here. The duvet cover looked new out of the packet. Even the furniture looked new compared to the tatty off-white wardrobe and chest of drawers in her daughter's room. Nothing was adding up.

Back downstairs, Sammi's mother still sat rocking. Someone had brought her a tea which steamed on the table in front of her. 'Mrs Jones?'

The woman looked up. Her eyes glazed like she'd been drugged. 'Yes.' Spoken in a barely perceptible whisper.

'I'm DI Jack Kent. Can I talk to you about Sammi?'

The woman nodded. Jack sat down on the settee next to her. 'I know this must be a shock, but can you tell me what happened this morning?' She took out her notebook and pen.

'There was a crash.'

'When was this? Do you know what time roughly?'

The woman stared at the large television that hung on the wall. 'The 3:20 at Kempton had just finished.'

A gambler then. Perhaps that explained the newfound wealth. The television looked new too.

'How was Sammi's health generally?'

'She was improving according to the GP. He thinks it's all in her head. Not walking and that.' The woman rubbed the plump skin on her arm. It was already an angry red.

'Can you tell me more about that?' Jack tried to hide the impatience from her voice.

'She's been ill since she was a child. She had leukaemia from the age of five. I thought I was going to lose her. But the doctors worked miracles.' Her face lit up at this.

'Go on.'

'They gave her the all-clear on her seventh birthday. She was fine for a couple of years. Although I panicked when she got even a slight cold.'

'I can imagine.'

'But then they were other things. She woke up one day with pins and needles in her legs. Then this spread to her arms. She used to have dreadful migraines too.' Jack noticed as she spoke about the illness, she became more confident. The timid, quiet voice had gone.

'Was this related to the cancer?'

'No. The doctors didn't think so. Though I don't even think they knew what it was.' She scratched at her arm again and it started to bleed.

'We'll need to look at Sammi's medical records. Can you tell me the name of your GP and how long you've been with them?'

'Years and years. It's Dr Marsh on the corner. She's amazing. Always gets us an appointment.'

'What school did Sammi attend?' Of course, the circumstances of the two girls lives would be different. There were no reasons to suspect a connection. Only the suddenness of their deaths and ongoing medical issues.

'The Academy on the High Street. It's okay. But they're

always threatening to fine me as though it's my fault Sammi is so ill and can't attend school.'

Jack noted this down. When she looked back up at Mrs Jones, she spotted a photograph in a silver frame on the sideboard behind her. She put down the notebook and went over to it. *Surely it couldn't be.* Holding up the photo, she asked, 'The man in the photo, who is he?'

TWENTY-FIVE

Sitting in the interview room, he shrieked, 'We weren't that friendly even. I don't know why she kept a photo of me.'

Jack wasn't convinced by Terry Doughty's act. Two teenage girls had died suddenly and he seemed to be the only link. Now what she needed was a confession or a motive. It seemed incredible that this truck driver could want to murder two young girls, one of whom was his daughter.

'Let's go back to Leia's death for a moment. We know she met with a dark-haired man on the day of her death.' Jack took a photographic still from the folder in front of her and placed it in front of Terry. 'This is you, isn't it?'

As if to make the point, Terry ran his hand through the mop of his dark brown hair. He lifted the photo. 'No, it's not.' His voice rose a pitch. 'I haven't a clue who that is.'

'I can tell you that we've trawled CCTV in the area and this...' Jack stabbed her finger at the photograph. '...is someone that doesn't want to be seen.' Georgia had checked every shop camera in the vicinity. Whoever the man was had left the scene with his collar turned up so they couldn't catch a glimpse of his face. But Terry matched the frame and height of the man.

Nadia interjected. 'We've spoken to the haulage firm. You weren't working on that day. You could have driven down to meet Leia. Poisoned her...'

'What?' He looked genuinely shocked. 'She was poisoned. How?'

'A mixture of drugs that weren't prescribed to her. Same as your wife. And, of course, you had every reason to kill her too.'

'Well, you're right about that.'

Jack raised her eyebrows. 'Sorry?'

'I did have every reason to kill that bitch, Gail. Not that I did. But Leia and this other girl. You can't really think I did that?'

They needed to come up with a motive. He was right. He had plenty of reasons for killing Gail. She hated him so much that she refused to let him see Leia and told everyone that would listen that he was dead. What possible motive did he have for killing the girls?

'When did you meet Mrs Jones and her daughter?' Maybe there was something in their relationship. She needed to dig further.

'About a year ago. Sammi was on the same ward as Leia. We got talking in the kitchen. We had a lot in common. Having daughters who were often sick, like.'

'And you kept seeing them?' Jack knew this from Mrs Jones. Every time he had a trip in the Midlands, he'd pop round. He'd even bring flowers and chocolates.

'I couldn't see Leia. The bitch put paid to that so I'd see Sammi and her mum instead. We got quite close.' He must have noticed the frown. 'Not like that. What do you take me for?'

'You won't be the first man to be attracted to a vulnerable woman.'

'Ellen Jones, vulnerable, you having a laugh.' Then he must have stopped to think about it. 'Okay, she did sometimes get upset and we did, well, have a cuddle. Once... Just once, mind, we ended up in bed.'

Of course Jack and Nadia already knew that. Ellen had told them. She'd also told them that she'd only slept with him when she was drunk and in need of some company. She soon found he had 'an unhealthy interest in Sammi'. He often asked about how she was, which doctors she was seeing. He even suggested new ones to try. Maybe that's what he got off on.

They just didn't have enough evidence to charge him. An hour later, Jack sat in DSI Campbell's office.

'Time's run out, Jack. The coroner wants to open the inquest.'

Time had run out on Terry's interview too. They had to release him. But it only made her more sure that Leia's death wasn't suicide or natural causes. They could hand over what they had already. The coroner would, no doubt, look at the reports from the police, social services and the medical practitioners and decide to adjourn the full inquest. It would be a better outcome than a week ago when there was a possibility that he'd go ahead with a full inquest with what he had. They needed more time to ensure the verdict was at least an open verdict or even a suspicious death.

'How's the court case going?' DSI Campbell changed the subject.

'The defence opens tomorrow. Nadia's not hundred per cent hopeful. The responses from Sara Millings could have been stronger. I'm kinda hoping Jacobs takes the stand and trips over his arrogance.'

Anthony nodded. 'You and me both.'

'I'll email you the full report on Leia Thompson, this afternoon. I don't think we've got time to do a paper copy.'

Jack waited to see if this annoyed her boss. He'd always

demanded one before, but he didn't respond. Perhaps he was starting to trust her, but it was more likely he had an appointment with a five iron.

Emily texted again that afternoon asking Jack if she fancied a meetup later. This was starting to annoy Jack. Why couldn't relationships be simple? Why was there always this to and fro like misdirections in drama? If you liked someone, you made time for them. You didn't just go hot and cold. But so many relationships that Jack encountered were toxic. Including her own parents. As a child, she always thought that despite her mother not enjoying climbing, or any outdoor activity, she loved Jack's father. Her father could be quite distant, but Jack always felt that she lived in a loving, comfortable home.

When her father died, everything changed. In her eyes, her mother seemed to get over his death quickly. Too quickly for someone that had lost the love of their life. She seemed to relish her newfound independence particularly at weekends. No longer did she have to go camping to mountain ranges, or, on the times she escaped these, no longer did she have to do the preparation. Her younger sister, who had appeared to enjoy the climbing trips, also found every excuse not to climb a mountain again. This had made Jack even more independent so maybe she should be grateful to them.

Jack's relationships had never run smoothly. She could blame the job and the weird hours, but it wasn't that. There were always extremes. She was aloof and didn't put in any effort, or she fell hard. Where she was aloof, she was able to maintain a string of one-night stands or serial encounters. Then there was Hannah who she completely fell for but whose death meant she would never know if this was reciprocal.

For some reason, she thought a relationship with Emily would work, but that had fallen flat. Perhaps it was time to put in some effort to find out why. Or she could take up Marcus's apparent offer of an affair, but that idea was completely ridiculous!

The rest of the afternoon and early evening was spent preparing her report for the coroner, while the rest of the team were following up on various leads. So much of investigating a case was to follow a line of inquiry that took you nowhere. A bit like those line mazes in kids' puzzle books. Very occasionally they led to something tangible.

The person in her team that Jack could trust to do this work was always going to be Georgia. The minute details of an investigation were her specialty; whether that was trawling CCTV or researching into someone's history or acquaintances, she was the best person for the job. So Jack wasn't surprised when Georgia appeared at her desk with a huge grin on her face. 'I've got to get home to put my kid to bed, but I think I might have found something about the doctors on the Thompson case.'

Jack's heart sank. She was hoping this might be a tie in for Terry Doughty – a chunk of tangible evidence that would tie in both cases. But, instead, this could pull them further away. She had to hear it though. 'Go on.'

'We know that the doctors regularly changed.'

And that Sammi Jones's didn't. 'Yes.'

'I can't find some of the names Gail gave us on the GMC database, and where they exist, they were only in Brum for a month or two or only worked for a short while before leaving the profession or leaving the country. They disappear from the records.'

How could multiple doctors disappear from official records? Doctors often left the profession, of course, but it seemed a coincidence that so many of Leia's doctors would have done so. Surely, they would have been reported missing if they simply vanished? Jack's blood ran cold. Had they been killed? Was whoever killed Leia an actual serial killer? Is that what Georgia was implying when she said they were missing?

Georgia must have spotted the colour run from her face. 'I don't think they're dead, just no longer practising. Am I okay to follow them up?'

'Yes, definitely.' Another thought crossed her mind. 'Did you find anything else out about the other sudden death cases?'

'There was no evidence that they'd been operated on. Not like Leia. I didn't take it any further as I didn't want to upset their families. It was a bit of a long shot.'

'See if they had any links with any of the missing doctors.'

Georgia made a note in her notebook and stood.

'And add Dr Sharma and Finn Locke to that list. Maybe he knew them as a student doctor or in some other way.'

They didn't have much else. Nadia was making a list of possible questions for Ellen Jones. The plan was to go and visit her in the morning. In the meantime, Miriam had been assigned as her FLO and was keeping in touch with regular updates on her behaviour. Ellen was also heavily sedated which made any prospect of an interview difficult. Jack finished the report and sent copies to DSI Campbell and the coroner, making it very clear that there would be an ongoing police investigation into the possible murder or manslaughter of Leia Thompson. She didn't state that there could be a link to at least one other girl's death, not wishing to jump the gun. Then she emailed Nadia to ask for the questions. Later that night, she would go through them and add to them, leaving Nadia free to attend court the next morning.

She had a bit of time free to meet Emily for a drink. Perhaps work would be more constructive knowing where she was with the whole relationship thing.

. . .

Emily had chosen the canteen at the hospital for coffee as her shift started at nine. It gave them half an hour. When she walked in, Jack spotted Emily straight away. She looked stunning even in scrubs. Her blonde hair was freshly washed, and she wore a hint of makeup. Jack wondered hopefully if this was for her benefit. She'd managed to wash her face and apply some deodorant in the women's toilet at the station. That was about it.

Jack sat down opposite Emily. Neither spoke for a moment. Eventually, Jack said, 'This is nice.' And they both laughed.

She took a deep breath. 'What have I done wrong?'

Putting her hand over Jack's, Emily said, 'What do you mean?'

'You went cold. I'm guessing I did something to upset or annoy you?'

'You're joking, aren't you?' Emily scowled.

'No. I'm deadly serious. One minute...' Jack moved closer so the only other person in the cafe, a young nurse, wouldn't hear what she said. 'One minute we were having great sex and enjoying each other's company. The next, I don't hear anything from you. You don't answer my texts...'

'I've been working. Maybe you're just too needy.'

Jack could feel her face redden. 'Needy? Me?'

'Well, we both knew that work was going to get in the way. Our jobs...'

'Yeah. I know that, but how hard is it to send a text or return a call. Clearly you're not bothered about me at all.' Jack felt like running.

Emily just grinned at her over her coffee cup. 'Actually, you make me very hot and bothered. We've only been seeing each other for a short time. Chill.'

She was right, of course. And for some reason, Jack had let her thoughts wonder to the future. She was rushing ahead and was bound to be disappointed. Chill wasn't a word in her vocabulary.

'Listen, Jack.' Emily took her hand again. 'I really like you and I do think if we take things slowly, we could have something more long term. But at the moment it is just, not casual, but not that serious either. If you get my drift.'

That was another issue. Jack had never actually lived with another woman, or man for that matter. Perhaps she'd hoped this would lead to something more permanent and she would get the chance to experience that. That might be the opposite of what Emily wanted, however. She was such a klutz and had the social skills of a gnat.

'Why don't we go away somewhere. I know I've mentioned it before, but let's book something. When my case has finished and before I have to shoot off to Nepal.' *If they were able to tie the case in a bow and this expedition ever got off the ground.* How could she make it sound so hopeful?

'I'd like that,' Emily said, nodding. 'But for now let's just enjoy each other's company when we can. I'm on days from tomorrow so how about I cook you something on Thursday evening.' She stood up and leant in until she could whisper in Jack's ear. 'And bring your toothbrush.'

TWENTY-SIX

Mary Stenner QC stood and addressed the court. 'I call Steph Bishop, Your Honour.'

A woman in her late thirties was ushered in and took her place in the witness box. Nadia knew that she was the cleaner at the block of student flats where Sara lived. A fact they'd finally been given when she was added to the witness list.

Asking her first question, Mary stood confidently and faced the jury, 'Mrs Bishop. Can you tell the jury how you know Sara Millings?'

'Yeah. I can. She's one of my kiddies, that's what I call them anyway, at the halls.'

'Halls?' Mary asked for clarification.

'The student flats that I clean. In fact, she's one of the nicer ones. Never much to do in her room.'

'Thank you.' Mary Stenner turned and waved towards Jacobs. 'And how do you know the defendant?'

'I seen him round. He was always on campus with those posh mates of his.'

'And where did you see them both together?'

'In the coffee shop just up the road from the halls. It was a

Monday. Cleaning always takes longer on a Monday as we don't clean on Sundays. Well, you can imagine. Anyway I like to treat myself to a coffee and a sandwich.'

'I'm sure you do. You were sitting near the two of them, I believe, and you could hear what they were saying.' A slight grin formed on Mary's face. She knew what was coming next. Nadia hated the pair of them for the fabrication but knew how this would play to the jury.

'I couldn't help it. I was sat behind her. Sara, I mean, and well, I couldn't quite believe what I was hearing.'

Mary held the lapels of her robe and leant in. 'Go on.'

'He mentioned sommat about what she'd consent to. And, oh my word, she said that she had certain... fantasies. I nearly spat out my sandwich.'

The look on the faces of the twelve jurors said it all. But this wasn't the end. Nadia knew Marcus had something up his sleeve to counter her lies.

It soon came to his turn. He rose slowly, turning over pages of his notes. Then he coughed, making sure all eyes were on him. Nadia knew a court case was pure theatre and Marcus was a principal actor. 'Can I call you Steph?'

The cleaner blushed. 'Yeah. That's my name.'

'Steph. Do you still work as a cleaner?'

'Well, er. What do you mean?'

Mary started to rise.

But Marcus continued before she could object. 'You resigned from your post, didn't you. When was it...?' He turned over the pages as though looking for a date.

'Two months ago. I, er, had an inheritance.'

'I'm sorry to hear that, who was it that died?' *No one, of course.* 'We can check.'

All eyes were on Steph as her face grew redder. 'It was my great-aunt. That's who it was.'

'You never did see Sara Millings or Steven Jacobs in a cafe, did you?' Nadia glanced at the jury. They were hanging on each word.

'Yeah, I did.'

'You never did see them and you need to be honest – you were paid to say that you did. Who paid you?'

'No one...' Steph looked from the judge to the jury. 'No one paid me.' Then she stared at the floor.

'No further questions, Your Honour.'

Nadia crossed her fingers. Was it too much to hope that this would have turned the jury back in their favour?

TWENTY-SEVEN

Jack reached for the coffee pot. She'd woken early and had time to use the Italian-style pot on the stove. It was always much nicer than an instant cup. The pot wasn't where she normally kept it on the windowsill near to the cooker. It wasn't on the draining board either, nor in the dishwasher. She eventually found it in the cupboard next to her mugs. Was she going mad?

Without another thought, she spooned a few teaspoons of her favourite coffee into the pot, added water and turned on the gas. Then she bit into some fresh strawberries and waited. She needed to understand what motivated Terry Doughty. Hopefully, she'd get more of a handle on him today when she spoke to Sammi's mum.

But she did have to consider what would lead Gail to proclaim that he was dead? Was it a toxic or abusive relationship? There wasn't any firm evidence of that in her mother's interviews. Gail clearly hated Terry, but there could be many reasons for that. The rumblings of a migraine clouded her thoughts.

. . .

An hour later and Jack was sitting on Ellen's sofa. She looked better today. Miriam had said that she'd slept well. The house was much tidier too. Jack wondered if this was the FLO's work.

'I'm sorry we have to do this, but we have to be sure that there's nothing suspicious about your daughter's death,' Jack began.

'She was so poorly. Always.' That explained it then. She was poorly and she died. Perhaps it was that simple. Jack looked up and noticed the photo of Terry had gone.

'What was the prognosis for Sammi?'

'Prognosis?'

'Outlook. In terms of her health.'

'I know what prognosis means. I mean, there wasn't one. The cancer stayed in remission. They didn't think the problems with her walking would last. She was doing okay apart from that.'

'Was she taking any medication?' Best to rule out any painkillers or antidepressants in case they found them in her system.

'No. Painkillers sometimes. But nothing else.'

'What sort of painkillers?'

'Oh, you know. Ones you get from the chemists. Co-Codamol, that kind of thing.' At least, Ellen wasn't scratching her arm today. It looked red and sore.

'And did she take them regularly?'

'Once in a while, when the leg and back pain got to her or when she was having a bad period. You know what that's like.'

Jack did. When she was training for a climb, her periods practically stopped, but the rest of the time they could be painful and heavy. 'When did you meet Terry Doughty?'

'It was at the hospital in April. A couple of years ago. I'm sure it was April. I'd just won a tidy packet on the National.' Definitely a gambler, then.

'And you saw him a lot after that?'

'No, not really. Occasionally, he'd be at the same hospital at the same time. Fate really.' Ellen smiled. 'Then when he was having problems with Gail, he got in touch more regularly. He missed his little 'un.'

Jack assumed she meant Leia. Although, she was hardly little. 'So, he came around a lot?'

'Once every couple of weeks, maybe. When he had a job near here.'

'How was Sammi's health during this time?'

'Well, it wasn't that great, to be honest. Probably coincided with her monthlies. She'd take to her bed which I think is why me and Terry got quite close. Bit of company for each other.' Another smile.

'And did he stay over? Did you give him a key, for example?' If he could let himself in then he could have the opportunity to poison Sammi. If she was poisoned, that is.

'Don't be daft. I hardly knew the bloke.'

That scuppered that idea.

'Oh, actually, I did once. He said he'd get me some groceries in while I was at my sister's, so I told him where the spare was.'

'And where do you keep the spare? Can you show me?'

It took her a couple of goes to get off the sofa. 'Yeah, follow me.'

Ellen walked into the kitchen, opened the back door and walked into the backyard. 'The gate isn't locked. The kids from next door only climb over it if it's locked.' The path to the entry from the other houses seemed to come through her garden so that was understandable. Ellen picked up a plant pot and sure enough there was a key. 'This fits the back door.'

'I'd stop doing that. If you want my professional opinion, it's not safe.'

Terry had opportunity then. He could easily have got in while they slept and put poison in Sammi's food or replaced her tablets with new ones. But why would he?

· · ·

After leaving Ellen's house, Jack spotted a message from her mother.

Call me.

She ignored it and instead contacted Dr Sharma. He was at the clinic and invited her over. Jack needed some insight into why Terry might want to hurt the girls and kill his wife. He was still their main suspect. Gail couldn't kill anyone else. She was dead. Georgia hadn't found any links with the doctors she was tracing or at least she hadn't brought any to her attention yet. And there was no apparent link between Finn and Sammi.

Kishran sat attentively, watching her. 'You want to know what causes a caregiver to fabricate an illness?'

'In your professional opinion, could a parent kill their own child and then go out of their way to kill again. This time someone outside of their family circle.'

He leant back in his chair. Jack imagined he used to wind up his teachers doing that. She was the one always looking out of the windows in school, but she recognised the type.

'Think of it like a vampire. You want a continuous supply of what you need to live. In a vampire's case, blood. In the carer's case, the attention that a sick child brings. All those visits to hospital with everyone asking if you're okay. Playing the martyr.'

'There's more to it though surely. And if you're getting attention, why kill them?'

'Good question. Maybe the child has discovered that you're hurting them? Maybe they're threatening to tell the other parent? Or maybe they need more of the poison to become sick and you accidentally give them too much?'

'So, it could be an accident.'

'Could be.' Every time he leant forward, Jack sat back. He always seemed to encroach on people's space. He wasn't doing it to her.

'Or it could be murder.'

'There are many cases where a caregiver has killed their child. Often, it's something as innocuous as salt poisoning. But it does happen. You tend to only hear of the brutal cases in the media. Where a father, for example, has shot his wife and children then turned the gun on himself.'

Of course, Jack had heard of examples of both but not directly worked on them. 'Did you meet Terry Doughty?' she asked.

'No. He was away working on the rigs when Leia was a patient. I did get the impression that her parents were not getting on at the time though.'

'Gail stopped him from seeing Leia. In fact, she told people he was dead. Is that what she told you?'

'No, she didn't, but she wasn't exactly enamoured with him. Called him all the names under the sun. Said he was a dreadful father.'

'Gail told everyone else he'd died. I'm surprised she didn't tell you and I, obviously, didn't get the opportunity to ask Leia whether she thought her father had died. I wouldn't have put it past Gail to do that.'

'I see. Leia always talked about her father with some affection. She was angry that he was away a lot and that he didn't help her gain her freedom. She felt trapped at home.' He rubbed his chin. 'Actually, that might explain why she fixated on me.'

'Fixated on you?' Jack dropped her pen. This was the first she'd heard of this. If he'd said Gail had fixated on him, then she'd already seen that.

'A lot of teenage girls are looking for father figures. Particularly the ones that come here. As you know, most of our patients are from wealthy families with fathers who work away a lot or spend excessive time at the office, so it's not surprising they look for a male role model. It's called transference.'

It was obvious he didn't mind being the father figure. In fact, teenage adulation was probably something he relished. Jack tried to not show her disdain. He may have even imagined Leia's fixation due to his own arrogance. 'How did Leia display this?'

'The fixation?' *Did he really grin?* 'Just by seeking me out. Particularly in the evenings when the other girls were in bed.'

'You stay here at night?' For some reason Jack had assumed he didn't work shifts and was just available to run therapy sessions during the day.

'I have an apartment in the eaves. I live on-site.' He started to drum his fingers on his desk. 'Of course, why would you know that?'

'And Leia would come to your apartment at night?' Now she was worried.

'No. Of course not. If that started happening, then I couldn't be her physician. No, I meant she would come to my office.'

'At night?'

'I often work late, Inspector. I spend most of the day organising group or individual therapy. It doesn't leave me with much time to keep the girl's records up to date. So, I often eat in my room then return to the office to work for a few hours.'

Jack nodded. Let him think that she believed him, at least. 'Can I see Leia's records? There might be something in them that would help us identify which of her parents was the abuser. If there was one.'

'I'm not sure they would help. I tend to use a shorthand that only a fellow professional would understand.'

This clearly meant not her. 'Perhaps you could interpret them for me? Could we book some time in this week?' She needed to either rule Terry in or out and she just didn't have enough evidence to charge him yet. It was frustrating. A session with Dr Sharma might just give her more to pinpoint him as the person that harmed Leia and then went on to hurt Sammi.

Georgia pulled Jack to one side when she got back to the station. Under her arm was her laptop. Her eyes shone with enthusiasm. Jack wondered how long it would take working for West Midlands Police to dull that spark.

'I've managed to get a contact at the GMC. They've told me that so many doctors ending practice at that point in their career is unusual. Junior doctors leave because of the intensive work-load and many retire early. But for those in the middle of their career, if they dislike working in hospitals, they tend to get jobs in private practice or become GPs. You might expect one doctor in a long string of doctors to go missing, but I've now counted at least seven.'

Georgia scrolled down her spreadsheet. Each of these doctors she'd highlighted yellow. What on earth was going on?

TWENTY-EIGHT

Steven Jacobs grinned when he placed his hand on the bible. Surely the jury spotted this. They must think, as Nadia did, that this guy was a vile, nasty human who'd raped at least one woman and, in all likelihood, more. Of course, because of the vagaries of British law, the jury did not know about Shelley.

Nadia glanced at Marcus. Did he look uneasy? Had his cool, composed veneer been fractured by the performance of his main witness? If anything, he looked tired, a little older maybe, but still in control. Unlike Sara Millings. She looked like a scared mouse.

The first questions from the defence were the usual *what is your name/address?* Steven stood composed in a blue two-piece suit, pale-blue shirt and a darker-blue tie. He probably wore brown shoes, the uniform of young male influencers, but these were hidden behind the witness box.

'How do you know Sara Millings?' Mary Stenner QC asked.

Nadia heard Sara take a deep breath behind her. Then felt her slowly exhaled breath on her neck.

Brushing a hand through his blond hair, Steven said, 'I'd

seen her around campus a few times. Thought she looked quite, well, up for it. Submissive, like.'

The eyes of the jury moved as one in the direction of Sara.

'Why were you on campus, Mr Jacobs? I believe you'd left your course a few months earlier.' It appeared Mary wanted to ask the difficult questions before Marcus did.

'You're right, it must seem a little odd, but I missed uni life. Yeah, I know I should have knuckled down.'

That lopsided grin again. Did he think it made him look charming? Nadia shivered.

'So, you liked to hang out with students. Go to the places they ate and drank,' Mary continued.

'Yes. That's right.'

'And you approached Sara Millings when?'

On the day you raped her, you little bastard, but you won't say that.

'The last week before Easter. We were in the same cafe. I told her that I liked the dress she was wearing. She was on her own, so I asked her to join me.'

'And what did she say?' Mary adjusted her wig slightly.

'She smiled that cute little smile of hers and played hard to get. It's what they all do.'

He was beginning to sound more like an incel by the minute. Nadia shuddered.

'All do?'

Steven coughed. 'Young women. They all play coy. Like they're not interested. When they're really gagging for it.'

Nadia spotted the flash of annoyance on Mary's face. He'd gone too far.

'And when did you see her again?'

'She gave me her phone number. We texted a few times. Then moved on to Discord.'

'Discord?'

'It's a chat server. We swapped videos and stuff.' That dreadful smile said it all.

'And stuff?'

'She sent me videos of herself and described her fantasies to me.'

Where is it? Where's the evidence? There wasn't any. Nothing on Sara's phone. The techs would have found it.

'What happened to the videos, Steven?'

Yes, Steven what happened to the videos.

'I got rid of them. After we met up. She asked me to. Said she'd only wanted to play once. So, of course, I did what she asked.'

And now he was trying to make himself out as the hero. Nadia sent a quick message to Marcus, hoping that the judge wasn't the type to frown upon mobile phone use in his courtroom.

> There weren't any messages from him on Sara's phone. We checked.

Forensics would have looked for deleted files. Sara had given over her phone without any pause. Nadia didn't think she was savvy enough to fool the professionals.

'You use the word *play*. What does that mean?'

Play. It sounded so innocent.

'When two or more people get together to practice kink, they have a play session. It's all very consensual. You decide what you're willing to do beforehand. Then you play it out for real but at any point she could have used her safe word.'

What was her safe word?

'Red. It was red.'

You never discussed kink, safe words. This is all bollocks.

'Did you meet Sara Millings at the coffee shop opposite the halls where Sara lived and discuss a play scene?'

'Yes, she told me that she'd had many fantasies. She wanted

me to use a knife. I have to say I was reticent. I've not done much knife play. I was concerned I would hurt her.'

'And yet you agreed to play out the scene?'

Now he looked down to the floor in mock shame. It made Nadia feel nauseous. God knows how Sara felt.

'I did. But I would have stopped whenever she said. But she egged me on. She enjoyed it. In fact, when the police turned up, I thought it was a joke at first. I thought maybe one of her friends or family had found out she was kinky and she was covering her back. It was crazy.'

Nadia had been there when he was first arrested. He had the same smug look on his face that he had now as though he was untouchable. As though he'd get away with it.

TWENTY-NINE

The next morning, Jack checked in with Miriam. She wanted to be sure Terry Doughty was still at the hostel. Her biggest fear was that he'd do a runner. Disappear back up to Scotland. Miriam described him as being in shock. Gail may have been his ex-wife, but he seemed to still have feelings for her. And the death of his daughter had shaken him to his core. Then there was the second death of the young girl he'd met at the hospital. Miriam said he'd acted like this was all happening to someone else, but he didn't look or act like the guilty party.

Of course, Jack knew this meant nothing. Anyone could hide the truth if they faced a court case and possible imprisonment. It wasn't true that a liar was easy to spot. That they'd look to the right or the left each time they were being dishonest. The prisons would be full in no time if that were the case.

As Jack ran another mile on the treadmill at the gym, using the rhythm of her run to centre her, she considered the evidence. Doughty had the opportunity to poison all the victims. He could be the killer. He could easily be seeking a narcissistic-type supply of dependency. Firstly, from his own family and then from Sammi's. But it wasn't a good fit as a jigsaw piece. He wasn't always present. As far as Jack could tell, he hadn't fully wormed his way into Sammi's family. He was on the periphery, and would someone who wanted to control another's actions work away all the time? Surely, they'd want to be present to see the results of their actions. Jack wasn't convinced. Digging deep, she picked up the pace to complete her stationary ten-mile run.

As she cooled down, she turned her attention to the other possible suspect. Finn definitely wanted to get closer to Leia. There was still a possibility that he killed Gail, but the deaths of Leia and Sammi were unlikely to be caused by him. He might have some medical knowledge, but why would he hurt young girls? Unless he got a thrill in watching them die. When she'd shown his picture to Sammi's mum, she hadn't got a clue who he was and Sammi never used the library. Jack felt ready to rule him out.

In the shower, she allowed her thoughts to return to the previous evening. A warm glow emanated from the pit of her stomach as she imagined Emily's fingertips exploring her body. Fortunately, her lover had chosen a pasta dish that was quick to cook or they wouldn't have eaten before heading to the bedroom. The distance between them bridged within an hour of them meeting again. Jack's heart quickened as she finished sponging off the last of the shower gel; she smiled and imagined herself back in Emily's soft embrace.

After her shower, Jack returned to her locker.

Jack, call me now, it's really important.

Jack sighed. Another message from her mum. She'd probably had a row with Clare. She just didn't have the energy for their drama. As they shared few interests, every conversation was a trial. Checking her watch, she could spare half an hour before getting into the office. Might as well get it out of the way and, at least, her sister would be unlikely to be there. Someone had to open the boutique she managed.

Her mum greeted her with a perfunctory kiss on the cheek. 'Finally,' she muttered. Jack noted that her cardigan was done up incorrectly. She was about to mention it as her mother rushed her into the living room. Her mum opened one of the drawers on the oak dresser, taking out a small piece of paper which she thrust into Jack's hand. 'I found this in one of your dad's old notebooks,' she said.

'Why were you looking through those?' Jack glanced at the piece of paper.

'Does it matter? Read it!'

The note was written in partially smudged black ink making the handwriting difficult to decipher.

> *I know what you did. Don't think I won't tell the police. Meet me as arranged. We need to talk.*

It wasn't signed.

Jack read it over and over. Was it meant for her father? And what was the secret? Her dad had been such an open book. He lived for climbing. Worked as a ranger in the Peak District so he could spend all of his time near crag. When he wasn't working, he was volunteering for Edale Mountain Rescue, saving other climbers. He had no time for secrets. It couldn't be an affair, he adored Mum.

'What do you think?' Her mother looked unsure. *Maybe that was it. An affair. But what would that have to do with the police?*

'Do you recognise the writing?' A woman's hand would be

neater. Wouldn't it? Perhaps it was sent by a distraught husband?

'No.' Her mum looked about to cry. 'But who writes these days? It's not something you notice, is it?'

It wasn't. But it could have been this secret that led to her father's death. 'I was right, wasn't I... all along?'

'What do you mean?' The colour drained from her mother's cheeks.

'Everyone told me to shut up. *Don't be ridiculous. Your father fell to his death. It can happen to any climber.*' Jack waved the message at her mother. 'But this proves it. I was right.'

'It doesn't prove anything. We don't even know it was written to your father.'

'Has Clare seen this?'

Her mum shook her head. That was proof enough to Jack that she thought that her father might have done something wrong.

'What are you going to do?' Her mum spoke in a whisper as though scared of the answer.

'I'll take it to work. See if there's anything present on it to find out who the sender was.' How she was going to do this, she didn't know. It wasn't as though this was part of an active case. The coroner had ruled her father's death an accident years ago.

'Good. I'm sure it will be nothing. A joke something like that.'

Why did she look so worried if it was a joke? 'Do you think Dad was seeing someone else?'

'No. Of course not. Why would you even think that?'

The ferocity of her mother's words only made Jack wonder if it was true.

'He wasn't working late or getting dressed up to go out?'

'For god's sake. You were there too. You know he was exactly the same as ever.'

Until the day he fell from a crag that he'd successfully climbed many times.

'Why were you looking through his journals, Mum?'

Her mother placed her hands flat on the dresser. Without looking at Jack, she said, 'I miss him.'

It had never occurred to her that her mother felt like that. It was stupid really. Jack missed her father every day. She missed the deep tone of his voice as he guided her through life. Whether it was while she was clinging to a mountain or trying to grasp some tricky bit of homework. When she climbed her first eight thousand metre, she heard his voice in her head willing her to take another step and then another. The day Hannah died, she would have stayed on the mountainside and died with her, if it hadn't been for her father's words: 'You carry on, Pet. You can do this.'

Sitting in the office, pretty much alone, allowed her mind to wonder from crag to the case and back again. Raven Tor, the nemesis in the background. The overhang shaped like a bird's beak, peering down, mocking her. It was the place both her father and a murderer she was chasing died. It was a mediocre piece of crag that held so much weight in her life.

Jack usually liked being on her own. Working early or late in the office meant she could get to grips with the puzzles in front of her. It was Georgia's day off and Nadia was in court. The other police officers working the case were doing door-to-door in Sammi's street. Maybe one of the neighbours saw someone enter the house through the back door? It could make all the difference. But no one had come forward and they'd spoken to most of the residents. It wasn't looking hopeful.

Firing up her laptop, Jack logged into the shared files.

Georgia had made copious notes about each of the missing consultants. She'd searched for them all without any luck. It was odd. None of them had been listed as missing. No relatives had filed a report. So where were they now? On a clean page in her notebook, Jack listed the names of the hospitals they'd last worked at. They were all in the West Midlands. The dates occurred after each other which could have some significance. It was too early to tell. Hospitals were like schools and police stations; there were always some staff that had remained there for a lifetime. If she could find someone that knew the doctors then they could tell her where they were or, at least, where they'd moved on to.

Mr Jarvis Taylor. He was the obvious one to start with. It wouldn't take long to get to Heartlands and meet with HR. She could be back before the end of the day when she'd asked the others to meet for a catch-up in the pub across the road.

Lois Sheering didn't seem that happy to meet with her. Jack had rarely heard a person emit so many sighs and tuts. Everything was too much trouble. 'We told the officer on the phone. Mr Taylor left in 2009. We don't have a forwarding address.'

'How old was he when he left you?'

Another tut. 'Thirty.'

'He was a surgical consultant at thirty. Isn't that unusual?'

Lois peered down her nose at the file. 'Not particularly. By all accounts he did very well. Good stats relating to his work.' She picked up a piece of paper. 'Excellent references.'

Tapping the tip of her pencil on her pad, Jack asked, 'And what hospital did he move on to again?'

'I don't know. It doesn't say.'

'So, here is, in your words, an excellent doctor with his career in front of him and he vanishes. But no one thinks this is odd.'

'I'm sure he just found work at another hospital and didn't bother to tell us. He handed in his resignation in a normal fashion. Or perhaps he decided that medicine just wasn't for him. It's not for everyone.' She clearly meant not for anyone that would do such a tacky job as being a police officer.

'Can you give me the name of someone in Paediatrics who might have worked here at the same time?'

A particularly loud tut this time. 'I don't think I can. Wouldn't that break some GDPR?'

'They can decide if they wish to speak to me. But this could be a serious missing person case. I do have to check.' Jack closed her notebook and crossed her legs. And waited.

Lois must have decided that the only way she was going to have some peace was to give her the list. Five minutes later, Jack left with a name. One of the hospital matriarchs. A matron on the children's ward.

Luckily, she was working today and without much cajoling, she agreed to meet with her. Jack found her in the playroom dropping off a young boy with the largest lower body cast that Jack had ever seen.

'Millie Agyepong?' Jack caught the matron's eye as she was about to leave the room.

'Yes. Can I help you?' Jack showed Millie her ID. The woman smiled. 'Come to my office. You can't hear yourself think in here.'

The matron's office was small but incredibly tidy. Patient files were neatly stacked and there were few personal items except for a small photograph of two young girls holding their mother's hand at the beach. 'My grandkids. Do you have children?'

'No. Not had that pleasure.'

Millie looked her up and down and laughed. 'Not surprised. Mind you, with those narrow hips, you'll probably need a caesarean.'

Jack winced. 'I'll bear that in mind.'

'So, what's that idiot of a husband been up to now?'

'I'm not here about your husband. I'm actually looking for one of your ex-colleagues.'

Raising her eyebrows, Millie said, 'Well, this is a first. The only time I normally see one of you lot is when he's done sommat daft. Like the time he ran over the neighbour's gnome with the car. But you don't need to know about that. Who you looking for?'

'Mr Jarvis Taylor. He was a...'

Millie leant forward, placing her folded arms on the desk. 'I tell you what he was – a bit of a lad. Just like my Derek.'

'You remember him then?'

She chuckled. 'I remember everyone who pass through my ward.'

'Do you know where he went? After he left, I mean.'

'Sure I do. Or, at least, where he said he was going. Denmark. He said he had a job there. I didn't believe him, mind. If you ask me, he got some girl in trouble and he just wanted to make a quick exit.'

Denmark? There was nothing in the notes from the GMC to say that. They mentioned a private clinic but little detail and then nothing. Maybe he never left at all. He might not be dead. He could have taken on a new identity and carried on treating Leia. But why would he do that?

THIRTY

One good thing about having another possible victim, it meant that the coroner was happy to open and adjourn Leia's inquest. It helped that the super had had a quiet word with him explaining Sammi's case, as Jack didn't want to officially include it in the paperwork. She felt vindicated. It was a small thing. She'd stuck to her guns by not completing a report until she was ready, despite the pressures. As a police officer, she was proud to have good instincts. It was a shame these didn't extend to her private life. Emily was off radar again leaving her feeling confused and a little bit grubby, used even. Was she just a sexual toy to be discarded when Emily was bored?

It didn't help that she hadn't slept well wondering what the note that her mother had found meant. It probably didn't even belong to her father. It wasn't addressed to him or signed. It could have been about anything. Even something quite mundane like a dispute with a neighbour over parking. She knew her dad could be quite forceful at times and he'd often shout first and regret later. Usually over the most ridiculous things, like someone leaving their shoes in the hall for him to fall over. But what if it was something more sinister? Something that led to his death?

There was only one place to go when she felt like this – the climbing school. Fortunately, Danny didn't have any other plans. None that couldn't be changed, at least. When she called him, she did hear Gemma, his wife, in the background saying something about a garden centre. No wonder Danny sounded relieved that she'd called. She arrived at the climbing school a few minutes before him, giving her time to check in the mirror for any outward signs of the increasing uneasiness she felt. Danny would be the first to pick up on this and she didn't want to face his twenty questions.

Within minutes of attempting a tricky boulder run, Jack felt better. Repeatedly slipping from the rock face at the same spot just pushed her on to concentrate harder.

After repeated attempts, she finally cracked the route across the boulder, Jack hung underneath the rock like a monkey on a tree limb. 'Did I ever tell you how much I hate bouldering?' Then she lowered herself back down to the crash mat where she sat for a moment stretching her shoulder muscles.

'Are you going to tell me now, what's bothering you?' Danny sat down next to her.

'What makes you think that something is bothering me?' You just can't keep secrets from Danny. He just looked at you with his doe-like eyes until you told him everything. Every little indiscretion you'd done since birth. He'd have made a good copper.

They sat in silence for a moment and then Jack cracked. 'It's Emily.' *Stick with that and you don't have to talk about your dad,* she thought.

'She messing you around again?' He didn't hide the tone in his voice. It was obvious he didn't particularly like her new girl-friend. But when did he like any of her love choices?

'She's probably busy with work.'

'I know she's a doctor, but she's got time to call or even text. You have time for her and you're equally as busy.' He was right, of course.

'We slept together Thursday and I haven't heard from her since.'

'Blokes do that. It doesn't mean they're not interested, just that they don't realise that women need some affirmation after sex. Blokes just need sleep.'

Was he seriously laughing at her?

He continued. 'I would have thought girls would know how women tick though. Maybe she's just not that into you?'

Thanks, Danny. Now she felt even worse. She bit her lip to stop herself from crying. It wasn't Emily that was on her mind. It was her father. Danny, being Danny, picked up that she was still upset and moved closer, putting his arm around her. Her head dropped onto his shoulder. He kissed the top of her head. 'She's not worth it, bab.'

A giggle formed in her chest. Danny's poor attempt at a Brummie accent lightened the mood. They were brought up a few miles from each other in the Peak District. Neither were native to Birmingham but now called it home. Their lives had intertwined over the years. Jack could barely remember a time when Danny wasn't around. He was her slightly older 'brother'. But she didn't want to share her dad's letter with him. Not yet, anyway. Maybe she was scared he'd know something about it?

Danny stood and got two coffees from the machine. Jack followed him to the benches where they sat in silence for a moment. 'How's the prep going for your climb?'

Perhaps he thought it was this that was also bothering her. 'We're getting there. Funding's still a worry.' She then told him in detail what concerned her about the climb until he began to yawn. She'd say anything as long as it wasn't about her father.

The reason she'd come to him for some support in the first place.

The next day, Jack was supposed to be going to her mother's for a roast dinner, but she decided she needed time outside to clear her head first. Shauna was moored near the Roundhouse so suggested that they both take a walk around Edgbaston Reservoir. It was less than a couple of miles' walk, but as Shauna wasn't a fan of any type of exercise, it was probably as long a route that she'd put up with without throwing her mate in the water. Every couple of metres, she did a quick jog to catch up with Jack's fast walk.

'Slow down, will ya,' Shauna panted, as if to prove a point. 'You're always tense when you go to meet the dragons. I don't know why you bother.'

She hadn't told Shauna that she was considering skipping seeing them. 'How's your new family getting on?' Not that she was gagging for another invite. Much as she loved Shauna's niece, she did feel a little like their unpaid babysitter.

'Okay. I'm not used to the attention.' Shauna tapped her on the arm. 'D'ya mind if I take Deanna with me next time I visit? I think if I keep going with you, then they'll reckon you're my partner and Deanna was upset about that.'

Phew. 'Not at all. Does she like kids?'

'Kids? We've not talked about them. Shit.' Shauna stopped in her tracks.

'What?'

'You don't think...?' She put her hands on her knees and bent over, panting.

'I'm sure she doesn't want them now. I was joking. I hadn't realised it bothered you that much.' Although, she would hold that piece of information for later.

They walked a little further. The thin, golden spire of the

Peace Pagoda came back into view. Jack changed the subject. 'Any news on Sammi Jones's test results?'

The autopsy had confirmed a similar medical history to Leia's. There were a number of operation scars. Sammi had had her appendix, spleen and gall bladder removed. She'd had other abdominal surgeries carried out. Without the organs, it was difficult to know whether these operations were necessary. Her medical records hadn't been released to them yet.

Shauna shook her head. 'Are you expecting an overdose like Leia's?'

'And possible ongoing poisoning. I'm expecting the medical history to be similar.'

'And you think it might be Leia's father that's responsible?'

'He's got the opportunity for her death, but like Leia, she's been ill a long time and he certainly wasn't around then. Could her medical conditions be real and unrelated to her death? I guess we won't know until we get her full medical history.'

Shauna strode towards a bench and sat down. She took a huge gulp of water from her flask. Jack sat down next to her. 'To be honest, there were more obvious signs of chronic illness in Sammi than Leia,' Shauna said. 'It looked as though she had ongoing symptoms of irritable bowel, for example. So, I guess, she could have been ill before Terry Doughty got his hands on her, if it was him. Do you have any other suspects?'

Staring across the lake, Jack thought about what she should tell Shauna. 'There's something odd about the medical practitioners that Leia saw. Some of them are missing.'

Shauna nearly choked on her water. 'Missing? Do we now have a serial medical killer on the loose and you didn't bother to tell me?' Her friend was smiling. She obviously thought this was a joke. 'I suppose it could be a doctor or a nurse that's responsible for all this.'

'No. I mean, possibly.' *What the hell did she think?* She wasn't even sure herself. This wasn't the movies. Sometimes there wasn't a logical explanation to a murder. More often than not, you came across the culprit by complete accident. And even then, the reasoning behind what they did never made sense. Why did a caretaker kill two young girls? Why did a mother fake her own daughter's abduction by hiding her under a family member's bed? 'I just think it's odd that we can't locate so many people in Leia's case. What do you think could have happened to seven doctors that seem to have vanished off the face of the earth?'

'Seriously?'

'Well, we haven't found them yet and they were never reported missing which you've got to admit is downright odd.'

The last place Jack wanted to be was her mother's kitchen but, in the end, she decided that she needed to see her mum again in case she had more to say about the note. But as much as she loved a roast dinner on a Sunday, she could do without the company of both her mother and sister. They didn't just gang up on her; they usually set on her like a pack of wild dogs each taking a morsel, before chewing and spitting it out.

'Mum says you've got a new girlfriend.' Clare didn't look up from stirring the gravy.

'Did she? Yeah, sort of, she's a doctor.' Jack took a slug of wine and waited for the comeback.

'That's nice. Hopefully this one will last longer than a week.' *And there it was.* 'You do worry her, you know, Mum, that is.'

Clare didn't have relationships. She had her business. Apparently, that made her more successful than Jack, who'd taken murderers off the streets of Birmingham and climbed the highest mountain in the world. She could have made some nasty comment about her sister being a spinster but couldn't be bothered. Instead she left her to prepare the gravy and went in search of her mother.

The living room door was shut. Jack opened the door and walked in expecting her mother to be tidying or plumping a cushion, but she found her sitting on the sofa dabbing her eyes with a tissue. She sat down next to her. 'Hey. What's up? This isn't like you. Has Clare said something?'

'Clare? No? I'm just feeling my age today.' Her mum stood. 'The chicken needs carving. Will you do it?'

'Sure.' Jack watched her mother leave the room knowing this wasn't about aches and pains. Had the letter bothered her that much? There was clearly more to it.

Conversation over the dinner table was its usual stilted. How was the shop going? Was Jack ready for the next expedition? Her mother saying that this should be the last one as she always worried about her climbing. Nothing out of the ordinary.

'I noticed you had the notebooks out?' Clare said, staring in the direction of her mother who carried on chewing her meat.

Eventually she said, 'I'm thinking of donating them to a museum. I mean your dad wasn't just a good climber, he did manage a fair few firsts in his career. They're just gathering dust in the garage.'

'I'd like them,' Jack said. She didn't have the space, but they were another link to her father. Maybe she'd learn more about the letter? Maybe there were other letters?

'Of course you can have them. I'll box them up for you.'

Clare dropped her cutlery. They rattled on her plate. 'Well, that's hardly fair.'

'Why, do *you* want them?' Jack knew that she didn't. She couldn't be more disinterested in Dad's climbing.

'No, but other climbers might want to read them. It's not just about you, Jack. Besides what have I got of Dad's?' She brushed a fake tear away with the back of her hand. 'He was my father too.'

'Jack can have them if she wants. Where would you put them, Clare? They'd sit gathering dust in your attic. At least Jack will read them.'

This is a first, Mum siding with me over Clare, Jack thought. It made her wonder whether there was something important in the journals. Something that her mother wanted her to read.

THIRTY-ONE

Reading the journals would have to wait for a day when she was less busy working a case and preparing for a major climb. She needed time to savour the words. If they were interesting enough, she might consider employing someone to write his memoirs. She pushed all thoughts that there might be other strange notes hidden amongst them to one side as she shut the door. Her head pounded. Maybe the migraines she was having were due to her eyesight.

The glasses. She'd forgotten about that detail. Leia had taken her glasses off at the cafe. Why? The only thing that made sense was that she wanted to look more attractive. She wouldn't have bothered doing that if she was meeting her father.

Jack had a sudden thought. Could that mean it was Finn she was meeting? Or was there someone else who Leia wanted to impress?

It took her half an hour to drive to the station. Whoever was with Leia shortly before her death was key, she was sure of it.

They'd just received a copy of Finn's working schedule. If they could rule him in or out that would help.

There. The date. He worked all day at the library. It was too far away from town for him not to be missed. He was also too young to have been responsible for the surgeries on Leia and there was no connection to Sammi. Jack was ready to rule him out.

Only then did she realise Jayden was standing next to her. 'Can I have a word, ma'am.'

'Ma'am?'

'Sorry, I know you're not the bloody queen. It's just... I want to thank you for putting me forward for the detective programme. I know I'll have to brush up on my studies, but...' Beaming, he couldn't look her in the eye.

'You deserve it. And if you need any help with studying, then I'm happy to oblige.'

He didn't move. 'Was there anything else?' Jack asked.

'Yeah, actually.' He put his rucksack down on the desk and lifted out his laptop. 'Me and Georgia have been following up on our missing doctors.'

'Great.' Jack leant in as he scrolled through his notes.

'We did like you suggested and visited each hospital to see if anyone remembered them.'

'And?'

'They did. Seemed all of them were remembered fondly as having a good rapport with patients and staff. Maybe not the hardest working, though.'

'And they all had reasons for leaving?'

'Yeah.' Jayden scrolled to a table at the end of his report. Either he, or more likely Georgia, had listed the destinations for each doctor. They had all gone to work in another country. Two had moved to Europe, one to Australia, one that Jack already knew about to Denmark, and the last to Sweden. They had also listed descriptions of each doctor, both physical and personal.

The height – six foot; hair colour – dark brown/black; body type – slender, all matched.

'They're the same person. So, someone, presumably another doctor, has taken over their identity when they went abroad.' It was obvious.

'Yeah. That's what me and Georgia think.'

'So what happened to the real doctors with those names? They must have qualified. You can't just turn up at a hospital under an assumed name and get a job.' This discovery threw up more questions than it did answers. 'You don't think we've got a serial killer of doctors on our hands?'

Jayden looked blank. It was a stupid question really. There was no getting away from the fact that there'd be bodies. Someone who was friends or family with these men would notice. But she just couldn't work out how they'd disappeared and been replaced by this other person. It was risky. Turning up at a new hospital using the name of another doctor. But if you moved around enough, the risk to being caught would be smaller. Jack wondered if the busy schedules and desperate need for staff would make the administration lax. Could the same thing happen in the police? Did anyone check past records other than a doctor's references? And did that bring Finn back into the picture? He'd done some training. Was it enough to enable him to pass as a doctor? Of course, he wasn't old enough. Unless he'd lied about his age as well as everything else. 'Thanks. You and Georgia have done some excellent work. You'll need to present it at Monday's meeting.' Jack needed time to think. This development could be momentous.

THIRTY-TWO

Courtrooms on a Monday were always busier. New cases were started. Magistrates were mopping up the detritus of the weekend. Bailing out drunks and Saturday-night fighters. Nadia thought they'd have their answer this week. Jacobs would be found guilty or innocent. The scales hung in the balance. She didn't dare guess.

Marcus didn't appear unduly bothered. He was eating a croissant, occasionally brushing the crumbs from his gown. He smiled at her. 'You look as though you have the weight of the world on your shoulders. How did the interviewing go?'

Nadia had spent the weekend speaking to more women students who'd lived in Sara's accommodation block over the years. 'A couple of them reported a possible stalker to the university. Nothing ever was done. They felt uncomfortable living there particularly on the ground floor.'

'What was the nature of the stalking?' He'd stopped eating now and was more attentive.

'One woman thought she'd seen someone staring into her bedroom on a few occasions late at night. Another said that she'd been followed home.'

'And these incidents weren't investigated?'

'Apparently the uni said they'd look into having extra outside lights fitted. They never did. They weren't even in the reports that I was given from the uni. Some of them did report to the police and it was misfiled by a junior officer. They were let down whichever way you look at it. And who knows, maybe Jacobs would have been caught before he attacked Sara and Shelley.' Nadia's stomach growled. She should have got some breakfast on the way to the courtroom. 'There was one woman who said that a man had tried to follow her into her flat one night. Her flatmates were in and heard her scream at him. When he saw that she wasn't alone he ran off.'

'Did she recognise him as Jacobs?'

'It was dark. It happened quickly. She wasn't sure. But I've got the names of the other women in the flat. I'm going to ring them in recess.'

Marcus glanced at his watch. 'We'd better get to the courtroom. Important day today.'

It was. Marcus was going to cross-examine Jacobs. Nadia hoped he'd convict himself with his sheer arrogance.

Steven Jacobs stood straight in the witness box. Hands behind his back facing the prosecution barrister, almost egging him on. He had the air of someone untouchable.

Marcus rose out of his seat, taking his time. They were like two boxers facing off before a bout. 'Steven, it's time to tell the truth. You raped Sara Millings on that night. The sex wasn't consensual or planned. You talked your way into her flat and held a knife to her throat. That's correct, isn't it?'

'I did not. This is all lies.'

Nadia wondered if Mary Stenner had spoken to him. Keep your chin up. Look confident but drop the cockiness, or you'll lose and go to prison.

'You said that you met Sara in a cafe, and you asked her to join you at your table. That she appeared to not be interested in you but gave you her phone number.'

'That's correct. Yes.'

'How many times did you speak on the phone or text during that time?' They'd checked her phone. There was no prior communication from Jacobs.

'Just a couple. Then we moved to Discord, like I said.' Sara didn't have the Discord app on her phone but could have used the web version. There was nothing in her laptop history though to suggest that.

'Where's the evidence of her messaging you? We don't have any screenshots. Nothing from your phone.' Marcus turned to the jury. 'Because it's a lie, isn't it? You only met Sara on the night you raped her.'

'She looks so innocent, doesn't she,' Jacobs sneered.

Marcus leant forward. 'I'm sorry. Could you repeat that.'

'There's loads of women into rough sex, BDSM... they look like butter wouldn't melt. She probably had a VPN. Did you think of that?'

He really must think we're all stupid. Of course a VPN would have been picked up by the police tech team. Marcus quickly came back with that retort. Maybe living with his rich, arrogant father had made Steven like this. But he was digging his own grave. It was a joy to watch. For the first time in the trial, Nadia found herself smiling.

'You said in your statement that Sara didn't use her safe word, *red*. Did she tell you to stop or say no to you at any time?' Marcus looked to the jury not to Jacobs. Every question he would be measuring their response.

'You don't understand how consent works. Women say no when they really mean yes all the time.'

'Do they? What do you think Sara meant?' This time he

stared directly at Jacobs, goading him into digging his own grave.

'It was all an act. Part of the role-play. She wasn't going to say yes. It was all a game. Part of her fantasy.'

'No!' Sara shouted. 'I'm sorry...he's lying.'

The judge interjected, 'Miss Millings, if you are going to interrupt, you'll have to leave the court.'

And so, it continued. For every question, Marcus Barnet QC put, Steven Jacobs replied with a sarcastic retort on the lines of 'she was so up for it'. It didn't matter Sara lacked confidence and conviction in her answers, Jacobs was convicting himself. The more Marcus pushed, the lower the defence barrister sunk in her chair. Why on earth did they put him on the stand?

Until finally, Marcus asked his final question. 'How much did you pay Steph Bishop to lie for you, Mr Jacobs?'

The judge intervened. 'Do you have evidence to support this?'

'I'll withdraw the question.' Marcus wrapped his gown around himself and sat down, smiling.

The defence rested. The summaries from each barrister were delivered. Marcus's with conviction, Mary's almost felt desperate; the damage had been done. The jury retired. Nadia hoped for a quick verdict.

THIRTY-THREE

Georgia and Jayden presented their report to the rest of the small team. The only one not present was Nadia, but Jack was hopeful now the defence was complete that she'd get her Sergeant back fully concentrating on this case.

The others seemed as confused as Jack was when presented with the information that a group of doctors had disappeared and were likely replaced with someone else. A cuckoo in the nest. It was bizarre. If it was the same person, then why didn't they use their real name? What did they gain from doing this?

Jayden explained it for the second time, after another officer asked why they'd gone missing again. 'The original doctor leaves to go abroad. The killer, if we can call him that, takes on his name and starts work at a hospital in the Midlands. He can only risk doing this for a short time.'

'Can we get their ID photos? The doctors who are working in the Midlands, I mean. If it's the same man...' Jameirah Kaur asked. She was one of the newer recruits, a neighbourhood police officer, drafted in to help after Sammi died.

'We've requested them. Should get them today. Of course, they could still be different people. Then our theory will be dead in the water,' Georgia continued. 'We do need to trace where each doctor was before these hospitals. We've had some limited information from the GMC, but it's Monday so we can start speaking to the HR departments, see if they can tell us anything more.'

'Great work. Yes, you and Jayden carry on with that.' Jack stood up next to the operations board. 'We need to check social media, LinkedIn for any more information about these seven men. We also need to see if we can trace their families. We don't have any missing persons reports so there may be an easy explanation, like they've moved abroad, as to how this mystery doctor took over their names to find work. But the other question we need to ask is why would they do that? Why would they need to pose themselves as another paediatrician and what were they doing? There's nothing to suggest that they weren't competent. But they did treat Leia Thompson on a number of different occasions. Her mother must have known that this was the same doctor with a different name, if that was the case. Why didn't she say anything? I'm happy to hear your views on this, however bizarre or extreme they may be. To be quite frank with you all, I'm at a loss here to explain any of it.'

Jayden put his hand up. Jack nodded to him to continue. 'In terms of this guy taking over other doctor's names, I can only think that he might have been sacked. We can work out a rough age from his description and the twelve years this deception covers, shall I look at the records kept by the GMC of doctors who've been struck off?'

'Good idea,' Jack replied.

'Also,' Jayden continued, 'and I know this will sound really odd, but this is beginning to sound like some kind of cult. Gail knew, presumably, that her daughter was been treated by a dodgy doctor and yet she continued to take her to see them. This was despite the fact that Leia didn't get much better. Who would do that? Unless she was herself vulnerable and under the spell, for want of a better word, of him. A bit like Rasputin. And yeah, I know that sounds ridiculous.'

'And what about Sammi in all this? We really need to know if she saw any of the same doctors.' Jack turned to Georgia. 'Have we had any of her medical records yet?'

Georgia shook her head. 'No, boss.'

'Right. This morning you can come with me and we'll visit Sammi's mother again.' Jack then gave the others their daily tasks. 'There is someone else that we need to look into. I don't want him knowing that we are doing that.' Jack brought up the photo and name of the person she was now convinced was the killer onto the board. 'Jayden, check out his past. I want to know every hospital he has worked in and whether he's linked to any of our missing doctors.'

They hadn't told Ellen Jones they were coming. She looked surprised to see them. The house was even more untidy than their first visit. Maybe Miriam had given up on trying to help her or was too busy supporting Terry. Ellen moved a pile of dirty plates and takeaway boxes from the settee. Georgia gingerly sat down. Jack stayed standing until Ellen moved the laundry off the only other seat in the room. Then she sat down on the well-worn settee next to Georgia. She muttered, 'I'm sorry about the mess. Since Sammi died...what's the point.'

'We need some information from you today. We need to find out what happened to Sammi and we need you to be honest with us.' Jack quickly thought about how tough she needed to be. 'If you're not honest, we may need to charge you with aiding and abetting.' She didn't say what with as she wasn't certain herself yet.

The colour drained from Ellen's face. 'Of course. Sammi just died. She was ill. I don't see what all the fuss is about.'

'We need to know who treated Sammi. Did she have a regular doctor?' Jack opened her notebook.

'We moved around a bit. Everybody does these days and we couldn't always afford the rent. But we kept the same GP. I've told you this.'

You gambled the money away, Jack thought, but would save that fact until she needed it. 'What about hospital doctors? Did Sammi have a regular paeds consultant?'

'No. She had different ones for her different conditions.' Ellen turned to Georgia. 'I don't know why they do that. You have to repeat all of the medical issues to each one. Wastes so much time.'

Georgia ignored her and just looked down at her pad. She wasn't getting any sympathy there.

'I'm going to ask you something now which may seem odd, but I want you to be honest with me.' Jack waited for Ellen to nod. 'Did Sammi see a regular doctor who may have used different names and worked in different hospitals?'

Ellen screwed up her eyebrows. 'Are you mad? Of course she didn't.'

You could hear it in her voice. Indignation mixed with horror, even a hint of anger. Jack knew she was lying. 'This person may have killed your daughter. Think very carefully before answering. As I've said, we could charge...'

'Why the hell would a doctor want to kill my daughter? This is ridiculous.' Ellen stood waving her arms around. 'You're barking mad. Get out of my house. Let me mourn my daughter in peace.'

Jack and Georgia stood to leave. There wasn't any point questioning her any longer and they couldn't caution her. They needed more evidence.

. . .

On reaching her car, Jack's phone started to buzz. It was Jayden. She put him on speakerphone so Georgia could hear. 'We've had the photo IDs from two of the hospitals. It's the same person.'

'Send me them to my phone.' Jack waited as the photos began to appear. They had their suspect now. They needed so much more to charge him. But it was becoming increasingly likely that she was right.

'I just don't get it, boss. What on earth was he doing to those girls?' Georgia hugged herself, no doubt thinking of her own daughter and all the trips to the hospital she needed to make.

'My guess is there are others.' Jack knew where to go next. 'We need to find them before he kills them too. But first let's rule out Leia's father.'

'If there're others that he's treating then there may be others that he's killed. We're going to need a bigger team to trawl through the records of all of the sudden death cases. I'm assuming that this is what you want me to do now.' Georgia didn't seem the least fazed by that.

'Yes.' Jack started her car. 'And keep checking the doctors. Share the work as much as you can. I feel dreadful for asking you to do this.'

They found him in the pub rather than the hostel, nursing a pint of Guinness. Jack wondered how long he'd been sitting here crying into his pint.

'I loved her, you know. Well, both of them. I had to work and all I knew was the rigs. Do you think if I'd been around more, she'd still be with us?'

'We'll never know the answer to that. But we think we might be near to finding out what happened to Leia...and Gail.' Jack placed her hand over his.

He nodded. 'Thank you.' He took another gulp of Guinness.

'I have got some questions for you though.' Jack sat back on her stool. These could rule him in or out. He might never know how important his answers were. 'The doctors that Leia saw. Did you meet all of them?'

He stopped turning his pint glass between his hands, the remains of the Guinness sloshing up the sides. 'No. Mainly the ones I took her to. In A&E, I mean. I'd get home from working away and she'd be laid up in bed in dreadful pain.'

He was squeezing the glass now, his knuckles turning white. Jack leant over and took the glass from him. Afraid it would shatter. 'So, you only saw A&E doctors? None of her consultants.'

'No. Gail dealt with all of that. She was always saying how much Leia was improving. And sometimes she did. I mean, she started walking again. Occasionally, it got so bad she needed the chair, but most of the time, she could walk unaided. But the pain. That always remained. And there were never any answers as to why she was like this. Those bloody doctors just kept shaking their heads as if they hadn't got a clue what was wrong with her.' He dropped his head. 'I should have pushed more. I know that now. But Gail was always blaming me. "If you weren't away at the rigs..." and she was right, wasn't she?' He hit the table with his fist. 'It was my fault Leia died. I didn't care enough.'

'If I'm honest, I think Gail was involved with your daughter's death. That's all I can say for now. You shouldn't blame yourself.' But she fully understood why he did.

Back at the station, new information came in quick and fast. The seven doctors were working abroad. They'd just left a month, two months, even a year, in one case, earlier than their imposter began work at the new hospital. So, of course, no one was searching for them. They were all alive and well. As her team contacted them that afternoon, each was shocked that they'd had their ID stolen. But there were clues that something was amiss. When Dr Dimitru applied for a new job in Greece, his CV was questioned. It was only when he produced his travel documents and contracts for work in other hospitals that he was allowed to practice.

'Whoever our perp is, he ran such a risk. I can't believe he got away with it for so long.' Georgia added the new information to her spreadsheet.

'And why did he stop? Risk of being found out?' He changed what he did, even his specialty. But he must have been close to being caught. Something had spooked him. Maybe someone who knew the doctor he was impersonating started work at the hospital? Maybe he found a better way to hide. He was careful. Jack had to give him that. All of the doctors that he chose had worked in different areas of the country, including Wales and Scotland. They'd never worked in the Midlands except the first one, Mr Jarvis. So the chance of someone knowing what they looked like was slim. In the ten years he'd kept up this ruse, he'd only worked for a few months at a time and then disappeared. Of course, there could have been others. Other mothers that he'd convinced to follow him. Other children he'd abused. They needed to keep digging. Needed as much evidence as they could find. The worry was he'd completely clam up when he was caught and they'd lose him.

'Why did you want to meet?' Shelley Anderson stirred her coffee before blowing on it and taking a sip. The coffee shop would be closing in an hour and was practically empty.

'The jury will be retiring about now and I wanted you to know that whatever happens, we will be prosecuting Jacobs for what he subjected you to.' But that was only part of the reason, she'd asked Shelley to meet her.

'I'd love to be there when you do it. I've been reading about the case in the papers. He's so smug about it all. Like all women are asking for it.'

It was likely to be his downfall in the end according to Nadia. If he'd played the innocent 'it was consensual' a little better, he might have got away with it.

Jack waited a moment. It was strange that Shelley bridged both cases. She'd seen it before on her last case. The killer had thrown Steven Jacobs's father off a balcony. Everyone talked about it being a small world. Everyone connected. It certainly felt like it. 'There's something else I want to talk to you about.'

THIRTY-FOUR

'All rise,' the usher said, and everyone in the courtroom stood.

The jury retired. Jacobs was escorted out of the dock. Nadia watched him stumble on one of the steps. As she turned to leave, she spotted Sara. She stood out of the way of the crowds of reporters and onlookers as they left the gallery. Then she strode up to Marcus. Nadia followed her.

'I just want to thank you,' Sara said, holding her coat in her arms. 'Whatever happens with the jury, that is.'

Nadia heard Marcus mutter something about being hopeful as he collected his papers together.

Then Sara turned to Nadia. Held out her arms and pulled her into a hug. 'I couldn't have done this without you.'

Nadia bit her lip. If only justice could be served. Was it too early to think so? This was her first big case as a lead officer. She'd hoped that it would feel different somehow. Help her to come to terms with her abuse. But it hadn't done that. There was still the verdict to come though. In hours or maybe even days.

Sara turned and followed the crowd out. Nadia spotted her

mother scooping her up as she left the courtroom. She was in safe hands.

'Fancy a drink?' Marcus asked, and then followed it with, 'Sorry you don't, do you.'

'I could have a tea or a Coke?'

'Here.' Marcus passed her some files. 'We'll drop these off at chambers and see if Jack is free to join us. We won't get a verdict today, but I'm parched.'

Nadia wondered why she felt resentment that he'd decided to include her boss.

THIRTY-FIVE

If Jack had any sense, she'd have ignored his call, but his exuberance was contagious.

'I've missed you.' His brown eyes sought hers before she could look away.

Nadia had left early with some excuse about needing to shop for her family. The look on her face said it all. *Be careful, boss.*

Jack didn't listen. In fact, she wasn't listening to Marcus either. Instead, she was breathing him in. Absorbing his energy. He was the opposite to the women in her life. They usually absorbed her strength. Lay in her arms. Expected her to take the lead. All except for Emily who was more than happy to be in control. Take some of the load, make some of the decisions.

Marcus had stopped talking. Waiting for her to speak and she had no idea what he'd been talking about. 'Sorry?' she muttered.

'I said.' He leant forward, his lower arms flat on the table. 'Is Shelley ready for the arrest? She knows that there'll be publicity. Not specifically naming her, but it will be in the press.'

Jack nodded, without saying anything about meeting her that evening. 'She knows. She just wants him to suffer.'

Marcus raised his glass. 'Don't you just love justice.'

He was being premature. They hadn't secured a conviction yet. But he was arrogant enough to think that he'd won. For a moment, Jack questioned what she saw in him. Just for a moment, then she caught his look again. That wicked glint in his eye. He brushed his fingertips across the back of her hand and she shivered. This was stupid. Get a grip. 'You really are an arrogant prick.'

'Moi?' Mock offence was his default pose.

'When are you going to invite me around for a meal with... what's her name?' Jack took a slurp of the wine. The acid burnt her throat. It wasn't even a good wine.

'I barely see her.' His chin fell to his chest, making Jack wonder if this was another load of bull. 'We work such long hours and now we're married, she treats me like her plaything. *Marcus, buy me this, buy that for the garden, it will look lovely.* I didn't expect to be spending my days off shopping.'

'What did you think? That you'd spend it in bed, having brunch at some bohemian cafe, then down the pub in the evening with your mates? Just wait until she wants kids.'

'I can't wait for kids. But she's more interested in buying clothes.' He waited for her response. She just raised her eyebrows.

'You need to go home. Come on, I'll hail you a cab.' Jack stood and he, like a sheep, followed.

The exit to the pub was a poorly lit side street. They'd only taken a few steps and Marcus put his arm around her. Leaning into him, Jack felt protected. Maybe it was his size. Marcus was a tall, muscular Black guy with shaven hair. He cut a strong figure in court in his wig and gown. Outside of court, in his sports Jag, he often got pulled over by the police. Jack knew he never made an issue out of it. Perhaps he should.

Before reaching the main road, Marcus stopped and turned to her. He took her face in his hands, lifting her chin. Then he kissed her on the lips. To her shame, she didn't back away or protest. Just kissed him back. She could almost see Shauna's face in front of her. *Don't be an idiot.*

Coming to her senses, Jack pulled away. 'I'll get you that cab.' Before Marcus could protest, she jogged to the main road, arm in the air until a taxi pulled up next to her.

'Shall we share?' Marcus held the door open.

She smiled. He wasn't to blame for her madness. 'It's fine. There's stuff I need to work on back at the office.' As he got in and slammed the door shut, she said, 'Let me know the verdict as soon as you get it.'

Walking back to the station, shame hit her. The attention she got from Marcus was nothing compared to how she felt about Emily. There was no way she was going to be taken in by him again. She pulled her jacket around her and concentrated on not bumping into the evening's revellers as they staggered from pub to club.

Then it struck her. Leia had wanted the attention of the person she sat with in the cafe. She took off her glasses and left them there. Glasses. She'd noticed a pair of glasses that were out of place. Left in plain sight. He'd taunted her with them. Another sign that she was right.

At the station, Jack read the reports as they were completed by her team. They were all working late and writing up the day's interviews. Each piece of evidence slotted into place. It was so obvious now what had happened. This vile creature had wormed his way into the lives of vulnerable women and abused their kids. She felt nausea spread through her body. Why had no one noticed before now?

Even Dr Jennifer Pride hadn't spotted what was happening

with all her knowledge of children's medicine. Jack trawled back through her notes. It seemed that unexplained pain and random symptoms weren't taken seriously. Young children didn't have the capacity to describe the pain, so were easily dismissed. Older children didn't have a voice either because everything was communicated through their parents. Teenagers, like those at the clinic, were seen as hysterical or hormonal.

Of course, they had some advocates like Amira Masih or Emily. Jack was sure her friend would listen. But the whole system: the NHS, social services, the police, education – all failed kids on a regular basis due to lack of staff or funding. Abuse in all its forms continued unabated.

It was time. She completed the search warrant paperwork and pressed Send.

THIRTY-SIX

Jack strode up to reception with an entourage of officers behind her.

'I've got a search warrant for the clinic. Is Dr Sharma here?'

Shelley shook her head. Jack had spoken to her over the phone the night before so she knew they were coming. 'I've no idea where he is. He left about five minutes ago without a word. Sorry I couldn't stop him.'

Jack sent half the team to search the office downstairs. She was more interested in searching his private office and bedroom. That's where she expected his secrets would be buried.

'I've found the keys for his quarters.'

There had to be a reason why he'd done what he did. Jack had lain awake the last couple of nights trying to find answers. Why would he poison and operate on young girls for no reason? How did he make their mothers complicit? Were there other girls involved? The top of his filing cabinet in his main office had other items on it. The glasses, a cuddly toy similar to the ones in Sammi's bedroom, a pencil case – all seemed so out of place, but she hadn't thought anything of it at the time. Perhaps she'd skipped over them as simply mementoes from his patients. Now she saw them for what they were – trophies.

Shelley had told her Kishran would spend hours upstairs in his study inside his flat. When there were problems late at night with the young women patients, she'd knock on the study door and wait for him to come and help. He'd always lock the door behind him, as though he kept the Crown Jewels in there.

Shelley took the key out of her trouser pocket and led them into the study. Inside were piles of notebooks. Piled up on the desk, on the floor and on the bookshelves. At first glance, there had to be hundreds of them. Jack picked up the one on the top of a pile on his desk. All the notebooks appeared to be the same: plain black, A4 size. She opened it. The first page had a name, Leia Thompson, and a date, March 2019–June 2019. The pages following were covered in notes. Measurements written in a spidery handwriting, almost indecipherable. There were drawings too. Not medical in nature. More infantile. A girl's body with scars scratched into the paper in red ink, maybe showing where incisions had been made. There were lists of medications too and notes made outlining the effects of each one.

Jack looked for answers, but all she had were more questions. It would take her officers months to read through all of the notebooks. Months to make any sense of it all. But she was sure of one thing. Leia and Sammi weren't the only victims of his abuse.

To confirm that, Shelley read out the front page of one of the books on the floor. *Rhona Miles, Sept 1998–Feb 1999.*

'Was she a patient here?' Jack asked.

Shelley shook her head. 'The clinic didn't open until 2018. I've never heard of her.'

Jack turned to Georgia. 'We need to get everything removed and catalogued. Can you and Jayden do that.'

In her gut she knew. All of these journals would document

the horror that each child went through. Of course, he moved from hospital to hospital gathering victims and vulnerable mothers. Carrying out unnecessary operations on their children, poisoning them. He probably chose only those girls with parents who were either distracted by their own issues or were addicted to the attention of having a sick child, like Gail. The clinic gave him some respite. He could operate without being under scrutiny. Blame everything on the young women's unhealthy minds. He was their confidant and abuser. They might never discover why. What he was trying to prove or disprove with his experiments. If that is what they were.

'We need to search the rest of the building.' Jack turned to Shelley. 'Is there anywhere else on site that we haven't seen yet?'

Shelley bit her lip. 'Oh god. I can't believe all of this was going on under our noses. But we were always so understaffed. So busy with the patients.' She wrung her hands. 'Other places...the girls' dormitories, the kitchen.'

'He's unlikely to have hidden anything there.' Jack stood and stretched her back. 'What about a garage?'

'There's a basement, but it's full of old furniture, files...stuff like that. I don't think anyone's been down there in years.'

'Show me.' Jack walked towards the door.

The basement, like the office upstairs, was locked. Shelley took the bunch of keys from her pocket. 'I think it's this one.' The door opened to a storeroom which was much as Shelley described.

At the back of the room were two tall, black filing cabinets. Jack pulled one of the drawers expecting it to be locked, but it slid open with ease. It was empty. She tried the rest to find the same. They didn't sit right in the room. They were too shiny.

Jack stepped back. The paint above them didn't quite match the rest of the wall.

'Help me move them,' she said.

Jack, Georgia and Shelley dragged the two cabinets away from a well-hidden door. Stepping forward, Jack turned the doorknob and opened it. The room was shrouded in darkness. A distinct smell of disinfectant wafted towards them.

Jack scrambled for the light switch. A loud, annoying hum ensued before the room was bathed in bright florescent light. It was an operating theatre. In the centre of the room sat a long stainless-steel table on wheels. Next to it, a trolley. Its drawers labelled with the names of medical instruments. Jack gasped. It was so similar to the basement in the children's hospital. Two sites. Could that possibly be the case? Had he abandoned one when he started work here? Or was he using both? Dr Kishran Sharma had continued to operate on these girls. Away from the prying eyes of other medical staff, he'd cut into their bodies for his own amusement and pleasure.

This was all the evidence they needed to put out a warrant for Dr Sharma's arrest. Jack called it in. Where the hell was he? Did he know they were coming for him?

THIRTY-SEVEN

Exhausted after completing the paperwork from the search of the clinic, Jack unlocked her front door, pushing it open. And then she froze. Something wasn't right. She stood rigid with the key still in the lock, door wide open, debating whether to shut it and run. Two sharp breaths and she shook her head. It was her imagination. She was off-kilter. Shaken by the discoveries of the day. Making stupid decisions. *Just relax.*

Taking the key out of the lock, she shut the door behind her, and what had bothered her came into focus. The door to the storage cupboard was wide open. She'd shut it that morning. She was sure of it. No one had keys to her flat. She didn't currently hire a cleaner as she was saving the pennies for her climb. Without a sound, she placed her bag on the floor, pulled off her shoes and took small, silent steps across the tiled hall. Just outside the cupboard, she stopped and listened. Nothing.

Turning back to switch the light on, she noticed the kitchen door was ajar and on the worksurface stood two bottles of water. There was no way she'd left them there. Her heart beat faster. She crept back towards the open cupboard door. Peering inside, she stopped for a moment to allow her eyes to adjust. She felt hot breath on the back of her neck. Somebody was behind her. She reared backwards, bringing her elbow up to connect with the person's covered face. They grabbed her arm, throwing her forward into the shelving containing her climbing gear. Hitting it with force, jarring her shoulder, she felt herself falling, grabbing at whatever she could. She landed on the floor and rolled onto her back, facing her attacker, ready.

As they lunged for her, she threw her leg up between their legs. They pulled back for a second, protecting their groin. Scrambling, her hand caught hold of something sharp, wrapped in cloth. Her hand ran down it until she felt the warm wood of the handle. The intruder managed to get their knees on top of her legs, pinning her to the floor. A scream formed in her throat as she was slapped across her face. It stung, but she ignored the pain and used the time to release the cloth.

'Bitch.'

She knew that voice. *Dr Kishran Sharma*. He must have known they were coming for him. As she struggled, he tightened his grip with his thighs. He grabbed at her throat with one hand. Then the other. Squeezing. *No air*. Gasping.

Her hand frantically fought with the cloth. It was finally free. She swung the ice pick. Heard the crunch as it hit bone. Blood splattered her face and arm. Then she swung a second time. Forcing the blade deeper into his back. He squealed and threw his arms behind him. Nearly wrenching the axe out of her hands. Jack swung for a third time. As he reared up, she caught the back of his head. A streak of blood arced across the wall. Kishran crumpled on top of her. Pinning her shoulder between the metal of a shelf and the floor. Jack screamed. A flash of stabbing pain shot through her back.

Kishran's body was wrenched off her, discarded. 'Is he dead?' She needed to know.

She tried to sit, and excruciating pain shot through her shoulder and arm causing her to nearly faint.

'Lie back down. The paramedics are on their way,' Emily said, but everything seemed off, blurred, indecipherable. Then she passed out.

THIRTY-EIGHT

'Have you reached a verdict on which you are all agreed?'

The jury foreman stood. 'We have, your honour.'

'On the count of rape, do you find the defendant guilty or not guilty?'

The foreman coughed. 'Guilty, Your Honour.'

Nadia covered her mouth with her hand and whispered, 'Yes.'

She glanced in the direction of Marcus, who simply smiled. She grinned back.

Sara was sitting next to her on the bench. Tears rolling down her face as her mother hugged her. Then Sara turned to Nadia. 'Thank you,' she said, and hugged her too.

The whole courtroom turned to watch Jacobs as he was led away out of the dock and back downstairs to the cells. His sentencing would be at a later date.

Nadia walked over to Marcus. For the first time that afternoon, he looked concerned. Worry lines etched into his forehead. 'What does Jack know?' he asked.

'She can't lift her arm above her head. Physio might help, but the scapula is broken and there's some tendon damage, possibly an issue with the rotator cuff, I think they said.' The doctor hadn't told Jack that there could be permanent damage. From what Nadia could gather, they neither wanted to down-play it or give her false hope.

'She's climbing a mountain in less than six months.' Marcus's statement sat heavily between them.

Eventually he tapped Nadia on the shoulder. 'Good result, by the way. When are you giving Jacobs the news that he's got to go through all this again with fresh charges?'

'Transport back to prison leaves in an hour. I thought I'd time it just before he's due to leave. Give him something to think about on the journey.' There were two claimants now. Shelley and another student who'd left the halls two years before. Nadia had spoken to her and got her statement that morning. The verdict couldn't have come at a better time.

'I might join you. If that's okay. I'd love to see the little rat in more agony.' Marcus placed the last files into his suitcase and followed Nadia out of the courtroom.

THIRTY-NINE

Shauna bounded into Jack's hospital room followed by Jack's mother. She leant down to hug her friend and stopped, realising she could do more damage to her already damaged left shoulder. Jack tried to sit up, grunting with the effort. 'Where're my clothes?'

'Why do you need those?' Her mother moved to the other side of the bed so she was standing in front of the bedside cabinet.

'I'm not sitting here another day. I can come back in for physio.' Jack swung her legs over the side of the bed and gingerly tried to stand. Her feet weren't the problem, but it was surprising how much pain affected her balance as she swayed.

Shauna sighed. 'Come on, mate. Give it another day or two, the docs know what they are doing.'

Every minute of the day and part of the night, Jack had been prodded and poked. Enough was enough. She didn't have an infection, her temperature, heart rate, main vitals were fine. Her shoulder would heal quicker with a good night's sleep. 'Move, Mother.'

'Jack, please.' Her mother stayed where she was, blocking

Jack from her clothes. 'Have you even thought about how you're going to get them on?'

'Well, to be honest, I was hoping you'd both help.' Jack looked from one to the other. Shauna had her arms crossed and didn't look in the mood to help anyone.

'I'll do it on my own then.' With her good arm, she pushed her mum to one side and opened the cupboard door. She was expecting to find her clothes, but, of course, they'd been taken by forensics. She still had to answer for killing Kishran Sharma, if that's who he really was, with an ice pick of all things. The Office of Police Conduct would have a field day with that one. 'I need something to wear.'

Emily chose that moment to come into the room. She must have taken one look at Jack and realised there was little point in arguing with her. 'I've got spare clothes in my locker. If you insist on leaving, that is.' She nodded towards Shauna. 'I'd rather you had a medical minder though. For the next day or so. We can take it in turns.'

'Sure.' Shauna agreed.

Emily pulled Jack into a carefully managed hug and whispered into her ear, 'You do what I tell you and stop working when I say, or else.'

Taking hold of Emily's elbow, Jack said, 'I will. I promise.'

Thirty-five minutes later, after a struggle to get Jack dressed, they got to the car park.

'I don't drive.' Shauna turned to Jack's mum. 'Can you drop us home?'

'I'm not going home.' Jack strode off towards her mother's car.

'What do you mean? I'm not taking you anywhere else.' Her mother's voice rose, but Jack strode on, stopping when she got to a blue Kia.

'If you won't take me to the station, I'll take the bus.'

The look on Jack's face must have spurred Shauna into action. 'I'll be with her. Stop her doing any more damage.'

They all got into the car. The station was only fifteen minutes away in good traffic. Jack's mother drove carefully, knowing any bumps might cause her daughter pain. 'I'm assuming the expedition is off. I'm so sorry, love.'

No one had come out with it. Jack knew they were all worried, the doctors, her friends, her family, that the damage would be permanent. Kishran had landed on top of her when he died. His weight slammed her against the floor and the edge of the shelves, pinning her by her shoulder. No one had said what she feared; she wouldn't be able to climb again.

Shauna squeezed her hand. Jack forced back the tears. They still needed the names of all the girls Dr Sharma had abused. Their families had to know the truth.

FORTY

Bella reached for the next dark-blue hold, grabbing it with her chubby hand. Jack tightened the belay to make sure she wouldn't fall far. Then Bella stretched a foot, scraping it off the foothold. She tried again. Success this time. She managed to push her body upwards.

'Well done, love!' her mother shouted from the sidelines.

After an initial spell in the office, Jack had spent a period of convalescence meeting colleagues for coffee and staying home reading through her father's journals. She still had regular calls with Sherpa Norbu and a television company to plan her climb of Kanchenjunga which had been postponed until the autumn. The plan was still to climb with her Sherpa colleagues as equals. Apart from that, she'd practically cocooned herself in her flat. Only leaving to attend work and physiotherapy sessions. She almost had full movement in her arm now. Almost wasn't good enough, though. She'd also found little in the journals to explain the strange letter her mother had given her.

What she did find was a story of the love her father had for his two daughters. Painstakingly he'd described their growth from toddlers into mountaineers. Pages were devoted to descriptions of their training. The successes:

Jack blazed across the mountain crag with no sense of fear. The route she took was the most perilous, yet her steps were assured and considered. Not one foot out of line, not one slip, her confidence grows daily. Clare follows suit. Always just one or two steps behind her sister.

And their failures:

Here's hoping that both my daughters grow at least another foot. There's such a limited number of routes I can give them. Jack's reach between holds is so restricted, I doubt she'll ever make it as a climber. Take today: she had to give up on the route I'd planned for her on Stanage. Three times she lost her footing on the same stretch. It's tragic to see.

Bella reached the summit of the beginner's climbing wall at the Rock Children's Climbing Centre. Jack carefully lowered her down. Michelle scooped her up and led her to the cafe area. Jack followed, taking a seat opposite the mother and daughter.

'She's really got a knack for climbing.' Jack sat back in her chair, hoping that Michelle would keep bringing Bella to the centre.

'Do you think so? That's amazing coming from you.' Michelle passed Bella her juice which she eagerly drank. 'What age were you, when you started climbing, I mean?'

'I don't honestly remember.' In the journals, Jack's dad described her as climbing before she could walk. Maybe that was true.

Michelle changed the subject. 'How're you and Emily getting on?'

Jack hadn't imagined that Shauna's sister would become as

much as a relationship counsellor as Shauna was. At least Michelle didn't laugh at her. 'We're going away for the weekend, so good, I guess.'

'Where?'

'Barmouth.' Jack couldn't believe that she was letting Emily drag her to the seaside, particularly in the height of summer.

Bella had finished her drink and was pulling on her mum's sleeve. Michelle ignored her. 'I read this morning about that poor woman who's just been released from prison. She hadn't even harmed her daughter. Was that your case?'

Jack simply nodded not wanting to be drawn into a conversation. Dr Kishran Sharma had harmed at least fourteen girls. Most of them were now well after escaping his care. He'd 'treated' them for a while and then tossed them aside. Leia and Sammi were the only ones that he had murdered. But one of the abused girls' mothers had been imprisoned for two years for physically harming her daughter. The case was reinvestigated by another team at West Midlands Police after it was discovered that Kishran was her daughter's doctor and she'd finally been released. At least some good could come of all this, some justice. Both her and her daughter were left with emotional scars though that could take years to heal.

Then there was Sammi's mother who they were still considering charging with assisting an offender. They were just waiting for the Crown Prosecution Service to make a decision as to how to proceed. Despite not being a mother, Jack couldn't comprehend how Gail or Ellen could have been taken in by Sharma. Ellen had said that he was the only one to understand her daughter's needs. She'd told Jack that he'd claimed to be 'misunderstood by the medical establishment' which had led to him being disciplined. This had meant that he had to practise surreptitiously. It was more likely, of course, that Jayden had been right and this was a case of cult-like infatuation.

Before Michelle could ask her more about the investigation,

Jack stood to leave. She had paperwork to sort, and she never liked discussing cases outside of work.

On the way to the station, she spotted Terry Doughty. He was walking from the hotel towards a lorry. Jack pulled over and watched him from a distance. His stride was assured. He was whistling. No signs of grief. It was like watching a completely different person.

There was nothing in Kishran Sharma's notebooks about killing Gail. And it wasn't his thing, harming the mothers. He saved his abuse for their innocent children. That didn't mean he didn't do it. But they'd never have solid proof. The drugs she ingested could have been in the house already. Anyone could have walked in and administered them and then drowned her in the bath. Jack had wondered if it was Finn, after his comments about Gail, but he was probably only interested in Leia as a friend and was just a socially awkward young man, not a killer.

Terry Doughty was a different matter.

He climbed into the cab of the lorry, no doubt about to drive back to Scotland. What could she do to stop him? Bring him in for questioning again? On what grounds? She watched him drive away, sighed and started her engine. Much as she wanted to arrest him, there was zero proof and she could be wrong, whatever she felt in her gut.

'Seventeen years,' Nadia said without looking up from her laptop.

'What?' Jack placed her jacket on the back of her chair wondering what her sergeant was referring to.

'Jacobs.' Nadia looked up. 'He got seventeen consecutive years.'

'Great. You must be really pleased. That's down to all your

hard work and tenacity. I'm so proud of you.' It was more than Jack had even hoped for. He'd got twelve years for the first sentence so he wouldn't be out for at least fifteen. She hoped the other prisoners would make his life hell.

'Are you coming to the super's leaving do later?'

Her shoulder ached. And she'd promised Emily a night in front of the television –popcorn and a movie. But Jack knew she'd have to show her face, shake hands with all the other high-ranking officers and lead the 'for he's a jolly good fellow' or she'd never live it down. 'Yeah. I'll be there. Let's raise a glass to your first big win.' She could even bring Emily with her. That would raise a few eyebrows.

Switching on her laptop, she turned to the next of Dr Sharma's scanned notebooks. This was exhibit number 231. She read the first page of notes.

Resilience. The more I cut, the deeper I connect to these girls. The more I understand what keeps them fighting. Young women are resilient to pain. Still, they function, eat, sleep and crave their freedom. No matter what they endure.
No longer should we worry about causing pain and discomfort in the process of treatment. Young bodies will cope and heal. I'm sure of it. This will pave the way for new treatments for illness and disease. My research will be applauded.

What she read disgusted and angered her. Jack didn't feel the least bit of remorse that she'd killed Dr Sharma. She'd discovered from his previous journals that he'd intentionally murdered both Leia and Sammi. Other girls had died by accidental overdose, but he'd given Leia and Sammi an overdose to keep them quiet. Leia, after finding out she was speaking to Finn, and Sammi, because she was asking too many questions. Sammi hadn't fallen for his charms.

This lack of remorse frightened her. Whoever he was – an

abuser, a physician, a psychopath – he was still a person. She'd been cleared by her peers of any wrongdoing. You could kill someone with an ice pick in self-defence, it seemed. The expected flashbacks, sleepless nights, didn't happen either and that's what worried her most.

She shook her head and turned to the next page of the journal documenting the operations he'd performed on a six-year-old girl. All unnecessary. The girl's mother claimed not to be aware of what Kishran Sharma had done. She knew him as Dr Mattu, a paediatrician at her local Leicestershire Hospital. Dr Mattu soon lost interest in her daughter, according to this particular journal. He'd moved on quickly to another place of work. The girl was now thirteen and still bore the scars of their meeting. Jack wouldn't give up until every child was found and every story documented. This was what she spent her lunchtimes and evenings pursuing. Sending her findings in weekly reports to Dr Pride, who'd promised to share them with her hospital trust with the hope that mistakes wouldn't be repeated.

He wasn't the first rogue surgeon and probably wouldn't be the last. But Jack would do everything in her power to stop this from happening again.

A LETTER FROM THE AUTHOR

Dear reader,

Huge thanks for reading *Broken Girls*. I hope you were hooked on Jack's journey. If you want to join other readers in hearing all about my new releases and bonus content, you can sign up here:

www.stormpublishing.co/nicky-downes

If you enjoyed this book and could spare a few moments to leave a review, that would be hugely appreciated. Even a short review can make all the difference in encouraging a reader to discover my books for the first time. Thank you so much!

As a reader of crime, I just love a new series to get my teeth into. This is just book two, there's plenty more to come and more secrets to unravel in the life of DI Jack Kent.

Thanks again for being part of this amazing journey with me and I hope you'll stay in touch – I have so many more stories and ideas to entertain you with!

Nicky

www.nickydownescrimeauthor.com

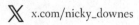 x.com/nicky_downes

ACKNOWLEDGEMENTS

Please only read these acknowledgements *after* you have read the book as they include spoilers!

People will often ask me what attracts me to write about the kind of gruesome crimes I describe in my novels. The answer is different for every book, but I wrote *Broken Girls* to highlight that crime is committed in the most unlikely places and by the most unlikely people. I have dedicated the book to my mum, Frances, who is a breast cancer survivor. Her surgeon was Ian Paterson. Ian Paterson is now serving twenty years in prison for carrying out unnecessary operations and surgeries that did not follow NHS guidelines on more than a thousand patients. Those unnecessary operations include the 'cleavage sparing' mastectomy he performed on my dear mum. We may never know how many deaths he is responsible for or precisely how many lives he ruined, but in 2017 he was finally brought to justice, which gives us some comfort.

I also want to dedicate this book to the fantastic staff in the NHS that have cared for my mum and wider family. We have one of the best health services in the world, despite its massive underfunding and understaffing. We must do all we can to defend it. I feel privileged, as an educator, to have been able to stand alongside health professionals this year in our joint fight for fair pay. It saddens me that those who care and educate are treated so poorly.

I am indebted to the various doctors and other health professionals who have answered all of my medical questions over the last year, including Dr Kim Pierson and Sian Aston. Their contributions have undoubtedly helped to make *Broken Girls* more accurate and realistic, but any errors that you detect in my description of medical procedures or in the use of medical terminology are entirely my own.

Finally, the team from Storm have been my guide and strongest supporter as I have worked on the book. I particularly want to thank my editor, Kate Smith, and publisher, Kathryn Taussig: I couldn't have written *Broken Girls* without you.

Thank you all!

Made in the USA
Coppell, TX
28 February 2024

29533482R00163